The Masquerading Magician

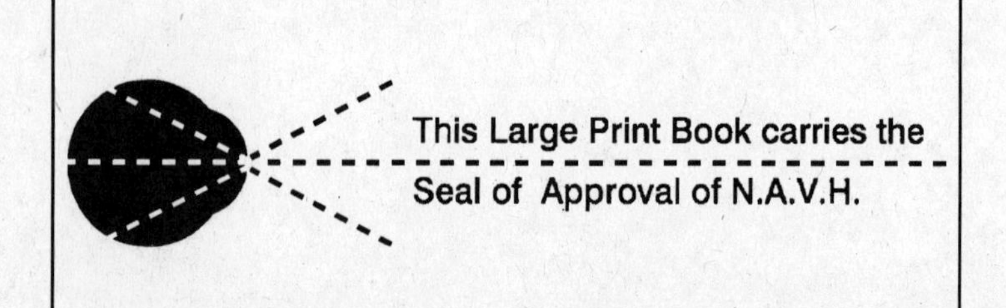
This Large Print Book carries the
Seal of Approval of N.A.V.H.

AN ACCIDENTAL ALCHEMIST MYSTERY

THE MASQUERADING MAGICIAN

GIGI PANDIAN

WHEELER PUBLISHING
A part of Gale, Cengage Learning

GALE
CENGAGE Learning

Farmington Hills, Mich • San Francisco • New York • Waterville, Maine
Meriden, Conn • Mason, Ohio • Chicago

An Accidental Alchemist Mystery.
Wheeler Publishing, a part of Gale, Cengage Learning.

This is a work of fiction. Names, characters, places, and incidents either are the product of the author's imagination or are used fictitiously, and any resemblance to actual persons, living or dead, business establishments, events, or locales is entirely coincidental.

Wheeler Publishing Large Print Cozy Mystery.
The text of this Large Print edition is unabridged.
Other aspects of the book may vary from the original edition.
Set in 16 pt. Plantin.

LIBRARY OF CONGRESS CATALOGING-IN-PUBLICATION DATA

Names: Pandian, Gigi, 1975– author.
Title: The masquerading magician / by Gigi Pandian.
Description: Large print edition. | Waterville, Maine : Wheeler Publishing, 2016. | © 2016 | Series: An accidental alchemist mystery | Series: Wheeler Publishing large print cozy mystery
Identifiers: LCCN 2015050972 | ISBN 9781410488978 (softcover) | ISBN 1410488977 (softcover)
Subjects: LCSH: Large type books. | GSAFD: Mystery fiction. | Fantasy fiction.
Classification: LCC PS3616.A367 M37 2016b | DDC 813/.6—dc23
LC record available at http://lccn.loc.gov/2015050972

Published in 2016 by arrangement with Midnight Ink, an imprint of Llewellyn Publications, Woodbury, MN 55125-2989

Printed in the United States of America
1 2 3 4 5 6 7 20 19 18 17 16

For the chemo nurses who
demolish cancer and raise spirits.

One

Persephone & Prometheus's Phantasmagoria: A Classic Magic Show in the Modern World.

The giant poster was illustrated in the style of Victorian Era stage magic posters. Two figures faced each other from opposite sides of a stage, the larger one in a tuxedo and top hat, the smaller impish figure in a devilish red suit. The taller tuxedoed figure held a wand pointed upward toward an ethereal floating figure. The devilish man held a ball of fire in his hand.

I smiled to myself as Max and I made our way through the lobby, my fingers looped through his. Some things had changed since the Victorian era. The tuxedo-clad magician in the poster was a woman. Prometheus and Persephone wcre a husband-and-wife magic act with equal billing.

Their style reminded me very much of posters of King of Cards Thurston and Carter the Great, both of whom used ghost and devil imagery in their posters and shows to illustrate the motif that they were magicians able to control the spirit world. The ambiance felt more like Paris in 1845, on the day Jean Eugène Robert-Houdin took to the stage at the newly built Palais-Royal theater with his ingenious mechanical inventions and masterful sleight of hand. But this was a small theater near Portland's Mt. Tabor, over 150 years later. Seeing that poster made me feel like I'd been transported back in time.

I should know. I attended Robert-Houdin's show over a century ago.

Though I look outwardly like a woman in her late twenties with trendy dyed-white hair who's named after her grandmother Zoe Faust, the truth is far different. Long before I bought a run-down house in Portland, Oregon, three months ago, I was born in Salem, Massachusetts. In 1676.

A shiver swept over me as a memory of a different time and place overtook me. Casually dressed Oregonians with cell phones in their pockets became formally attired members of society who would remember this performance for a lifetime.

Breathe, Zoe.

I willed myself to remember it wasn't a taut corset constricting my breathing, but my own nerves. I had thought tonight's opening performance would be the perfect way to spend time with Max after he'd been away, but could I trust myself with him? I couldn't tell him the truth about my past, no matter how much I wanted to. Maybe this had been a terrible idea.

Max pulled me toward the ticket-taker. I was holding up the line. I took one last look at the floor-to-ceiling poster in the lobby. Though the artist had done a wonderful job projecting the ghostly feel of the first phantasmagoria acts, down to faux-faded edges, there was a twenty-first-century addition: across the bottom, a garish yellow stripe contained a warning to theater patrons that any attempt to photograph the show with cell phones or other recording devices would result in expulsion from the theater.

I didn't have time to think more about whether I'd made a mistake coming here tonight. Almost as soon as we found our seats, the lights went down. The dramatic opening of Carl Orff's *Carmina Burana* sounded from speakers overhead. The music was in the spirit of the era they were invoking, even though it hadn't been composed until the 1930s. A spark appeared in the far corner of the darkened stage. It was barely noticeable at first, but a moment later, flames erupted from the back of the stage.

A wave of murmurs and stifled exclamations rippled across the rows of the theater. Max swung his head around, presumably looking for the fire alarm.

"Relax," I whispered.

"There's no way this little theater is safe for this kind of fire," he whispered back. "We need to —"

"It's only an illusion." I put my hand on his arm. "I promise."

Max's reaction didn't surprise me. No matter if he was on duty as a detective or not, he was always looking out for others. He settled back into his seat and gave me a sheepish grin before turning his attention back to the stage.

The flames followed a course, like dominoes. The tiny spark that had ignited in one corner of the stage as a slow simmer was now a full-blown fire that followed the path of a rope that appeared on the stage floor. The flames then snaked upward in a renewed fit of energy, as if being chased, jumping to a hanging spiderweb made of rope. The flames followed the woven web, tracing the intricate pattern like rabid mice in a maze.

I inhaled deeply, making sure I was right that this was only an illusion. I didn't smell fire. Smoke and mirrors. Or, more accurately, glass and lighting.

As the false flames approached the middle of the web suspended over the back of the stage, the music swelled, culminating in a crash of cymbals at the moment the fire reached the center.

"Ladies and gentlemen," a disembodied woman's voice boomed from offstage. "This display of fire is the handiwork of Prometheus. Never fear. I know how to handle him."

The illusory flames extinguished as abruptly as if a tidal wave had blanketed the stage. A small man dressed in a bright-red tuxedo, with spiky red hair that resembled bursts of flame, walked out onto the naked stage.

"Persephone," he said in a more powerful voice than his slight frame suggested, "you're no fun." He turned toward the audience, raising his hand to the side of his mouth as if about to impart a secret. "Don't mind her. But don't be too hard on her either. I'd be in a grumpy mood too, if I had to spend time in the Underworld."

He turned his head toward the darkness offstage, the direction from which the disembodied woman's voice had come. I knew that's where he wanted us to look, so

I looked elsewhere, wondering what would come at us next. I tilted my head upward, toward the lights above the stage.

And froze.

It had definitely been a mistake to come here tonight.

Prometheus turned back to the audience, but my own eyes darted back to the catwalk of lighting equipment above the stage as my hands gripped the armrests. I couldn't believe what I was seeing. No, that's not true. I completely believed it. I didn't *want* to believe it.

Max leaned over and whispered into my ear, "What's the matter? Were you wrong about this being an illusion?"

I shook my head. "Just my imagination," I whispered. I forced myself to pull my gaze from the catwalk. To look away from Dorian. Things could get very ugly if I called attention to the interloper.

My friend stood in the shadows high above the stage, watching the show from above like Quasimodo or the Phantom of the Opera. It wasn't that he didn't have the money to buy a ticket and sit in a proper seat. Dorian Robert-Houdin couldn't show himself in public. He was a gargoyle, once made of stone before he was unintentionally brought to life 150 years ago by Jean

Eugène Robert-Houdin, the "Father of Modern Magic" in more ways than anyone realized.

What was Dorian thinking? What if someone saw him?

I felt an overwhelming urge to protect him. Should I act? What could I do? He and I were two misfits, surprised to find ourselves partly immortal through alchemy. I'd accidentally unlocked alchemy's greatest secret, the Elixir of Life, at the turn of the eighteenth-century. The years that followed were filled with crushing pain from the loss of those I'd loved, but also unsurpassable joy from the time I'd been able to spend with them. In the last three months, Max and Dorian had quickly become important to me. How could I deal with Dorian without alerting Max to the existence of a living gargoyle?

I glanced around the theater. The thudding of my heart filled my ears as loudly as the cymbals that had sounded moments before. It faded ever so slightly as I realized that nobody else had noticed the three-and-a-half-foot gargoyle watching from above. All eyes were focused on the stage. Thank God the entertaining performance was holding the audience's attention. So far. Prometheus was still speaking, carrying on the silly patter that's essential for a successful stage magician to master. *Carmina Burana* continued to play in the background, its intense vocals adding effective background suspense, but the volume had lowered as the magician spoke.

I pulled my eyes from Dorian as a woman in a black tuxedo stepped into view. She crossed her arms and raised a theatrically painted eyebrow at Prometheus.

In lacquered black high-heeled shoes that shone brightly under the spotlight, she stood more than six feet tall. Instead of the typical leotard or evening gown you'd expect to see on most women on the stage of a magic show, she wore a tailored tuxedo with tails down to her knees. Sleek brown curls adorned her head in the heavily styled waves popular in the 1920s, and bright red lipstick made full lips stand out on a pale face. If it had been a century ago, I would have described her face as handsome. Broad-shouldered and bold, she held herself confidently. With a top hat in her hands, she was elegance itself.

"I am Persephone," her voice boomed. "Perhaps you've heard of me. I'm Queen of the Underworld. But don't worry. I'm also the Goddess of Spring Growth. We Greek gods are difficult to pin down, I know. Since this week marks the first week of spring, you get to see a benevolent Persephone tonight. It's Prometheus you need to worry about. But I'll protect you from his fire-starter tendencies."

"She's quite dramatic, isn't she?" Prometheus said, stepping forward out of the shadows. If ever there was a contrasting duo, it was the two figures on the stage. Where Persephone was large and powerful, Prometheus was a puny wisp of a man. Not frail, though. Even from where I sat several rows back, I could tell he had the lithe body of an acrobat. That was good. The audience would want to keep an eye on him instead of looking around — and up.

"I'm warning you, Prometheus," Persephone said. "No fire games for these good people tonight. They've come to see a classic magic show. I will impress them with my prestidigitation."

Prometheus snapped his fingers. A crackle far greater than the sound of snapping fingers echoed as a burst of flame shot from his fingertips. Simultaneously, a roar of flames surged through the stalk of a potted fennel plant in the back of the stage. The flames stretched upward.

It was only a matter of time before people in the audience looked up and saw Dorian.

If he was spotted, would he have the sense to stand perfectly still and pretend to be a stone gargoyle placed there as a joke? Or would he try to run? I hoped it wasn't the latter. Dorian was no longer the swift creature he'd once been. His body was slowly returning to stone. This night was a rare break for me from my research and experimentation with the secrets of *Non Degenera Alchemia — Not Untrue Alchemy —* the book Dorian hoped could save his life. He'd stowed away in a crate from France just to find me, but three months of alchemy work had yielded few results. After so many decades of denying my gifts, my gifts were now denying me.

I'd discovered a quick fix, a Tea of Ashes that temporarily reversed his deterioration. But if I failed to find a permanent solution, a fate much worse than death awaited my friend. Soon, Dorian would be fully awake but trapped in an unmoving stone body — and I didn't know if the condition could be reversed.

I stole another glance at Dorian. He was no longer stock still. I let out a breath of relief as I saw him inching slowly along the catwalk toward the wings. At least, that's what he was trying to do. One of his claws caught in the metal latticework. It was the foot that had been giving him trouble. He tugged at his leg with his hands. My chest tightened when I saw what was happening.

Dorian's clawed hands flailed as he lost his balance. I clutched the armrest, expecting to see him fall onto the stage in front of over a hundred onlookers.

Two

On the stage, Prometheus's illusory flames flickered and grew. High above, Dorian's hands flailed wildly at his sides.

I held my breath and considered what sort of distraction I could create to prevent people from noticing a three-and-a-half-foot gargoyle crashing into the audience.

Before I could act, Dorian caught hold of a metal railing and steadied himself. He stood perfectly still. If anyone looked up, they would assume he was simply a stone gargoyle. A carving that resembled the "thinker" gargoyle of Notre Dame de Paris, with wings folded behind broad shoulders and small horns poking out on top of his head, was certainly an odd choice for a catwalk decoration, but everyone knew theater folk were an eccentric bunch, right?

I swallowed hard. How could he be here? Dorian knew how important it was that he not be seen. It was difficult enough to keep his existence a secret without him appearing above the crowd of a sold-out show.

I also understood the impulse. The gargoyle was homesick. He couldn't resist the lure of a magic show with posters showing a classic performance more reminiscent of Belle Époque era Paris than dot-com era Vegas.

Persephone pointed a red-tipped finger at Prometheus. The fennel flames extinguished. Like a phoenix rising from the flames as it renewed itself, a metal tree sprouted from the top of Prometheus's head, pushing through his spiky crimson-tipped hair. The trunk inched upward, and green leaves emerged from the trunk.

"What are you doing?" Prometheus sputtered, holding onto his head as if the roots of the tree pained him as the metal branches continued to grow. "Fire is supposed to bring death and destruction, not *renewal.*"

"Is it not all connected?" Persephone replied. "Your fire fed the soil for this tree to grow. This is your own doing."

Prometheus moaned as the mechanical tree grew slowly but methodically until it was over a foot high. Prometheus shook his head, causing a few of the false leaves to fall to the stage floor. In place of the leaves was an orange. Persephone walked across the stage, the tail of her black tuxedo flapping behind her, and plucked the orange from the two-foot tree now sitting atop her partner's head. This illusion was one that Jean Eugène Robert-Houdin had created — as Dorian must have realized too. That's why we were here on opening night. I wanted to see a classic stage show like the ones I remembered from a distant past, from a happy time that had been far too brief. I couldn't fault Dorian for wanting the same thing, especially since the gargoyle had a stronger connection to the great magician than anyone.

The posters hadn't been misleading. The suspense here was much more subtle than most modern shows I'd seen, building slowly and holding our attention with wonder rather than demanding it with glitz.

Of course, I couldn't tell my date that I'd actually seen the illusion performed by its original inventor well over a century ago.

Perhaps coming here tonight had been a bad idea. Perhaps it had *all* been an awful idea.

I couldn't worry about that now. I was too terrified that someone would see Dorian. I felt the warm pressure of the heavy gold locket I wore on a chain around my neck. I couldn't let this happen. *Not again.*

It was times like these I felt foolish for thinking I could have a normal life here in Portland. But I was so tired of running. Finding a community where I fit in seemed too good to be true. As did meeting a man whose herbal gardening skills rivaled mine and was handsome and intriguing to boot. Max Liu was dangerous for the same reason that he wasn't dangerous. He was simultaneously alluring and safe. A rational detective who'd learned the teachings of his grandmother, an herbalist and apothecary in China. He was in his early forties, single after his wife died years ago. Losing her caused him to live his life in the present rather than the past, and part of this mantra made him avoid all talk of the past. It was one of the reasons it was easy to spend time with him. He didn't push me to open up about a past I could never make him understand.

But I knew Max and I would never work in the long run, because even if he accepted me for who I was, he would continue to age naturally while I never would. Yet, I could imagine myself comfortably settling into life with him and the many friends I'd made here in a short time.

Persephone bantered with the crowd while she peeled the orange she'd plucked from the miraculous orange tree. This wasn't as elaborate an illusion as Robert-Houdin's original, but the audience was captivated. Persephone threw the peeled orange into the audience. A young man I knew caught the fruit.

"It's real!" he shouted, holding up the orange.

My young neighbor Brixton was attending the show with his friends, sitting several rows in front of me and Max. Dorian had gotten both of us excited about the classic magic act, and Brixton had convinced his friends Ethan and Veronica to attend the show.

Fourteen-year-old Brixton was the one person in Portland who'd learned my secret and Dorian's. It hadn't been on purpose, and I'd been terribly worried about it at first, until events that winter had cemented his loyalty. At first he'd tried to convince Ethan and Veronica that he'd really seen a living gargoyle, but that was long behind us. I hoped.

"May I ask," Persephone said, "if there is someone here tonight who would like to escape from Prometheus's trickery? I can send you away to the Underworld, where you will be safe." She paced the length of the stage, the spotlight following her deliberate steps. "In this early part of the evening, the spirits are only strong enough to carry one of you. I'll do my best to protect the rest of you. A volunteer?"

"Brixton volunteers!" Ethan shouted, raising Brixton's arm for him. Brixton snatched it back and scowled at Ethan.

"Thank you, my young friends," Prometheus cut in, "but in this modern age, unfortunately I must insist on a volunteer who is at least eighteen." The mechanical orange tree was now gone from his head. I didn't see it anywhere. We'd all been paying attention to Persephone.

"How about closer to eighty?" The spotlight followed the voice and came to rest on two elderly men. A bulky man with gray hair and huge black eyebrows was grinning and pointing at his friend, a skinny throwback to the 1960s in a white kurta shirt and with long white hair pulled into a ponytail.

Persephone ushered the smaller man to the stage and asked him his name.

"Wallace," he said with a calm voice that struck me as out of place on the dramatic stage. "Wallace Mason." He wore the Indian-style cotton shirt over faded jeans and sandals. While most of the audience had dressed up, he looked like a man who thought the embroidered neckline on his shirt *was* dressing up.

Persephone continued an easygoing patter with the crowd, the spotlight remaining on her while Prometheus prepped the man. A minute later, the stage lights flickered. As they did so, an astringent scent assaulted my nostrils.

"The spirits are ready," Persephone said. "They have sent ether to carry my friend here to safety." She raised her arms, and Wallace Mason began to float. His white hair fell free of its ponytail and flowed past his shoulders. As his feet left the stage, the image of a flowing evening gown appeared over his clothing. The audience laughed.

"Forgive the spirits," Persephone said. "They think women are most worthy of saving."

I knew what was happening. I'd seen various versions of the Floating Lady illusion over the years. All of them involved someone — or their image — hovering high above the stage. Unfortunately, it was the worst possible illusion for keeping Dorian hidden from view. One of the audience members was sure to spot him.

The theater plunged into darkness. All that was visible was the ghostly, floating form of a confused man — and, for anyone who looked up, the shocked gargoyle above him.

A ripple of murmurs from the crowd followed. I looked around to see what people were looking at. When I looked back up, Dorian was gone.

I jerked my head around, searching for the gargoyle. Since a hefty stone gargoyle hadn't crashed onto the stage or into the audience, that meant Dorian must have freed his foot and scampered to safety. I hadn't imagined his presence, had I?

Max put his hand on my arm. "Don't worry," he whispered. "He's not going to fall."

I tensed, then realized Max was talking not about the missing gargoyle but the volunteer floating above the stage.

"I'm just tired," I whispered back. Max knew how hard I'd been working lately. He was under the illusion I was busy with my job and fixing up my crumbling house, not my true actions of working to save Dorian's life. Lying to those you care about is one price to pay for immortality.

I forced my shoulders to relax. Once Max's attention was back to the illusion, I looked up, toward the spot where I'd seen Dorian earlier. There was still no gargoyle. Only the ghostly image of the volunteer in a superimposed evening gown. Wallace Mason's floating image reached the catwalk — and disappeared into the ether.

The lights went out again. A moment later, Prometheus and Persephone stood in the center of the stage, the volunteer in between them. The magicians took his hands in theirs, raised their arms above their heads, and gave deep bows. I applauded enthusiastically, clapping as much for Dorian's escape as for the illusion.

During the brief intermission, I excused myself to use the restroom, when in truth I wanted to make sure there was no sign of Dorian. I knew Dorian, so I knew the types of places he liked to hide. There was no balcony in this theater, so I went to the adjacent alley but saw no sign of him. Hitching up my dress, I climbed the fire escape to the roof. No sign of him there either. I hadn't found him when the sound of accordion music wafted up through the vents, signaling that it was time to return to our seats. *Where was Dorian?* I reached my seat as the lights were falling.

"I really wish you'd leave your cell phone on," Max said, looking slightly annoyed.

"Didn't you see the signs in the lobby? Using a cell phone here is punishable by death." At least that got a smile out of him.

For the rest of the act, the magicians told the story of Persephone's powers as the Goddess of Spring Growth, who possessed the ability to bring the dead back to the living. A good story is one of the secrets of a successful magic show. Illusions are simply tricks if they don't tell a story. *Persephone & Prometheus's Phantasmagoria* was a dark fairy tale. The magicians knew how to lead their audience where they wanted them to go. I wished I could relax and enjoy the show.

When the lights went up at the end of the performance, I turned to Max, trying to think of how to excuse myself to look for my living gargoyle.

Max and I had met that winter, the very day I moved to Portland. It was now the start of spring, and Max had missed the first blooming flowers while he'd been out of the country in China to celebrate his grandfather's 100th birthday. When he'd returned a few weeks ago, there had been a change in him. He said he'd been busy with a case at work, but was that all it was? Going to the magic show together was our first date in over a month. But if Dorian was stuck somewhere because of his unmoving stone leg, unable to make it home . . .

"How about I make us a pot of tea back

at my place," Max said. "I brought back some oolong tea from China with a flavor that's the most perfect blend of peaches and honey I've ever encountered."

The warmth in his dark brown eyes as he talked about one of his passions made me temporarily forget about Dorian. Max's straight black hair flopped at an angle over his forehead, reaching past his eyebrows. The unkempt look was sexy, but also unlike him. What had happened in China?

"I'm really tired," I said. "I know we haven't had a chance to catch up much —"

"Yeah, you've been distracted for half the night."

"I'm sorry, Max. I —"

"It's okay, Zoe," he said with a smile that didn't reach his eyes. "Besides, I'm sleep-deprived from a case I'm working."

I looked down at the green silk dress I hadn't worn in years. I'd pulled it out especially for this evening that I'd wanted to be special. The dress was one of the few items of clothing that hadn't been ruined when part of my roof collapsed during a brutal winter storm, only saved because it had been in storage in my Airstream trailer. The material was only slightly disheveled from my rooftop jaunt. I'm used to being careful with clothes, a habit from a time when they weren't so easily replaced. Max had dressed up too, in a slim-fitting black suit and the black-and-white wingtips I loved.

"It's supposed to be a gorgeous weekend," I said. "Why don't you come over for a barbeque in my garden tomorrow afternoon?"

At that suggestion, Max's withdrawn expression transformed into a genuine smile.

And so it was that instead of staying out with a man with whom I could never be completely honest, no matter how much I wanted to, I went home to a crumbling house where I hoped a gargoyle with a failing stone body would be waiting for me.

Three

I drove through the Hawthorne district of northeast Portland and eased my old truck into the driveway. I sighed as I looked at the gaping hole in the roof, covered with a tarp that flapped in the wind. One day I'd have time to fix the old Craftsman house.

A skinny figure dressed in jeans and a hideous velvet smoking jacket was waiting for me in front of the house.

"Zoe!" Brixton said. "It took you long enough. You *have* to listen to this."

Since Brixton wasn't my kid, I hadn't been expecting to see him in my house at ten o'clock at night.

"One minute, Brixton. Let's get inside. What are you wearing? You look like Hugh Hefner."

"Who?"

"Never mind."

I stepped across the creaking porch and opened the front door of my house. The diffuse light from a gold-colored Chinese lantern illuminated the corner of the living room, casting a mix of light and shadows across my green velvet couch and Dorian's stack of library books, which was nearly as tall as he was.

"Dorian?" I called out after Brixton closed the door.

A light peeked through the kitchen door, and I heard a rhythmic scraping sound.

I pushed through the swinging door and found Dorian stirring a steaming pot. As usual, the gargoyle stood on a stepping stool to reach the stove. He'd become a chef after serving as a companion to a blind former chef in Paris, who believed Dorian to be a disfigured man. Now the gargoyle was my roommate. A secret one who didn't need a bedroom, but a roommate nonetheless.

I was glad to see him safe, but his calm countenance made me question what I thought I'd seen that night. A flash of irritation rose within me. I'd been abrupt with Max because I was worried about Dorian, and here he was acting as if nothing had happened.

"You're all right, Dorian?"

"Ce n'est rien," Dorian said, continuing to stir the pot. "It is nothing. My leg merely stiffened from standing still above the stage

for so long."

"You shouldn't have been there in the first place! What were you thinking?"

"Hey," Brixton said. "Didn't you hear me outside? Don't you want to hear this?"

"I have lived safely in the shadows for over one hundred and fifty years," Dorian said in his thick French accent, ignoring Brixton as well as he turned to face me. "I know what I am doing."

"But you've never had your body start reverting to stone before." I studied Dorian's legs. His left leg was a darker gray than the rest of his body and hung at an awkward angle with his clawed foot turned outward. Something was happening that we didn't yet understand. "You almost fell. And anyone could have seen you."

"Yet I did not fall, nor did anyone see me." He turned back to the stove and switched off the gas flame.

"You were at the show?" Brixton asked.

"It was not remarkable, yet it had some high points. Now will you fetch three mugs?"

The sulking teenager obliged, shoving his cell phone into his pocket and selecting three handmade pieces of pottery, painted with vibrant reds and oranges. I'd bought the mugs in 1960s New Mexico from the craftswoman who made them. I smiled to myself in spite of the situation. I had a small collection of mugs, but those were the ones most people were drawn to. They were my favorites as well. The craftswoman had instilled a loving energy into the clay, transforming a lump of raw materials into something both beautiful and functional. I thought of craftspeople like her as artisan alchemists.

Dorian poured the thick steaming liquid from his pot into the three mugs. He gave a start when he looked up at Brixton. "What is this vulgar jacket you are wearing?"

"Like it?" Brixton asked, his earlier agitation suddenly forgotten. "Veronica thought we should dress up for the show. I found this in the back of my mom's closet."

"Hmm . . ." Dorian handed Brixton his mug.

Brixton took a sip. "I don't know how he makes hot chocolate taste so good without milk or sugar."

"Cocoa elixir?" Dorian looked at me with innocent black eyes that wouldn't have been out of place on a puppy dog. "I know you have been feeling sick. *Alors,* I made your favorite."

"It's a good thing you're such a good cook," I said, accepting the mug. "You know how to bribe me." I took a sip of the rich, chocolatey drink. It had hints of coconut and cinnamon. "See, I've already nearly forgotten you almost got yourself found out tonight."

Dorian grinned and jumped down from the stool. He stumbled, but caught himself before he fell flat on the linoleum floor. *"Merde,"* he mumbled.

"You're due for another infusion of alchemy," I said, knowing better than to ask if he was all right. "The garden is doing well enough that I've got plenty of plants to create salts for your Tea of Ashes."

"I much prefer the flavor of my cocoa elixir," Dorian said.

Using a combination of mercury and sulfur, I was able to turn my hand-grown plants into a salt-like ash through an alchemical transformation described in Dorian's peculiar alchemy book, *Non Degenera Alchemia.* Salt was one of the three essential elements for alchemists. Mercury is the spirit, sulfur the soul, and salt the body. Dorian's soul and spirit were intact. It was his body that was failing him. My Tea of Ashes worked by temporarily fooling Dorian's body into thinking it had been rejuvenated with a true alchemical salt.

Alchemy is usually a long, drawn-out

process. It can't be rushed. The discipline of alchemy strives to turn the impure into something pure, be it transmuting lead into gold or turning a failing body into an immortal one. It's as much about the alchemist as it is the ingredients. It's a personal transformation, done in isolation in one's own laboratory while following a series of natural steps that transform the elements. Using earth, air, water, and fire, you calcinate, dissolve, separate, conjoin, ferment, distill, and coagulate. You get out what you put into it. And alchemical transformations of the body can't be transferred to others — a lesson I learned the hard way a long time ago.

That's the way alchemy is *supposed* to work.

But the book that brought Dorian to life wasn't like that. *Non Degenera Alchemia* was backward alchemy, a dangerous alchemical idea that involved quick fixes. I speculated that's why the title wasn't simply *True Alchemy,* but instead the convoluted double-negative *Not Untrue Alchemy.* Drawing upon external life forces to shortcut nature, backward alchemy was the antithesis of true alchemy. The "death rotation" described in the book's coded illustrations and Latin text told of backward actions that took minutes instead of months, and began, rather than ended, with fire.

The quick fixes in the book showed me that I could use my energy, along with that of the plants I'd lovingly tended in my garden, to hastily produce the end product of ashes. But it wasn't a permanent fix. I had only scratched the surface in my understanding of the book.

"Is there enough for seconds?" Brixton asked.

Dorian smiled and topped off Brixton's cocoa. "It is too bad the magicians selected the orange tree automaton," he said.

"I thought that was pretty cool," Brixton said. "That was a real orange that grew from the metal tree."

"It was nicely done," I agreed. "You take offense that they stole the idea from the great Jean Eugène Robert-Houdin?"

"*Non.* I would have much preferred them to have re-created Father's pastry chef automaton."

"Of course you would," I said, barely able to suppress a smile.

"Bon soir, mes amis," Dorian said, leaving his empty mug on the counter. He limped out of the kitchen. I presumed he was heading out on his nightly excursion. Since it wasn't a good idea for him to go out during

the day, when it would be too easy for people to see him, he explored the city and surrounding forests at night. Lately his nocturnal jaunts had been limited because a portion of the city's forests had been overrun by treasure hunters. The brutal winter storm that wrecked my roof had also caused a mudslide that unearthed a portion of hidden jewels from a decades-old train heist. Poor Dorian now had to share the woods with clandestine treasure hunters.

"That was weird," Brixton said.

So much of my life was weird that I couldn't be sure which part he was referring to.

"Doesn't he always insist on cleaning up 'his' kitchen?" Brixton continued.

"I think he's embarrassed that we saw him lose control of his body."

"That's exactly why I thought you'd want to hear this." Brixton attempted to raise an eyebrow enigmatically, but ended up lifting both of them.

"Right! You wanted to tell me something. Sorry, Brix. What is it?"

"The magician Prometheus" — he paused for dramatic effect — *"is an alchemist."*

I let out my breath and smiled. Brixton had an active imagination. Ever since he'd broken into my house and learned I was an alchemist, he'd seen alchemists everywhere. Well, perhaps not *everywhere.* But it had happened on more than one occasion.

"Don't you see?" Brixton said. "He could help you!"

Brixton knew I'd accidentally discovered the Elixir of Life in my twenties. Aside from my hair, which had turned white centuries ago, the Elixir prevented me from aging. He also knew alchemists weren't exactly immortal. Even though some of us have unlocked the secrets that transform energy into eternal life, we're flesh and blood and can be sickened or injured. With my herbal skills, sickness is less of an issue, but I have several scars that remind me how precarious life is.

It was typical of the young that Brixton had never asked me when and where I was born. He knew I used to run a shop in Paris in the early 1900s before returning home to the US and traveling around the country in my 1942 Chevy truck and my 1950 Airstream trailer. He'd never asked, as Dorian had, for the details of my birth and upbringing, so he didn't know I'd been born in Salem Village in 1676, or that because of my way with herbs and plants, I'd been accused of witchcraft at sixteen. Both I and the world had come far since then.

"Oh, Brix —"

"Why are you looking at me like that?" Brixton asked. "I'm telling you —"

"The same way you told me about Mrs. Andrews?"

"That was different." He scowled and busied himself with the mug of cocoa.

Brixton had sworn that one of our neighbors hadn't aged in ten years, from Brixton's first memories at age four to his current age of fourteen. I'd taken him seriously — only to find out the woman had gotten plastic surgery.

"And Jonas Latham?" I said.

Brixton scowled again. "Even though I wasn't right about him being an alchemist, I was right that he was up to something."

While riding his bike to my house, Brixton had noticed a man carrying laboratory supplies that looked similar to my alchemy vessels. As the man slipped into his garage, Brixton caught a glimpse of his "alchemy" lab.

Again, I'd given Brixton the benefit of the doubt. When I went to investigate, the police were at the man's house, arresting him. Brixton claimed it was a witch hunt and that the police had arrested him for being an alchemist. I asked Max about it, inquiring as a curious neighbor. It turned out the man had been running a meth lab in his garage.

A woman who had plastic surgery. Then a man dealing drugs.

"All right, Brixton. What is it this time?"

Four

"Um . . ." Brixton appeared suddenly fascinated with the crisscrossed scratches in the linoleum floor.

"Brix."

"Well, the thing is . . . He looks really familiar."

"*He looks really familiar?* That's all you've got this time?"

"This isn't like the meth dealer or Mrs. Andrews."

"You probably saw posters of the magic show online before it came to Portland," I pointed out.

"Would you let me finish? The magician is familiar from *history.* I swear I've seen him in a history book." He paused to lift the last coconut cookie from the magic-lamp-shaped cookie jar on the counter and pop it into his mouth.

"A former president, perhaps?"

"Not funny, Zoe. Not funny. I'm being

serious!" With a mouthful of gooey cookie in his mouth, Brixton wasn't making his case very effectively. "You didn't recognize him? There's not, like, a registry of alchemists?"

"It doesn't work like that."

"Well, it should. How am I supposed to remember everyone I've seen in a history book?"

"If this man is an alchemist who's discovered the Elixir of Life, do you really think he'd choose a profession where he could be famous? Wouldn't that make it much more difficult for him to keep his secret?"

"I know you've been good at making sure you never get publicity or anything, but there are a lot of people with bigger egos than yours. People who want the attention. And don't you remember how he said he needed a volunteer of legal age 'in these modern times,' like he'd known *previous* times?"

I frowned. The magic show that night was straight out of the 1800s, it had sparked an uncomfortable sense of familiarity, and Prometheus clearly enjoyed the spotlight. Was it possible Brixton was right this time? I shook my head. "Living out of the spotlight isn't a matter of personal preference," I said. "It's about survival."

"Immortals are always famous in the movies —"

"Exactly. In the movies. Not in real life. There are only a handful of alchemists out there who've succeeded in extending their lives. They stay so well-hidden that I haven't managed to find a single one since I started looking earlier this year."

"Which is totally why it's awesome that an alchemist is here in town. You should invite him over to the teashop."

Brixton was right that I needed help, but if he was also right about this man being a figure from history, that meant this alchemist was a dangerous wild card. Before approaching him, I needed to know more. Not only whether Prometheus could be an alchemist, but if he could be trusted.

I tried to think about how best to explain my concerns, but Brixton was no longer paying attention to me. "That's weird," he said, staring at the screen of his phone.

"What?"

"Nothing. Just a website that got hacked." He tucked the phone into the pocket of his jeans.

"Don't go anywhere," I said. "I'll be right back."

I climbed two flights of stairs to reach my attic office. A three-foot section of the roof was missing, but had been patched with a quick fix — like everything else in my life these days. The attic flooring below the rooftop hole had collapsed too. The gaping hole, located directly above my bedroom closet, was now covered with a sturdy wooden plank and a Qalicheh Persian rug.

A combination of plastic, plywood, and decorative coverings kept the rain out until I could reverse Dorian's deterioration and resume work on the fixer-upper house. Saving Dorian's life was a bigger priority than saving the house from dry rot. Besides, this hole in the roof provided an easier way for Dorian to come and go from the house without being seen. Unlike the rooftop opening he used to squeeze through, this one was large enough that he could maneuver through it and replace the tarp even with a stiff leg.

With the storm damage, my attic office rivaled the basement alchemy lab as a work-in-progress. The top of the Craftsman house contained my public persona; the lower regions hid my private one: Zoe Faust, the twenty-eight-year-old proprietor of the online secondhand shop Elixir, a descendant of the woman who'd started an apothecary shop named Elixir in Paris in 1872; and Zoe Faust, the 340-year-old alchemist who'd accidentally discovered the Elixir of Life 312 years ago, and who ran an online business because she was no good at transmuting lead into gold.

Stepping past a collection of antique books on herbal remedies, a row of Japanese puzzle boxes, and the articulated skeleton of a pelican, I grabbed my laptop computer. When I entered the kitchen a minute later, the fridge door stood open but Brixton was nowhere to be seen.

Then the crown of his head popped into view from where he stood behind the fridge door, and he kicked the door shut with his foot. In each hand he was balancing a stainless-steel storage container with a platter of treats on top.

"The desserts wouldn't have run away in the few moments you took to come back for them," I commented.

"Yeah, that coconut cookie made me wicked hungry and I couldn't decide what I wanted. It's cool, right? Dorian said there was more than you two could eat."

I lifted the more precariously-perched platter with my free hand and led the way to the dining table.

"I already looked them up while we were at the theater," Brixton said. "I knew that magician looked familiar as soon as I saw him, but it wasn't until the intermission that I could use my phone without Veronica punching me. But then I couldn't find you to tell you. Anyway, the magicians Prometheus and Persephone are a married couple, Peter and Penelope Silverman. They didn't announce their secret identities or anything."

"Now you think they're *both* alchemists?"

He shrugged. "I only recognized Prometheus, but who knows? That's why you should look into it. With two alchemists helping you, that could totally save Dorian."

I opened the laptop while Brixton inhaled a piece of chocolate zucchini bread. Peter Silverman's website bio was short, but as a magician he was well-known enough that an online encyclopedia had listings for both himself and Penelope, who was both his wife and magic show partner. They were both in their early fifties, and Peter was the child of Marge and Herb Silverman of Silver Springs, Ohio. Penelope Silverman, *née* Fitzgerald, began her career as a circus performer and she'd been an expert lion tamer and knife thrower before she ran away from the circus to become a magician.

Peter and Penelope met in Las Vegas, where they each had their own stage show. Penelope's page had a photograph from her solo show, and Peter's showed an illustrated poster of their joint *Phantasmagoria* act, similar to the one I'd seen that night. Before the two met, both of them were struggling, performing only as opening acts or at hotels nobody sober would stay at. About five years ago, they'd become the marginally successful team of Persephone & Prometheus. There was nothing controversial except for one thing: Peter had once punched a theater patron for taking a photo of the show.

I looked again at the poster illustrations. Their likenesses were approximate, but not photographic quality. There were no photographs on either their own website *or* the external listings. That was odd. I typed in an image search. Hundreds of images of Penelope popped up, most of them showing her as a young woman in a skimpy costume with a whip. Though Penelope was stunning in her fifties, she'd aged normally.

But I couldn't find a single photograph of Peter Silverman.

"What is it?" Brixton asked.

"Nothing." I tried one more quick search, finding more of the same. Penelope had several social media accounts, but Peter had none.

"What are you looking at?"

I closed the laptop. "I'm sure your mom is worried that you're not home yet. Let me put your bike in the back of the truck and give you a ride home."

It was a fifteen-minute drive to the cottage where Brixton and his mother were staying while Blue was gone. Brixton slipped on headphones as soon as he sat down in the passenger seat, which was fine with me. I needed time to think.

Peter Silverman was hiding something. That didn't necessarily mean he was an alchemist. In fact, it was more likely to mean any one of a dozen other things that had nothing to do with alchemy. Maybe he'd changed his name to get away from a life of crime. Or perhaps he was running away from alimony payments. I briefly considered that he could be a hero in the Witness Protection Program, but they'd never let him appear on stage.

Whatever it was, it couldn't be good.

After I dropped Brixton off at the cottage, I selected one of my favorite songs to listen to on the drive home. I had installed a compact cassette player in the early 1970s, about thirty years after buying the truck. I had a sentimental attachment to the countless mixed tapes I'd made myself for my long drives across the country, so I'd never upgraded. I found the cassette that included "Accidental Life," a 1950s song by an artist who called himself The Philosopher. It combined a spiritual sound with the danceable rock rhythms gaining popularity in the fifties. What I loved most about it was how The Philosopher used his deep, soulful voice to tell the story of a man who wandered the earth for a thousand years. It wasn't only the lyrics that spoke to me; there are some voices that simply feel like home.

The song ended long before I pulled into the driveway. I drove the rest of the way home through side streets, enjoying the late-night silence. In the driveway, I took a moment to breathe in the crisp night air. The spring scents of cherry blossoms, daffodils, and hyacinths came on a gust of wind.

Inside, I walked through the house to check that all the doors and windows were locked. After being burglarized shortly after I bought the house, it had become my nightly ritual. Despite the break-in, this dilapidated house felt like a real home. Aside from my Airstream trailer that I'd lived out of for decades, this was the first place that had felt like home in the last century.

Just as I was about to turn off the kitchen

light, I spotted a wooden spoon that had fallen in the crack between the Wedgewood oven and counter. I reached it easily enough, but paused before washing it. The scent of vanilla, cloves, and cardamom wafted up from the spoon, along with a scent I couldn't place. Though I'd been cooking for many more years than Dorian, he was the one who knew how to bring different flavors together in unexpected, complementary ways. Once I came to think of myself as worthy of a good life, I began using vegetables, herbs, and spices to make healthful meals. But my own purpose of cooking was to be healthy, not necessarily to enjoy the taste. Though I know how to dry high-quality herbs and spices for my alchemical transformations, and can create healing tinctures, teas, and salves, before Dorian entered my life I'd never thought about using the same ingredients to transform simple foods into heavenly masterpieces. My little gargoyle gourmet was a culinary alchemist.

These days, I'm considered a vegan. When I began eating a plant-based diet around the turn of the twentieth century, it was known as a Pythagorean diet, named for the mathematician Pythagoras, who advocated eliminating animal products from one's diet. Dorian was horrified when he learned I didn't stock bacon, butter, and heavy cream as kitchen staples. He'd been taught to cook with the traditional French methods, so learning to cook with the ingredients in my kitchen had been an adjustment. He rose to the challenge, though, and now declared that his vegan creations were the most impressive gastronomic feats in this hemisphere. Not only the best *vegan* creations, but the most delectable foods, *period.* I never said he was modest.

Dorian was still off on a nocturnal walk. He didn't need sleep, so after his nightly walks he spent the hours before sunrise baking pastries at Blue Sky Teas, slipping out before anyone saw him. Baking vegan treats for the local teashop was Dorian's contribution to our household expenses. Because nobody could know he existed, I was his front. Everyone besides Dorian and Brixton thought I was the chef who rose before dawn to bake fresh breads and delicacies. I hated all the lies I had to tell to fit into normal society, but this untruth provided a reasonable explanation for why I'd been so tired lately. With that thought, I yawned.

My last stop of the night was the basement. When I opened the door I kept locked at all times, my senses perked up. The second yawn that had been about to surface disappeared, replaced with a surge of adrenaline.

"Dorian?" I called out.

Silence.

I descended the stairs.

Standing on the bottom step, I had a full view of the room. The scent of home-brewed beer that had been so strong when I moved in had been gone for months, as were the putrid scents of my earlier failed experiments. After accidentally poisoning myself, I was now rigorous in my cleaning and storage of alchemical ingredients, and I kept the room locked at all times. Yet the harsh scent of sulfur dominated the basement. How could that be?

I stepped farther into the room, thinking I must have been so tired I couldn't smell straight. This wasn't sulfur. It was the pungent scent of cloves. No, that couldn't be right either. It must have been mold from an old book. Figuring out which one wasn't important right now. I had enough mysteries to deal with without worrying about the natural decomposition of an antique book. Besides, I couldn't be sure what I smelled. The only thing I felt sure of that night was that the perplexing odor came from a bookshelf in the far corner. I paused before turning off the light, with one last thought flitting through my mind: how strange it was that the scent seemed to be getting sweeter, rather than more foul, with age.

FIVE

When I walked into my kitchen sanctuary shortly after sunrise, Dorian was already there, wearing an apron and standing tall on his stepping stool as he fixed himself an espresso. I took a deep breath and savored the energizing scents surrounding me. A bowl of freshly made wild blackberry compote mingled with the fragrances of yeast from a loaf of sourdough bread in the oven and freshly ground French roast coffee beans. Next to the espresso machine sat two grinders, one for coffee beans and one for aromatic spices.

I tugged at the sleeve of my blouse, which was poking out from an ill-fitted sweater. I hated nearly all of the new clothing that I'd picked up at a local secondhand shop after my clothes were ruined. I supposed it was better the splintered wood had fallen into my closet rather than my bed, but I was unhappy nonetheless. I've never gotten used to wearing off-the-rack clothes. Even when ready-to-wear clothing supposedly fits properly, no two bodies are alike; it's impossible to get a perfect fit without tailoring.

I hitched up my high-waisted, oversize jeans to avoid tripping, but my superficial concerns were forgotten as soon as my gaze fell to Dorian's left foot. Not only was it fully stone, but another claw had broken off. Would it grow back after I healed him?

"Morning, Dorian," I said, hesitating to mention his foot. I also thought better of mentioning the fact that there was a chance there might be another alchemist in town. It was much more likely that Peter Silverman was a criminal hiding from his past; that would explain why he hated photographs and shunned social media. Dorian had a habit of overreacting.

"If you visit Blue Sky Teas today," he said, tamping down the coffee grounds, "you will see a new cake named after Brixton. I found a large patch of 'wild treasure' blackberries, which the boy loves. Brixton's Blackberry Bread will be on the menu." He turned from the espresso machine and his black eyes grew wide. "*Mon dieu.* I thought you were a morning person."

"That bad, huh?" I hadn't lived with another person in nearly a century. I wasn't used to making myself presentable before breakfast. I ran my fingers through my tangled hair. I gave a start as a clump of hair pulled out into my hand. *It was happening again.* I quickly tossed the hair ball into the trash. Thankfully, Dorian didn't appear to have noticed.

"I would be happy to make you an espresso. Perhaps one that is *très petite*?"

Dorian had ordered the espresso maker on my credit card — without asking me. Since I don't drink coffee, the existence of the contraption caused people to think I had a "friend" who stayed overnight. Brixton's efforts had cemented the gossip that I had a secret French boyfriend. Before he realized he needed to protect Dorian from the world, he'd tried to expose the gargoyle. Though I'd foiled Brixton's attempts to share a video of Dorian, he'd gotten a voice recording of Dorian's deep French-accented voice that he shared with his friends. I couldn't completely deny the existence of a Frenchman, so I made up a story about a platonic friend who was disfigured and therefore shy of meeting anyone new. It was a messy lie, and one I hadn't wanted to tell, but I'd had to act on the spur of the moment to protect Dorian. I especially hated that Max thought I was keeping a male friend from him, though technically that was the case.

"Thanks, but I'll stick with tea." Since the plants and drugs I put into my body affect me so strongly, I've never been able to drink coffee. Decaf would work, but then what's the point? The amount of caffeine in black tea, green tea, or chocolate gives me a boost without turning me into a Berserker. I got myself a glass of water and turned back to the sickly gargoyle. Even though the transformation was hurting me in ways that scared me, I knew what I had to do. "I'll do another plant transformation today, to make your Tea of Ashes."

"*Non.*"

"What do you mean, *no*? Your foot —"

"It is killing you, Zoe." He stepped, rather than hopped, down from the stepping stool. "You think I cannot see what is happening to you? I can no longer ask you to do this for me."

"You're not asking. I'm offering."

The gargoyle's gray lips quivered. "I do not wish us both to die."

"*Neither* of us is going to die," I said firmly. I didn't think it would help anything to mention the fact that if I died it would be a natural death — nothing compared to Dorian's tragic fate of being alive yet trapped in unmoving stone.

"You are a good woman, Zoe. I thank you for trying."

"Dorian —"

"Un moment." He opened the oven door and placed the loaf of bread onto a wooden cutting board. "Do you not wish to tend to your *potager*?"

Though he suggested it to avoid a painful subject, he was right that I wanted to check on my backyard vegetable garden.

"I will be in the dining room with breakfast and the newspaper," Dorian said. "If you wish to join me and speak of other things, I would be happy to save some bread for you."

Denial wasn't healthy, but who was I to judge? I'd done it myself for decades. I desperately wanted to be able to heal Dorian, but after I'd run from alchemy for so long, I didn't know if I alone was capable of that. Was it worth it to speak with the stage magician, just in case Brixton was right?

I left Dorian to his espresso and zucchini bread and went to check on my two gardens: the indoor window-box herb garden and the edible plants in the backyard. Though I'd started my new garden in the midst of a cold and rainy Portland winter, I knew how to coax the best out of plants. Because I wanted to get a good volume in a short amount of time to create Dorian's Tea of Ashes, I'd planted several quick-growing herbs and vegetables, including lemon balm, parsley, leaf lettuces, spinach, sorrel, nettles, and fennel. Most of them could easily take over the garden if not harvested, but that wasn't a problem. The thriving plants gave me a few minutes of peace, but they didn't tell me what I should do about approaching Peter Silverman.

After making sure the plants were tended, I made myself a green smoothie in my vintage Vitamix with greens from the garden plus a green apple for sweetness and a knob of ginger for kick. I wholeheartedly believe that both cars and blenders were perfected in the 1940s. In the modern world of disposable everything, I missed the time when things were built to last.

I found Dorian sitting at the dining table, an empty espresso mug at his side and flaky crumbs from the freshly baked bread scattered across the entire table. Ever the gentleman, he'd saved a quarter of the small loaf on a plate for me.

Directly in front of him were *Le Monde* and two local newspapers. He'd been obsessively reading every word of *Le Monde* for months, ever since the French paper reported gold thefts from European museums. It was an important story to follow because Dorian and I believed the "thefts" not to be thefts at all, but rather the handiwork of unscrupulous alchemists who'd died centuries ago but left false gold behind. Unlike real gold that could be created by true alchemists, the shortcuts of backward alchemy could be used to create false gold. Because intent is important in alchemical transformations, and the intentions of these backward alchemists weren't pure, their false gold was now turning to dust. There hadn't been any recent developments, but after so many years living itinerantly, I enjoyed having newspapers delivered to my doorstep.

"Good riddance!" Dorian declared.

"Did I miss something?"

"This local newspaper reports the last of the treasure hunters have left. My woods can now go back to normal."

The woods near River View Cemetery were one of Dorian's favorite places for nocturnal exploration, and it caused him grief that so many interlopers were sneaking around "his" domain.

"Did someone find the hoard?" I asked.

"That does not appear to be the case." He chortled.

"What's so funny?" I looked over his shoulder. "*THREE INJURED IN FALL NEAR RIVER VIEW CEMETERY.* That headline doesn't sound very amusing to me."

"Not that dreary article." Dorian pointed a claw at another column. "The gossip columnist is much more dramatic, writing of monsoons and masterminds. *Écoute.*"

LAKE LOOT TREASURE HUNTERS GIVE UP HOPE. Amateur treasure hunters from throughout the Pacific Northwest flooded to Portland in February, after monsoon-like rains led to the discovery of jewels from a 1969 train robbery. Two months later, those treasure hunters have abandoned their quest. Graphic images of injuries sustained by three men caught in a second landslide were leaked to the press. Since then, no treasure hunters have been seen on the hillside.

A source close to the police department told this reporter that the photographs were purposefully released to scare other amateur treasure hunters away from exploring the cordoned-off area still considered a high risk for landslides.

"What else does the columnist say of interest? Mmm . . . *Oui . . . Bon.*"

I took the newspaper from his hands.

"I was reading!" he protested.

"You stopped reading aloud. Let me do it."

In 1969, mastermind Franklin Thorne robbed the wealthy Lake family's private train car and killed guard Arnold Burke. Thorne was subsequently killed in a shoot-out with the police. Since the brazen train heist, the stolen jewels, dubbed the Lake Loot, remained elusive . . . until February of this year, when torrential rains caused a landslide in the hills near River View Cemetery. Days later, a sapphire necklace from the robbery was discovered near the Willamette River by two boys playing at the river's edge. Since the boys found this small portion of the Lake Loot, treasure hunters flocked to the area.

"Zoe," Dorian cut in.

I looked up.

He held out a clawed hand. "May I?"

"What's the matter with how I'm reading it?"

"Your voice lacks a certain *je ne sais quoi.*"

"I'm not reading melodramatically enough for you?"

Dorian blinked at me. "It is a dramatic

story. It calls for a dramatic reading."

"Here." I handed over the newspaper.

Worried about another landslide, authorities blocked off the area and declared they would arrest anyone caught trespassing. But the lure of missing train-heist loot was too great. This announcement was clearly a misstep, one that simply caused the treasure hunters to return under cover of darkness, under more dangerous conditions that led to three men sustaining critical injuries. Was it the thrill of the chase that lured Oregonians to danger? If found, the distinctive jewels must be returned to their rightful owners, the Lake family, who have offered a small reward. Julian Lake, the 80-year-old survivor of the 1969 robbery, had no comment on recent developments . . .

"That's not the end. Why did you stop reading?"

"Forty-six years," Dorian murmured. "People speak of this as if it is a long time!" He tossed aside the newspaper and cleared the table.

It was time for me to descend the stairs to my basement alchemy lab. Dorian may object to my continued production of his tea, but I wasn't about to let him simply return to stone. Instead of turning on the overhead light, I lit an oil lamp. It put me in a better frame of mind to practice alchemy.

But instead of peace, I felt confusion. The scent from the night before had vanished. It must have been my overly active imagination. Since I'm not a night person, I must have been too tired to think straight. I wished that my own body's reaction to creating Dorian's Tea of Ashes was nothing but my imagination. I was much sicker than I wanted to admit to either Dorian or to myself. If I didn't find a true solution, soon I would waste away as completely as the plants I was about to turn to ash.

Six

Inside my makeshift alchemy lab, I tried to focus. In the past three months, I'd made fourteen glass vessels explode, sent seven streams of green liquid shooting up to the ceiling — with a stiff neck from cleaning the ceiling to prove it — and had created four tinctures with scents so noxious I couldn't use the basement for days.

This wasn't how things were supposed to go.

In the eighty years since I'd pulled away from practicing alchemy, I'd lost my touch. Big time. Processes that were once second nature to me were now faded memories. When I recalled those years working side by side with my beloved Ambrose, my partner in both life and in alchemy for four decades, I felt as if I was watching an out-of-focus film about someone else's life. I'd continued working with herbs for food and herbal remedies, so my gardens always thrived, my dried herbs transformed boring soups into vibrant ones, and my tinctures and teas were effective remedies.

As for the more complex transformations I'd rejected for causing more grief than joy, such as unleashing the philosopher's stone — that's where I was blocked. I was unable to reach the white phase of a transformation where new energy rises from the ashes.

I reached for the locket I kept close but rarely opened. It was enough to feel the carved gold. I already knew every detail of the two faces inside, one a miniature portrait from 1701, the other a black-and-white photograph from 1904.

It didn't matter whether I worked in my alchemy lab with the plant transformations that used to come so easily to me, or whether I sat at my dining table surrounded by books that could shed light on the coded instructions in *Not Untrue Alchemy.* Nothing was coming back to me.

In the past three months, since meeting my unique friend, I hadn't made nearly as much progress on his strange alchemy book as I'd hoped. Perhaps my biggest failing was that I no longer knew how to find any true alchemists. I had wasted quite a bit of time that winter trying to find someone who could help, only to come up empty. I'd never finished my alchemical training, so there were missing gaps in my knowledge of the history of alchemy.

The thing about alchemists is that they love codes. After reading every word of the book myself and having the Latin translated by an expert, I felt I knew less than I did when I started. The Latin clearly stated that to reinforce the words, the practitioner must look to the pictures.

Retired chemistry professor Ivan Danko was helping me translate the coded messages hidden in the woodcut illustrations of the book. But despite his passion for alchemy as a precursor to modern chemistry, his assistance wasn't the same as having a true alchemist at my side. Ivan thought of our work as a scholarly exercise to understand history. He didn't know the true reason for my interest, nor did he know that alchemy was real. It was understandable that he devoted more time to his own historical research than to helping me with *Not Untrue Alchemy*.

And because I had to use so much strength to create the "quick fix" Tea of Ashes that kept Dorian alive in the short term, I didn't have the time and energy to fully devote myself to the larger issue of a solution that could cure the gargoyle for good. I knew there was a better solution within reach, though. I pulled Dorian's book from the shelf. It fell open to the same page it always did. The page with the Latin that had brought Dorian to life. *The book had to hold the key.*

This image of a basilisk had always disturbed me. The creature with the head of a bird and the body of a serpent was nothing unusual in coded alchemical illustrations, but this basilisk was different. His serpent's tail was wound counterclockwise and hung down at an unnatural angle. Yet instead of writhing in pain, the creature was void of expression. *Too* void; he was dead. His stiff body clung to the sole turret that remained in a wasteland of castle ruins. Through the union of a bird and a dragon, the basilisk symbolized the blending of mercury and sulfur.

I was distracted by a sweet scent. I glanced around my lab, wondering where it could be coming from. I looked up to the ceiling, where some of my exploding experiments were still embedded, looking rather like constellations. It was a fitting image, since alchemists look to the planets in the heavens for guidance about when to begin different transformations. I wondered if any flowers had germinated on the ceiling and made a mental note to take care of that. But for now, I turned back to the book.

Birds are highly symbolic to alchemists, because an egg is the perfect vessel, hermetically sealed and representing the whole universe. Different birds symbolized different alchemical processes. For example, a self-sacrificing pelican signified distillation, and a phoenix represented the final phase that produced the philosopher's stone. In this way, alchemists could instill their teachings in codes that could be passed down through illustrated books that only the initiated would understand. During the height of alchemy in the Middle Ages, coded messages carved into public buildings were the norm.

Other animals were used in alchemical codes as well. Toads symbolized the First Matter (itself a riddle), and bees signaled purification and rebirth. However, the bees in this book didn't seem to have gotten the message. In the woodcut illustrations in *Non Degenera Alchemia,* the skies were full of bees swarming in a counterclockwise direction, with rogue bees stinging the eyes of the people and animals on the ground. I shivered.

I turned the page to get away from the disturbing basilisk illustration, only to come to an even more disturbing one. This page showed the Black Dragon, which symbolized death and decay, and was a code for antimony. Antimony was Isaac Newton's favorite substance, because of its starlike crystal shape, which he thought could explain light and the universe. This Black Dragon was picking his way through another set of ruins. Death surrounded him, yet he appeared to be alive. Fierce flames escaped the dragon's mouth. I slammed the book shut, wondering if I was subconsciously avoiding working with it because of its psychological effect on me.

Something had to change. I couldn't keep this up much longer.

The book had shaken my ability to focus, so it would be pointless to either work in the lab or try to translate the obscure symbols in the book's woodcut illustrations. A knot formed in my stomach as the images from Dorian's book swirled through my mind. I had to get out of the house. *Away from the book.*

I nearly ran from the house as I left to take a walk to clear my head. I walked through Lone Fir Cemetery, a peaceful park not far from my house. I couldn't stop thinking about the strange scent from my bookshelf. I knew I must have imagined it.

Books might become moldy and begin to smell stale, but not sweet. And even if my plant transformations had resulted in plant seedlings sprouting in the basement, they wouldn't give off the aroma I'd smelled. Clove-scented honey. *That's* what the sweet scent had been! The scents of spring that surrounded me in the cemetery made it impossible to ignore the memory.

I hurried home and went straight to the bookshelf in the locked basement. I again pulled *Not Untrue Alchemy* from the shelf. I brought the pages to my nose and breathed deeply. I inhaled the musty, woody aroma that I found in most centuries-old books. Underneath the obvious was the distinct scent of honey. This was where the scent was coming from. *Dorian's book.*

I've worked with a lot of old books, but I'd never encountered anything like this morphing sweet scent. I wondered if Ivan had.

I hadn't seen Ivan in several weeks. He'd come down with pneumonia at the tail end of winter, which hit him hard because he suffered from a degenerative illness. He didn't like to talk about the specifics, so I didn't know what was wrong with him. After getting back on his feet, he'd been intent on making up for lost time in his own research.

I'd brought him a healing garlic tincture when he was sick, but I had respected his wishes and left him in peace to catch up on his own research now that he was well. But this wasn't the time to be polite. If Dorian's book was truly *changing,* this was a breakthrough I couldn't ignore.

I reached for my phone.

"Dobrý den," Ivan's voice said on the other end of the line, and when I identified myself he switched to English. "I'm so glad you called, Zoe," he said in his Czech accent. "I wanted to thank you for the tincture you brought me when I was sick."

"I hope it helped."

"Do you want to know something about being Czech?" he asked. "People often think my accent sounds Transylvanian. They encourage me to dress up as Dracula for Halloween. Especially a young girl who lives next door to me. Her name is Sara. She wears a scarf around her neck each day. I thought it was a fashion statement for a seven-year-old finding herself, but I learned from her mother it was because she was protecting herself from Dracula. One night, when her parents did not realize what she was doing, she watched an old black-and-white Dracula movie, and it made her think she lived next door to a vampire."

With Ivan's graying hair and scruffy beard, I couldn't imagine him as the romantic Hollywood version of Dracula. But there was a stoic strength to Ivan. He didn't dwell on his health problems, instead undertaking an ambitious research project he wanted to finish before he died. His light blue eyes always shone with intelligence and determination. No, I couldn't see him as Dracula. But I could see him as Vlad the Impaler.

"Thanks to your garlic tincture," he continued, "Sara says there's no way I could be Dracula."

I laughed. "I hope it helped your infection too."

"That it did. *Děkuju.* I'm back to work on my book. Sara has christened herself my research assistant, fetching me the books in my home library I can no longer climb to retrieve."

"About your library," I said, "I have a question for you." I paused and chose my words carefully. "Have you ever encountered an old alchemy book that smelled sweet, compared to the more typical moldy smell?"

He chuckled. "Once, at the Klementinum, a patron was banned for sprinkling a rosewater perfume on a foul-smelling book."

"What about the scent of honey?"

"Honey?" Ivan hesitated, and when he

resumed, there was a change in his voice that caused my skin to prickle. "It's curious that you mention honey. I think I may have something that would interest you."

I gripped the phone. "You have a book like that?"

"I remember it because of the unnerving nature of the woodcut illustration." He paused, and I could picture him shuddering. "I hadn't thought of it until you mentioned honey, but now I see it clearly in my mind." As he spoke, the tone of his voice changed from casual to agitated. "Perhaps it's best to leave it alone."

"Why?" I asked, the tenor of my own voice reacting to his worry.

"It's an image I don't know that I will ever forget, Zoe," Ivan said hesitantly. "I don't know if you want to see this."

SEVEN

I assured Ivan that I could handle looking at a disturbing image. He told me he was at Blue Sky Teas and had his research with him on his laptop, so I told him I'd be right there.

The teashop was on Hawthorne, walking distance from my house. My mind always calmed down several notches as I walked through the door beneath the sign that read "*There is no trouble so great or grave that cannot be diminished by a nice cup of tea* — Bernard-Paul Heroux." Inside, a weeping fig tree stretched up to the high ceiling, casting peaceful shadows across the redwood tree-ring tabletops.

A woman in her late twenties rushed out from behind the counter so quickly her blond braids whipped around her head.

"Zoe!" Brixton's mom stood on the balls of her bare feet and threw her arms around me. "You really outdid yourself with today's treats. Can I double my order for weekend mornings? I'm nearly out of these oatmeal cakes. Who knew so many people would think vegan food was so tasty?"

"Definitely," I said, looking around at the long line of patrons. Dorian would be thrilled.

Blue Sky Teas was started by our mutual friend Blue, who'd been cleared of a murder charge but was currently serving a short jail sentence for a previous crime. During Blue's absence, Brixton's young mom, Heather, was keeping Blue Sky Teas open for limited hours, which helped both women. Heather was trying to become a professional painter. She had the talent to pull it off, but she hadn't made much money at it yet. I was surprised Brixton wasn't helping her today. It was midmorning on a Saturday, so maybe he was still asleep. When I was young, there was no way a fourteen-year-old kid would be allowed to sleep in. Then again, when I was young, fourteen-year-old's weren't thought of as kids.

Brixton and Heather used to live only a few blocks away, but they were now living temporarily at Blue's cottage in a field on the outskirts of Portland. At the cottage, Heather had more space for her painting.

The recent floods that had swept through Portland inspired her to create a new series of paintings featuring water, and the cottage was strewn with painted canvasses in various stages of completion. Brixton had a stepdad, too, who he adored, but I hadn't met the man. Abel was out of town for work most of the time. The nature of his work hadn't been volunteered, so I hadn't enquired.

Heather retreated behind the counter, and I joined Ivan at a table near the window. A quart-size mason jar filled with yellow daffodils and white trillium declared that spring had begun. The vase of wildflowers dominated the table, dwarfing the emaciated man sitting there.

Ivan Danko hadn't been this small a man when I'd met him earlier that winter. Although his ongoing illness seemed stable, his recent bout of pneumonia had taken its toll. His blue eyes had a cast of gray, and his short beard was ragged. He'd barely touched his breakfast.

"I thought I had an image of the book on my laptop," Ivan said after we exchanged pleasantries, "but I was mistaken. I'm sorry to have sent you on a fool's errand."

My heart sank. Each time I thought I was coming close to a breakthrough with Dorian's book, something got in my way. It was as if the universe was teasing me. "Do you remember anything about it?"

"I don't know exactly how to explain it," Ivan said. "It would be easiest to show you."

I stared at him. "Wait, I thought you didn't have it."

"Not here. In my home library. I'm nearly done with my tea. Do you want to accompany me back to my house?"

"I'll get my tea to go."

Ivan lived in a small house on the north side of Hawthorne Boulevard. We walked to his home, breathing in the sweet scents of plum and cherry trees, newly blossoming as spring took hold after an especially brutal winter. I made an effort not to speed up our leisurely pace to the brisk walking I preferred, since I knew Ivan hadn't been well.

One look at his house made it clear that the retired professor of chemistry was a scholar. Ivan had transformed the largest room of his house into an alchemy library. He was writing a book about the unsung heroes of science — scientists who experimented with alchemy as part of their work. Isaac Newton was one of the more famous scientists who conducted alchemical experiments. Knowing how men of science viewed alchemy, Newton had hidden his work, yet he felt it was important enough to continue in secret.

Finishing his academic book on unsung scientists who worked on alchemy was Ivan's goal before he died. I was again struck by the collection he'd amassed.

"It's here somewhere," he said, rooting around in a stack of papers on a side table. "Now if only I could remember where I put it . . ."

While he searched, I looked around the room. The oak bookshelves had been custom-made to fit into the dimensions of the room, including a low bookshelf that ran underneath the window that dominated one wall. The window looked out onto evergreen trees that towered over the house, making this the perfect room for contemplative research. On the window sill were several photos, including a recent one of him and Max smiling as they held giant beer steins. The two men were friends who'd met as regulars at Blue Sky Teas.

A photo album lay open on Ivan's desk. An enlarged photograph showed Ivan as a young man. I stepped closer to his desk to take a better look at the photograph. Ivan was pictured with two other men in Staromestske Namesti, the historic Old

Town Square in Prague, in front of the famous astrological clock. He wore a beard even then, and his hair was just as unkempt. The buttons of his white dress shirt were mismatched. I smiled, amused to see he'd always been an absentminded professor.

Ivan reached across me and closed the album.

"I've never asked you why you left Prague," I said. "Wouldn't it have been easier to write this book there, in the heart of alchemical history?"

He looked to the photo album, a mixture of joy and sadness on his face. "Too many painful memories. Someone so young will not fully understand —"

"I thought you said I was an old soul."

Ivan gave me a sad smile. "Before I came to be at peace with my illness, I behaved quite foolishly. I tell people my condition made it necessary for me to take early retirement. This is true — up to a point. Had I acted better, the university would have kept me on as a professor emeritus, with my office and research privileges." He closed his eyes and was lost in thought for a few moments. "But that choice was taken away from me, by my own actions. I couldn't accept that I was losing control of my body. I'd like to blame it on the illness affecting my mind, but that would be a lie; my mind is as sharp as it ever was."

"Which is its own curse," I murmured. "You're fully aware that your body is failing and everything that means."

Ivan's eyes lit up. "You do understand."

I thought of Dorian but didn't speak. I took Ivan's hand, which was far too frail for someone in his mid-fifties, and squeezed it gently.

"I was angry," Ivan said. "I lashed out at everyone around me and went down a self-destructive path. I went back-and-forth between looking for false cures and drowning myself with alcohol. The university asked me to take an early retirement, to avoid a scandal. It was too painful to stay in Prague, where I spent so many happy years in my youth. And I did not wish the people who knew me before to see this is what I became. In this modern age, research is possible anywhere."

"It's not the same."

"I had the choice of staying in Prague but being too angry to do my research, or going somewhere else where I could focus completely on my book before I die." He cleared his throat and looked away. I gave him space, but he didn't need long. "Ah! Here it is."

I took a piece of paper from his hands. Not only was it a printout of a scanned copy, but it was the image of a secondary source, not an original alchemy book. The top half of the page contained explanatory text in German, and the lower half showed a poor-quality photograph of an illustration in an alchemy book. The yellowed page looked like a woodcut, as was common for alchemical reproductions. Though the image was blurred, I made out the central image of a cherubic angel trapped in a prison of flames, with bees circling above in a counterclockwise circle.

Backward alchemy.

I felt myself shaking with fear and excitement as I took in all the details. On the edge of the image, outside the flames, two men were dressed as jesters. Though the book had been damaged, the image was clear enough to reveal that the bees were stinging the men's eyes.

The bees in Dorian's alchemy book were used in a similarly unsettling way. But here in this image, there was something more. I realized why Ivan had said the image was so disturbing. The hair on my arms stood up as my gaze fell to the eyes of the angel. The absolute horror in her eyes cut through my core, bridging the gap between the printed page and the ground beneath my feet.

"I told you it was alarming," Ivan said. "It is much worse than any horror movie, no?"

It had always amazed me how much life artists could breathe into an image, even when all they had was a knife and a piece of wood. "Why did my question make you think of this illustration?"

"Honey," Ivan said. "The scent of honey. This is a book *about* alchemy, not an original alchemy book itself. The author of this scholarly book made a notation that when working with this alchemy book, he detected the scent of honey. Apparently, honey was used as a preservative. Counterintuitive, but alchemists have always been known for being ahead of their time."

"Where did this book come from?" I asked. Ivan and the author's theory of honey as a preservative didn't ring true, but something was going on.

"The academic text is in a German university archive," Ivan said, "but unfortunately the original source is unknown. The woodcut illustration was found as three single sheets of paper in a French bookshop."

I nodded. "From the blackened edges, it's clear the book was badly damaged."

"Ah!" Ivan said. "That's what I thought myself at first. But take a closer look. This photograph is of the three pages *together.*"

I squinted. "They're overlaid," I whispered.

"Alchemists and their codes," Ivan said. "Here, the author notes that the flames were from a subsequent page, yet when the pages are placed together, the flames trace the edges of the angel."

The way the images were overlaid created a *new* meaning. Was it on purpose? Or by accident? Looking more closely at the photographic image on the page, it looked as if the paper had been scorched at the edges. And were those granules of soot? Without the original, there was no way to tell.

"Can you read me the rest of the text?" I asked. I'm good at picking up languages, but I never learned German. To blend in completely — to hide in plain sight — I've found it best to become fluent in a handful of languages, rather than gaining a superficial understanding of many more. Along with a deep understanding of a few languages, I'm good at picking up the local vernacular of a certain time and place. Unlike some alchemists I've known who would cling to outdated speech patterns, I've adapted.

Ivan explained that the rest of the text on

the page theorized that the image was a warning about the dangers of alchemy. I knew better. This image told of backward alchemy's death rotation. Ivan knew of my "scholarly" interest in it, but he hadn't connected this illustration with backward alchemy. I shouldn't have been surprised; it was an obscure subject, even for alchemists and alchemy scholars. His oversight drove home the fact that Ivan's help wasn't enough. I needed to find someone familiar with backward alchemy. I needed to find a true alchemist. The magician Prometheus?

"The passage ends," Ivan said, "by noting that half of the angel's body is stone."

I gave a start, and my eyes grew wide as I looked to the lower half of the angel's body. This was one thing the scholar was right about. With the blurry quality of the photograph I hadn't noticed before, but now that I looked for it, it was obvious. The angel's legs fused into a stone boulder, the two becoming one. She was trapped by her own body.

It was exactly what was happening to Dorian.

My phone buzzed, startling me out of the disturbing implications of this new information. A text message from Brixton popped up on my phone, saying there was an emergency and I had to get back right away.

WHAT EMERGENCY? I texted back.

He didn't reply. I called him. He hated talking on the phone, so I didn't expect him to answer. But he did.

"Zoe! He's here!"

"Who's *where*?"

"Get over to your house."

"Who —"

"It's the magician! I knew I was right. He's an alchemist — and he's right here —"

"He came to see me?" How would he know where I lived? And more importantly, *why* would he seek me out?

"No. He's a *criminal,* Zoe. He's —"

My blood went cold. "Brix, if he's breaking into the house" — the line went dead — "call the police," I said to dead air.

I tried to calm my breathing. One day that boy was going to cry wolf one too many times . . . But I'd never forgive myself if this was something real. I'd given Brixton a key to my house when he'd stayed with me for a few days. He rarely used it after that, but what if he was at the house and the magician-alchemist was trying to get inside? All I knew was that Peter Silverman was a criminal of some kind. And a kid wasn't going to stop him.

EIGHT

NOTRE DAME DE PARIS, 1845

Someone must have broken into the room and switched documents. Surely that was the only explanation for the content of the papers strewn across the architect's desk.

Eugène Viollet-le-Duc frowned. He looked from old architectural drawings of Notre Dame de Paris to sketches of the cathedral over the centuries. These records couldn't be right, could they? Yet Viollet-le-Duc could not fathom the purpose of such a deception.

The world-renowned architect and artist had been hired along with Jean-Baptiste-Antoine Lassus to restore the grand cathedral. To Viollet-le-Duc, "restore" was a broad term. He had plans to bring the outdated building into the nineteenth century. He dreamed of simultaneously restoring the previous glory of the cathedral and adding modern flourishes to show the new generation how glorious the Paris institution truly was.

To ensure his own additions would be perfectly integrated, the architect gathered official historical records and sought out artists' renditions of the cathedral over the centuries.

Now that he had both sets of records before him, something wasn't right.

The cathedral's construction had begun in 1163, and modifications had continued for centuries. The prolonged construction was due to both expanding the site's glory to God and taking advantage of new advances in architecture. Viollet-le-Duc planned to use modern architectural styles and techniques, as his predecessors had done with their own generations' discoveries. There was also more to be done than restoration and expansion. There was also rebuilding sections that had been destroyed. During the French Revolution of the previous century, which had ended shortly before his birth, the revolutionaries had destroyed anything they felt symbolized nobility. Religious symbols of the Kings of Judah on the façade of Notre Dame had been mistaken for Kings of France, and therefore defaced.

Yet if he could believe the drawings

made by multiple artists, the old carvings on the façade hadn't simply been vandalized. At different points in the cathedral's history, the carvings on the façade had been altered to give them new meaning.

That meant not all of the destruction had been done to deface the monument, as he'd been led to believe.

Viollet-le-Duc hastily unfurled the official plans and sketches in his possession. None of them showed the strange writing carved into the facade. He turned his attention back to the drawings that showed the real carvings. With a magnifying lens, he looked more closely. *Riddles.* These words made no sense. What a strange thing!

And what was this? He looked more closely, focusing the magnifying lens. A drawing of the cathedral before the French Revolution showed a man holding a book. The stone book bore the Latin words *Non Degenera Alchemia.*

Viollet-le-Duc chuckled to himself. Stonemasons often bemoaned that they were uncredited for their efforts. To be remembered, they would sometimes carve representations of themselves into their work. The stone carvers who worked on this section of Notre Dame must have had a good sense of humor. They had put their own secret joke in a place that would be seen by scores of people. He appreciated the effort, and regretted that he was obliged to restore that section to its original meaning.

Suddenly seized with inspiration, he cleared the desk and sat down with his notebook open in front of him. With an expert hand, he began to sketch. A winged creature took form beneath his pen. This was no angel; it was a gargoyle.

He paused, picturing the current cathedral in his mind. Weathered stone gargoyles already surrounded much of the old church. Though far enough from the ground that one had to squint to see their details, those gargoyles had always inspired his imagination. It was a shame that their function as waterspouts also meant they naturally crumbled within decades rather than centuries. He wished to carve larger chimeras that could be appreciated both from the street below and up close. Grotesques that would not be hindered by being functional waterspouts. Viollet-le-Duc imagined a gallery high atop the cathedral, where commoners could climb to view the splendid city and also get a closer look at the architectural details of the cathedral itself. High above the stonemasons' alchemy joke, this would be his Gallery of Chimeras.

Nine

When I reached the sidewalk in front of my house, the first thing that came into view was the rooftop tarp that covered the hole Dorian used to climb out from the attic. Since his stone form had been carved as a prototype for a statue on the gallery of gargoyles that adorned Notre Dame, he felt most natural coming and going through the opening high above the ground.

Rushing up to the house, I found Brixton sitting on the bench on my porch, calmly strumming his guitar. There was no emergency in sight.

"It's *him,* Zoe." Brixton set his guitar aside and picked up a hardbound book with library markings on the spine. "Prometheus. The alchemist."

I groaned. "Brixton! I don't have time for more theories. I was in the middle of something import—" I broke off when I saw the page he'd turned to. Brixton was holding the old library book open to a page with a photograph of the man we knew to be Peter Silverman. I lifted the book from his hands.

"The website where I first saw his picture is still down," Brixton said, "so I went to the library and got a library card to check this out to show you."

On the page was a photograph of the stage magician I'd seen last night. He looked roughly the same age he was now, around fifty, but with a different hairstyle and mustache. There was something eerily disturbing about this photograph. Something I couldn't quite put my finger on, but it wiped the smile off my face. I've never been a fan of mustaches, but that wasn't it. In this closeup photograph, the man I knew as the magician Prometheus stared past the camera with vacant eyes that sent a shiver down my spine.

"He's *dead,*" I whispered, realizing what was wrong with the photograph. "This photograph was taken after he was dead."

"He was supposedly killed in a shootout with the police, after he killed some guy during a robbery."

I flipped to the cover of the frayed hardback book. It was a book about infamous Portland murderers throughout history. Brixton wasn't simply claiming Peter Silverman was an alchemist. The man in this photograph was a *murderer.*

The caption read: *Franklin Thorne, killed by Oregon state troopers in 1969.*

1969. *Nearly 50 years ago.* The murderous magician hadn't aged a day.

"I told you he's an alchemist," Brixton said. "He must have found the Elixir of Life like you did, so he wasn't really dead. Just pretending. Now you know he really could help you with Dorian's book! I told you my idea for a database of alchemists was a good one. It would have saved me from getting a library card."

I shook my head. "The magician from last night's show must be related to this man. I'm sorry I doubted that you recognized him, but you can trust me on this point. The simplest explanation is usually the right one."

I've been around long enough to know the most straightforward answer is almost always the right one. *Almost* being the key word. But I didn't want to admit my doubts to Brixton. It was still much more likely that the magician was simply related to this infamous murderer. Striking resemblances occur within families. That reality is why people readily accepted that I'm the granddaughter of a woman who looked remarkably like me. That's much more believable to people than the truth that I'm the same woman. But what if my secret situation was true for this man, too?

Brixton took the book back. "I looked up more about Franklin Thorne while waiting for you to get here. Truly, they're not related. This guy Thorne didn't have any family."

Franklin Thorne. Why did that name sound familiar?

"The Lake Loot!" I cried.

"Yeah. Duh."

The missing train heist loot had recently been discovered. That's what must have brought Peter Silverman to town.

I made Brixton wait while I looked it up myself. As far as I could tell, Brixton was right that the two men weren't related. And neither had any connection to alchemy.

"A publicity hoax!" I said. "Maybe he cultivated the look. It would be great publicity for a guy who goes by the stage name Prometheus to pretend to be immortal."

"He couldn't have altered this library book," Brixton said. "The pages are all faded."

"No, and he probably wouldn't have gone to all the trouble," I whispered. I knew it was technically possible to create an illusion with so many layers of complexity, but a hidden library book didn't make any sense. Why go to the effort? "Wait, you said at first you remembered this man from a history book, and then realized you originally saw this photo on a website?"

"Yeah, that Murderous Portland site I follow."

After being trapped by a real murderer earlier in the year, Brixton had given up on daring activities, such as the B&E that had caused him to meet me and Dorian. In place of this risky hobby, he'd taken to the more macabre, but safer, activity of learning about Portland's murderous history. He was enamored with a website set up by a graduate student at Portland State that was devoted to Portland's seedy past, from its founding in the 1840s through the end of the twentieth century. Brixton had seemed most interested in the earlier Wild West era, but apparently he'd read about more recent crimes as well.

"But the site was hacked and it's still down," Brixton continued. "What's the matter?"

"That's an awfully big coincidence for the site to be down as soon as Peter Silverman arrived in town. I don't like it. If this was a publicity stunt, Prometheus would want to get the photograph out all over the Internet. But instead, the biggest site that makes his photo available is down. It's as if he *doesn't* want to be found."

"That's what I said," Brixton grumbled. "It's like you're not even listening to me."

Brixton had cried wolf twice in as many months, but that's not what made me skeptical. It was the fact that alchemists were so few in number. Even when I'd been studying alchemy, before I ran from it, I knew very few people who'd discovered its secrets. Granted, I knew fewer alchemists than my male counterparts did. Aside from Nicolas and Perenelle Flamel, most were skeptical of female alchemists. I'd apprenticed to Nicolas at the start of the eighteenth century, two hundred years after he and his wife had faked their own deaths in Paris. Because he was a cautious man who valued his privacy, even Nicolas didn't know many true alchemists. And I'd lost track of the Flamels in 1704. I didn't even know if they were still alive.

There had once been a larger number of practicing alchemists. However, even in periods of time where there had been a flurry of alchemical interest and activity, few people unlocked the secrets of alchemy. Most alchemists died either accidentally poisoning themselves in their laboratories or naturally of old age. Very few of us had found the Elixir of Life. There were more plausible explanations as to why Peter Silverman resembled Franklin Thorne.

Still, there was no way the complexity of a publicity stunt included altering obscure library books. There was more going on here than I understood.

"Shouldn't you be getting over to the teashop to help your mom?"

Brixton rolled his eyes, but he stood up and slung the guitar over his back. He paused before hopping onto his bike. "You know you're wearing Mom Jeans, right?" he said.

"That bad?"

"Worse. So much worse."

That was the last straw. My bank account was too low to commission the tailored clothing I was used to, I didn't want to put in the hours required to sew myself clothing from scratch, and I doubted I could afford anything decent from a department store — not to mention the fact that I didn't understand the social mores of shopping in a multi-floor department store inside a mall. That was one modern invention I'd only watched from afar. One of the few times I'd ventured inside a mall, my senses had been assaulted by a barrage of perfumes and powders that the "helpful" sales clerks wanted to show me. I fled before making it through the cosmetics section. But I was only putting off the inevitable. I was too old to get better at transmuting lead into gold, but learning how to shop in a mall had to be marginally easier. Didn't it? As soon as I figured out how to save Dorian, I would reinvent myself.

"I'll look after the library book," I said. As soon as Brixton disappeared down the driveway, I hopped into my truck. I had my own destination to reach. I didn't know what to make of the alchemical woodcut that showed an angel turning to stone, but there was something much more immediate I could do.

The library's newspaper archives were extensive. I had no trouble finding scans of the original newspaper editions from the spring of 1969, when the infamous train robbery had taken place.

In the days following the crime that had killed guard Arnold Burke — and resulted in the thief's death as well — the local newspapers reported on different aspects of the train heist. Several reporters quoted conflicting accounts of the heist from eyewitnesses, one reporter wrote a profile of the heroic guard, and an enterprising investigative journalist dug into the past of Franklin Thorne so quickly that his story appeared the day after the heist. There was also speculation about what would have driven Thorne, a toy maker, to become a thief. The most widely accepted explanation was that the Thorne family had once been quite wealthy, but had fallen on hard times a generation before. As wide-ranging as the stories were, all of the reporters agreed on one thing: aside from a childless older sister, Franklin Thorne had no family.

I read through newspaper stories from the first few days after the theft and shootings, then I rested my head on the library table and closed my eyes. The fake wood surface smelled of plastic and bleach. Peter Silverman, aka stage magician Prometheus, aka murderous thief Franklin Thorne, had nothing to do with me. He wasn't here to find a fellow alchemist. He was here to retrieve riches he stole decades ago, now that renewed interest meant that someone else could get their hands on it.

I lifted my head, and my hand moved instinctively back to the archives. I stopped myself. *Peter Silverman isn't your problem, Zoe.*

But if Brixton was right, could he be my solution?

TEN

"Why are you sitting on the sofa in your *imperméable*?" asked my gargoyle, his dark gray brows drawn together.

"I was all set to go out and confront a problem, until I thought better of it." I sat stiffly on the green velvet couch, my silver raincoat buttoned over my awkward clothing and the keys to my truck in my hands.

If Peter Silverman was a murderer who was back in town to find the loot he thought was lost, why would he admit to being an alchemist? Even if I could get him to open up to me, was an alliance with a dangerous alchemist worth the risk? I've survived for centuries because I listen to my intuition. And my intuition was screaming at me that I should steer clear of Peter Silverman. But at the same time, if his help could save Dorian's life . . .

Dorian hopped up on the couch next to me. His feet didn't touch the ground. "I suppose it is too much to ask an alchemist to avoid speaking in riddles."

"I don't mean to be enigmatic. Take a look at this book." I lifted the library book from the coffee table and opened it to the bookmarked page.

"The Fire God magician," Dorian remarked. "Prometheus. I would not have thought him good enough to merit being featured in a book. It is an unflattering photograph, no?"

"Take a look at the title of the book. It's a book about Portland's infamous murderers."

Dorian's snout twitched as he looked from the front cover to the information about the photograph. "But this is . . . How is this possible? It says this man was killed by *les flics* in 1969."

"I think he's an alchemist. A real one who's discovered the Elixir of Life." Something was wrong with that picture, though. Alchemists aren't immortal. If he was truly dead, as this picture indicated, there were only two ways he could have come back to life. One, he could have faked his death in the first place. Two, it was possible he could have used backward alchemy, the same unnatural alchemy that had brought Dorian to life and was now killing him.

"*C'est vrai?* Is it true? But this is wonderful! You have had such difficulty locating another true alchemist all these months. Monsieur Danko means to help you, yet he is not a true alchemist, and cannot know your true mission. Why is your face grave, Zoe? Working with a learned alchemist who may have been alive longer than you, this could help you decipher my book, no?"

"He's a *murderer,* Dorian."

Dorian waved his hand through the air. "You fail to see the big picture. Ah! I am settling into American life so well that I am using American idioms! Did you hear?"

I sighed. "I'm glad you're feeling more at home in Portland, but the big picture generally includes staying *far away* from murderers who the police felt necessary to shoot several times."

"Yes, but —" He broke off. "*Attendez.* Why did he come back?"

"Look at his name."

"Franklin Thorne? Ah! He is the man who stole the Lake Loot that has enticed these meddlesome treasure hunters."

"He would have been forced to leave town quickly at the time, unable to get the loot without being found out. But now that enough time has passed, he most likely wants to retrieve the rest of it before someone else finds it, since part of the stash has already been discovered."

"*Mais,* why would he care for jewels?" Dorian asked. "He could simply make gold."

"As you've seen, not all alchemists are good at transmuting lead into gold."

Dorian frowned. "I thought you were a special case."

"It's a huge depletion of energy for anyone. It's the level of difficulty to complete the transformation, and how quickly we recover, that's personal. But we're getting off track. Dorian — if he truly died in that shoot-out, and it's the same man we saw on stage last night, he had to use unnatural means to bring himself back from the dead. He would have to be using backward alchemy."

"That is even better! He might understand my book." Dorian grinned, his wings wriggling in his excitement.

"If he doesn't steal it first." My hand flew to my mouth. I hadn't realized the implication of my words until I'd spoken them out loud. There was *another* reason besides the valuable jewelry that could have lured an alchemist who practiced backward alchemy to Portland in the first place. "An immoral alchemist," I said slowly, "might want *Not*

Untrue Alchemy to use himself."

Dorian gaped at me, his dark gray tongue hanging over his light-gray little teeth. "You think," he said, "he is here to steal my book?"

I shook my head, shaking free of my confused thoughts. "I can't see how it's possible. Even if he knew of the book's existence, there's no way for him to know it's here." Alchemists can't sense each other from afar. Up close, there are subtle cues, mostly inadvertent slipups that show we were alive during periods of time we couldn't possibly have otherwise experienced. It's not like we're surrounded by an aura that other alchemists can see.

"The scent of the book is most strong," Dorian said. "Could he have sensed it that way? I have never smelled anything like the strange scents in this book. And as a chef, I have smelled many things."

"The sweet scents in the book aren't unique. It's only odd that they're coming from an antique book."

"I believe you are correct," Dorian said. "I cannot imagine my book is what drew him here."

"The much more plausible explanation," I said, "is that he's simply here to find the rest of the jewels that washed up in that mudslide along the Willamette."

"Alors," Dorian said, purposefully widening his liquidy black eyes so he looked like a teddy bear gargoyle, "he is merely trying to find what is rightfully his. That does not sound like such a bad man."

"Dorian!"

"Yes, yes, the murders he committed —"

"Sounds like it was only one accidental murder." I cringed. Was I trying to excuse him?

Dorian's wings slumped. "I am sorry to pressure you into speaking with the alchemist, my friend. I wish for no harm to come to you. Yet if there is a way this man can help me without hurting yourself, do you not wish to explore it?"

"Of course."

"*Bon.* We can at least hear his side of the story."

"We?"

Dorian looked up at me with innocent eyes. "Alchemists who have discovered the Elixir of Life would not be afraid of me. I am going with you."

Eleven

An hour later, I dropped a hefty duffle bag at my feet and glanced around.

We would have been there sooner, but Dorian insisted on cooking us an early lunch to "keep our energy up." I didn't object as soon as I tasted his newest version of macaroni and "cheese" made from cashew cream.

"We're alone," I said as I unzipped the duffle bag. Sweat trickled down the side of my temple. That gargoyle was heavy. "But you should hurry."

"Mais oui." Dorian stepped out of the bag, asking for my assistance with his left foot, then got straight to work on the lock in front of us. He had it open in less than a minute.

"Merde," he whispered. "I do not think I will be able to relock this door from the inside."

"As long as we can get back out, that's fine with me."

I grimaced at the sound of the door's screaming hinges, even though rationally I knew that we didn't need to be quiet. Not yet. The front of the theater was locked up. The staff and performers hadn't yet arrived to prepare for that evening's performance. I'd had Dorian pick the lock of the side door, located on a deserted alley that led to a backstage area.

With the dexterity of Dorian's clawed fingertips, it was like having my own personal locksmith. I thought of him as a "locksmith" rather than "burglar" because my intentions were pure — I wasn't planning on stealing anything. I wanted to take a look around to see if anything suggested these magicians were more than they seemed. Before confronting a potential murderer and showing that I knew his secret, I insisted we do reconnaissance. This was a long shot, since alchemists know how to be careful. But at the same time, since nobody expects alchemy to be real, it's tempting to let your guard down. That's what I was hoping Prometheus, aka Peter Silverman, had done.

Dorian could see in the dark, so he didn't need to turn on any lights. I, however, did. At least, if I was going to be of any use. But I found there was already a light burning.

"Zoe!" Dorian whispered in the deep, gravelly voice he erroneously believed was quiet enough not to be overheard. "We are not alone!"

"It's okay, Dorian. It's a Ghost Light." I pointed at the solitary bulb on a standing lamp in the center of the stage. It didn't mean someone was inside the theater. The theater tradition was an old one. The solitary burning bulb was meant to ward off ghosts. Or to protect the safety of anyone working late. The rationale depended on who you asked. The point was that it was an old tradition no longer needed with modern lighting. A few theaters still used it, but it would be second nature to someone who had worked in the theater a hundred years ago.

Dorian didn't notice my worry. He got to work exploring the theater by the light of the unadorned, ghostly bulb.

"Everything is locked!" he declared indignantly.

"Isn't that what I brought you along for? It was difficult lugging you inside that bag. I think you've been eating too many of the pastries you're cooking for Blue Sky Teas."

Dorian wrinkled his snout at me. "An important role of the chef is to taste his own creations! How else would culinary progress be made? Especially with these complicated vegan rules you impose."

"How can you say the rules are complicated? The only rule is no animal products."

"Semantics," Dorian mumbled. "*Alors,* these are locks beyond what my claws can unlock. I cannot imagine what foul magic lurks beyond these chains."

I knelt down to inspect the chain wrapped around a traveling trunk, then eyed the dramatic little gargoyle. "They're performers, Dorian. You know very well from your father that stage magicians are careful to protect their illusions. All this tells us is that they're magicians who create their own illusions. Which we already knew from seeing their show." I wished I was as confident as my words indicated.

I walked around the trunks, crates, and cabinets that had been locked with complex sets of metal chains. They were perhaps a bit on the paranoid side, but nothing out of the ordinary for stage magicians.

In the 1800s, several famous magicians stole cutting-edge acts from each other. Many magicians filed patents for their inventions, such as the Ghost, but spies infiltrated crews to gain enough knowledge to pretend they'd invented similar illusions on their own. I must have been lost in my memories, because I didn't hear anything until a voice rang out.

"Who left the lights on?" A deep female voice echoed through the theater.

"Perhaps it was the ghost," a male voice answered.

Dorian and I slunk into the shadows at the back of the stage as Prometheus and Persephone, sans costumes, strode down the center aisle toward us. If they turned on any spotlights, we'd be seen. I pulled Dorian behind a section of curtain and opened a fold just enough to peer out.

"Very funny, darling," Penelope said.

Peter shrugged. "I don't remember doing it, but you're right. It was probably me. Old habits . . ."

I felt my heart racing. *Old habits.*

"I thought you were over the need to leave a light on for the ghosts of the theater."

The two magicians hopped up onto the stage, just a few yards away from us. Though they were both dressed casually in paint-stained jeans, their hairstyles were already in place for their characters that night. Penelope's highly stylized curls pressed along the sides of her face, and Peter's flame-inspired spikes were stiff enough to impale someone.

Peter ran his hand across the edge of a

beaten-up trunk wrapped in chains. "Being back in Portland has brought back a lot of memories, Pen."

Dorian tugged at my hand. The magicians were close enough to us that I dared not whisper a reply, or even shift to look at him.

"Nobody has messed with these locks," Penelope said. "I don't know why you insist on locking up *everything* like this. It takes so long to open."

"You know why."

"I swear," Penelope said, "I'd like to clock the person who started that damn rumor about 'The Scottish Play' being cursed and Gaston Leroux for writing *The Phantom of the Opera.*"

"Right. Let's focus. We don't have much time. The crew will be here soon. Let's get this trunk open and get out of here."

So Peter didn't trust the crew. I thought about the illusions the magicians had performed. Though the tricks were detailed and involved precision, they didn't require many players to implement them. I'd learned from Dorian (who'd learned from his father) that there were many ways to perform the same trick. Instead of using complicated rigging as some performers did, the illusions I'd seen the previous night involved ingenious tricks of light. The magicians hadn't used real fire, so they could have made do with one or two local stagehands.

Penelope opened two combination locks that held the chains in place around the storage trunk.

"Just one more —" Peter broke off. "Did you hear something?"

"The ghost, perhaps?"

"I'm serious, Pen. I think I heard something."

"I wish you didn't have to be so secretive."

Peter stood still for a moment, listening, then sighed. "You're right. It must be getting to me. I must have imagined the sound."

Only he hadn't imagined it. Dorian pointed up toward the catwalk above the stage. Two figures, barely visible in the shadows, were making their way across the walkway that held the stage lights.

TWELVE

The area above the stage was cast in shadows, and I couldn't make out the faces of the two figures who crept along the catwalk. Yet from the glimpses I caught of the long-haired man, he looked vaguely familiar.

As he stepped past a set of metal lights and into the dim glow cast by the Ghost Light, I got a better look at his face. I stifled my gasp. It was the elderly volunteer from the show the previous night. Wallace Mason, who'd played the Floating Lady!

Between Peter and Penelope's strange actions and the lurking figures above us, I was more confused than ever. What was going on here? Stage show "volunteers" were often planted in the audience, themselves performers who were part of a show. It was an easy way to be sure the volunteer would behave exactly as they were supposed to in a complex illusion. But Wallace and his accomplice weren't revealing themselves to

Peter and Penelope. They weren't part of the act.

As soon as Peter lifted the lid of the trunk, I temporarily forgot about the men spying on the magicians. Stuck to the inside of the trunk's lid was a poster for the Queen of Magic, Adelaide Herrmann. That's who Persephone had reminded me of the previous night. Adelaide Herrmann was the first famous female magician who had equal billing. Along with her husband, Alexander Herrmann, she had captivated audiences across Europe and America in the late 1800s.

The two magicians removed a child-size backpack from the trunk, secured the lock, then left. A heavy door clanked shut. It echoed through the empty theater.

Dorian and I didn't dare move. Any sound we made would alert the other intruders to our presence.

"They're gone," a somber voice said from above.

"Shhh."

"You're too careful."

"And you're not careful enough. I bet they've got it with them. There's no use staying here."

"We might as well look around. Since we're here."

The men climbed down from the rafters. They made enough noise on the rungs of the narrow metal stairs that Dorian and I nodded at each other and crept from our hiding spot behind the curtains. Dorian scampered toward the back door, but I hung back when I saw what he'd left in his wake. Another small piece from his left foot had fallen off and was rolling along the floorboards. Another claw? I had no idea if stone claws could grow back on their own, so I ran after it. If I was able to save Dorian's life, I wanted him to be as whole as possible.

Where had it gone? Footsteps sounded behind me. I didn't have time to find it.

I caught up with Dorian just inside the back door. He climbed back into the duffel bag just as the lights clicked on above us.

"I *told you* I heard something," Peter's voice said. I turned and saw him and Penelope staring at me and Dorian.

"What have you got there?" Penelope asked, indicating the lumpy sack that contained Dorian.

"She's stolen something. Only I can't tell *what* would be that shape."

"Stolen?" I said. "I wouldn't dream of it. I knocked and nobody answered, so when I found the door open —"

"The door is locked," Penelope said.

"Maybe one of your crew forgot to lock up," I said. "It was wide open. Try it yourself."

"Why would we do that?" Peter said. "If it's unlocked, all it means is that you're a good burglar. Pen, why don't you search her for lock picks."

Penelope crossed her arms and leaned against the black wall. She smiled as if she was watching an amusing television show she wasn't participating in. "If she's that good, Peter, I'll never find the lock pics. They could be under a fake scar, hidden in her mouth. She might even have swallowed them if she's a regurgitator."

Dorian made a gagging noise as she spoke the word "regurgitate."

I quickly coughed to cover up the sound, but Penelope looked to the duffel bag.

"I'm terribly curious," she said, "about what you've got in the bag. We like our possessions to remain inside the theater. I'm sure you understand."

"I'm sorry. I think we got off on the wrong foot. I live locally and run an online business called Elixir. We've got lots of really cool antiques that I thought could serve as props in your stage show. I brought over one of my statues to show you. Just to give you a sense of the kind of things I've got."

I hoped Dorian was up for playing dead as a stone gargoyle. I unzipped the bag. Inside I found a stone gargoyle, his snout flared more than usual and his face set in an angry scowl.

"Remarkable," Penelope said. "Peter, are you looking at this?"

He wasn't. He was tapping the screen of his phone. "Elixir, huh. This is your website?" He held up the screen.

"That's right."

"You expect us to believe you make a living off this site? It's not even mobile friendly."

"I set it up before smartphones," I said.

"How is that possible? You can't be older than twenty-five."

"I'm twenty-eight, actually." That was the age I was when I accidentally discovered the Elixir of Life.

"We'll take him," Penelope said.

"What?"

"The gargoyle. The reason you're here. We'll take him."

"Oh! Oh. This is an example. A prototype. He's not for sale. You can order a custom carving through me, to your specifications."

"We like this one."

"Great. I can have one made that looks

identical." I named a price, hoping it would be too high.

"Perfect."

"Perfect?"

"Is there a problem?" Penelope asked.

"Of course not," I stammered, thinking I would have been better off letting them think I was a thief. Where was I going to find someone who could make a cast of Dorian? "I'll come by on Monday with some paperwork and to discuss materials options."

"We look forward to it," Peter said.

I cringed when the exit door squealed as I departed, even though there was no longer any need for secrecy. In the alley, I hesitated. Why hadn't they called the police? Isn't that what people would do if they found a burglar in their place of business? Unless they really did have something to hide.

But there was something more important than worrying about the magicians' motives. To hide, Dorian had turned himself completely to stone. Would he be able to bring himself back to life?

As I lugged the duffel bag to my car, I got my answer. The bag kicked me.

"That hurt," I said.

"Not as much as it's going to hurt me to have a plaster cast made of my body," the bag mumbled.

"You're lucky they didn't see you moving."

An older woman passing by on the sidewalk gave me a strange look. Better wait until we were inside the car to say anything else. I squeezed the bag into the space in front of the passenger seat on the floor of the pickup truck. Once we were both safely inside, I leaned over and unzipped a few inches. A pouting gargoyle looked up at me.

"You okay?"

"Why," he said thoughtfully, "did they not call the police when they saw you inside their theater?"

"That's what I was wondering."

"And why did you not tell Monsieur Silverman you know him to be an alchemist? This was the point of our expedition!"

"Hey, what are you doing? You need to stay inside the bag until we get home."

"I am attempting not to get out of the bag, but to stretch. I cannot move my legs."

My own legs felt weak at that news. "Let me get you home."

"Non!"

"What do you mean, *no*?"

"Do not worry about my present state. It is not what happens to me *today* that matters. The feeling is already beginning to return to my legs." He wriggled inside the bag. "It becomes more difficult each time, Zoe. You must confront the magician."

"You're forgetting something."

"I forget nothing. I simply do not say everything at once. I am a civilized Frenchman," added the face peeking out from the old duffel bag.

"The two intruders," I said.

"Yes. I recognized them as the volunteers from the performance last night."

"There was only one volunteer. The man with the long gray hair was The Floating Lady."

"The other man," Dorian said, "was the friend with whom he sat in the audience."

Where had the other trespassers gone? What were they after? And what was the item Peter and Penelope had removed from the trunk that Wallace and the other man had noted? *I bet they've got it with them,* he had said.

"I'm not going to rush off and confront anyone without knowing what's going on," I said. "I've got a better idea."

Dorian didn't experience heat and coldness the same way people do, so I left him inside my locked truck, hoping he didn't stretch so forcefully that he'd rock the truck and draw attention to himself.

I was in luck. The box office was opening. Opening night had been sold out, but I hoped the early box office hours meant there were still tickets left. I approached the ticket office and bought myself a ticket for that night's performance.

Thirteen

It had been a long day already, but it was only mid-afternoon when I heaved the heavy duffle bag containing Dorian up my driveway. I set it down abruptly when I saw who was waiting for me at my front door with a bag of groceries in his hand.

"Max!"

"I thought you forgot about me and our barbeque plans."

"Of course I didn't forget about you," I lied. I had missed Max while he was gone in China more than I'd imagined I would, but now that he was back, I didn't have time for him. Dorian's dilemma was taking up all of my energy — both mental and physical. I felt a wave of anger, immediately followed by guilt for being so selfish. It wasn't Dorian's fault. I wished the world was a different place, one where I could tell Max where I'd been. One where I could have brought him with me. I knew he'd be able to help, and more importantly, he would understand me on the deeper level I wanted. Maybe I could —

"Did you want to say something else?" he asked. "Your expression —"

I shook my head. "I feel bad that I lost track of the time. That's all. You know how I get caught up in nature when I go on a walk."

"You drove up, Zoe."

"Of course." *Damn.* "That's because I drove to River View Cemetery to go for a walk *there.* I like some variety."

Max's relaxed stance stiffened. "I thought most of that place was roped off after the mudslides. It's dangerous up there."

God, I was awful at lying. I kept digging myself deeper and deeper. "It's so beautiful there. And only part of it is cordoned off."

"You didn't go to the unstable steep parts, did you?" Max asked as he came down the porch steps, a grave look on his face. I knew he was conditioned to be a stickler for law and order, but the concern on his face was far greater than the situation called for.

"Why the third degree?" I eased the heavy bag containing Dorian onto the front lawn.

"It's nothing. Can I help you with that . . . sack?"

"I'm fine. It's just one of my antiques. I

was having it cleaned. I, um, picked it up on my way home." I needed to change the subject. "Let's see what you brought with you."

"Fresh from the farmer's market." Beet greens poked out over the edge of the brown paper bag he held. Several bunches of asparagus rested on top, and I spotted purple garlic and Brussels sprouts underneath. It was a bountiful spring harvest.

"I'm glad you brought food. Since I lost track of time, I didn't have a chance to go to the market."

"And this," he said as he handed me a bag of fragrant tea, "is the tea I mentioned last night. Hey, are you okay?"

I self-consciously tucked my hair behind an ear, careful not to tug too hard and pull out any more clumps. "What do you mean?"

"Last night, I thought it was the light of the theater, but you've got dark circles under your eyes. And your skin is pale."

I inspected the bag of tea, ignoring Max's skeptical gaze. "It's spring. I've got allergies. Nothing to worry about."

"This is the tea I brought back from China, but I'm getting my own spring garden started now, even though it's a little late. You'll find that one of the nice things about living in Portland is that we get enough rain that plants often thrive even during extended vacations."

I smiled at Max. "My secret is elderberry. You know it looks out for the other plants, to help them out." I turned to look fondly at the plant that used to be thought of as a garden's "protector," then looked at Max with equal fondness. "I'm glad you're back. And I'm glad you're here." I'd told him far too many lies in the last five minutes, but that statement was true. Even though I couldn't tell him as much as I wanted to, his very presence was comforting. I held out hope that one day I'd be able to tell him more.

"I missed sitting with you in my garden," he said softly.

"While the sun set."

"Then watching the night-blooming jasmine come to life."

"You know," I said, "you never revealed your secret for getting it to bloom off-season."

"You want to know all my secrets?"

"A little mystery is a good thing, but you could at least tell me how your grandfather's birthday party was."

"Didn't I? I told you he appreciated having his far-flung family gather around him one last time."

"But what about *you*? How was the visit for you?"

"Visiting China. It was . . . Let's just say it's relaxing to be home, Zoe." He took a step toward me, then abruptly jerked back. "What the — ? Is that a battery-operated antique?"

"What are you talking about?"

"Your sack. It made a noise."

"There might be something else in the bag. Something with, er, batteries, like you said. I'd better get this bag inside. You can take the food into the kitchen." I sighed. "I'll meet you there in a minute." I let Max into the house before stepping back outside to retrieve Dorian.

"Set me in front of the hearth," the sack whispered as I heaved it up the porch steps.

"I'm taking you to the basement," I whispered back.

"I wish to stay upstairs," he whined.

I closed the rickety front door behind us. "That's not a good idea, Dorian."

"I do not trust that man in my kitchen."

"Did you say something?" Max called from the kitchen, poking his head into the living room through the swinging door.

"Just the creaking floors." I waited until Max disappeared back into the kitchen, then lifted Dorian's stone form from the bag and set him in front of the fireplace. It was a spot he liked, because even in his stone form he could see everything. I didn't feel good about leaving him in stone form for too long, but I couldn't have an argument with Max there.

When I stepped into the kitchen, the farmer's market vegetables were stacked on the kitchen countertop and Max was holding a mason jar containing one of my latest transformations — a sun-infused healing lemon balm tea I was drinking daily to stave off the effects of helping to cure Dorian.

"It's a solar infusion," I said.

He raised an eyebrow.

"Steeping dried herbs in the sun, rather than the kitchen, to unleash their healing powers," I explained. Alchemy draws upon all the forces of nature, the planets being some of the strongest forces. Alchemists generally consult planetary alignments before they begin any transformative processes. The more complex the operation, or the greater the desired impact, the more important that alignment becomes. Each planet also has an associated metal, such as lead for Saturn, quicksilver for Mercury, silver for the moon, and gold for the Sun.

"I know what a solar infusion is. My grandmother did something similar when I was a kid. You'd get along great with my extended family. It's never made sense to me why it's worth all the effort. Especially moon infusions she'd steep under a full moon, thinking it was possible to harness the moon's power."

"Max. You make your own tea. You have one of the most unique gardens I've ever seen. And not two minutes ago we talked about night-blooming plants!" If my hair wasn't so weak from the backward alchemy quick fix I'd been performing, I would have tugged at my hair in frustration.

"That's different."

"Is it?"

In Max, I saw someone who'd once believed in all the possibilities of the world, but who couldn't break free from what he'd become. I hadn't realized it so clearly until that very moment. Max was walking on a tightrope, caught between two worlds: his childhood, with his herbalist grandmother who was an apothecary, and his adult life, working as a detective with a set of procedural and scientific rules that dictated his understanding of rationality. I knew it was nearly impossible to change a person if they weren't ready to change, but I believed Max could recapture the openness he'd once known. It didn't have to be a choice between two extremes. Once he realized that, I could open up to him, and we might have a chance for a future together.

I took the mason jar from his hands and set it back on the counter.

"Can we change the subject?" Max asked.

"What did you have in mind?"

"As lovely and complicated as this solar infusion of herbs is, it's not anywhere near as lovely and complicated as the woman in front of me." Max stepped closer and ran his finger along my jaw. His breath smelled of fresh lavender and peppermint.

Max's dark eyes were different than those of anyone I'd ever known, because of what they showed me about his soul. I've known a lot of people in my lifetime. Faces blur together in my memories, but I've never forgotten people's eyes. Before the advent of photography, it was usually only wealthier people who had their likenesses captured through portraits, so I didn't retain physical reminders of many of the people I'd known. I remembered their eyes not because of a unique color or shape, but because eyes are tied to an outward expression that people themselves are unaware of.

"Last night," Max continued, "I was hoping that we could pick up where we left off."

"I'd like that."

For a fraction of a second, I was self-conscious about my cracked lips and frumpy clothing. But with his eyes locked on mine as he stroked my cheek, I quickly forgot all about my own failings.

A faint knocking sounded. The front door? I couldn't be entirely certain it wasn't my imagination. Max either didn't hear it or chose to ignore it as well.

"Yo, Zoe!" Brixton's voice called from the backyard. "You in there?"

I pulled away from Max.

"I thought we were barbequing for just the two of us," he said.

"I thought so too." I opened the back door of the house, on the far end of the kitchen.

Brixton and his friends Ethan and Veronica stood in my backyard garden. Veronica's gangly frame towered over the boys. Her sleek black hair flowed past her shoulders, and I was pleased that she looked much more comfortable in her skin than she had even months before when I'd first met her.

"Hi, Ms. Faust, Mr. Liu," she said.

"What's up?" I asked.

"Your face is flushed," Brixton said. "Are you feeling sicker?"

"Sicker?" Max asked.

"He must mean my allergies." I turned back to the kids. "Max and I were just getting a barbeque started."

"I love barbeque," Ethan said.

Veronica elbowed him.

Max laughed. "There's plenty."

The miniature charcoal grill I kept in my trailer was only big enough to cook for two at a time, but there was enough food in my kitchen to feed an army, along with their counterparts. I asked Max to get the grill started while I collected ready-to-eat goodies. I pulled a carafe of iced tea from the fridge, selected an assortment of nut milk cheeses and breads, and washed an assortment of vegetables.

Because of Dorian, I kept my curtains drawn most of the time. Now that he was hiding in his stone form, I pulled open the kitchen curtains. I looked out the kitchen window and watched as Max began grilling two dozen asparagus spears along with full garlic heads wrapped in aluminum foil.

I was about to leave the kitchen to carry statue-Dorian into the basement so he could change out of his stone form, when Veronica opened the back door. She joined me inside while the boys stayed outside with Max.

"Now that Blue Sky Teas is serving my cooking," I said to her, "I can't figure out your real motive for coming over."

Veronica blushed. "We didn't come over *just* for food."

"No?"

"Brix knows you've been working too hard lately," Veronica explained. "What with getting up in the middle of the night to cook for Blue Sky Teas and managing your online business, Brix said you were bummed you didn't have time to fix up your spring garden like you wanted to."

"That's why he invited you two over?"

She gave a shy smile. "Yeah, but he also promised Ethan you'd cook for us. Your pastries are so popular at Blue Sky Teas that they're usually gone by the time we wake up on the weekend."

"Ah." I looked on through the window as Brixton pulled back a giant stalk of fennel and let it go, snapping it directly into Ethan's face. I'd taught Brixton enough about gardening and plants for him to know the weed-like plant was hearty enough for roughhousing. He wouldn't dare mess with the dwarf lemon trees that were still finding their footing.

"Really?" Ethan said to Brixton, then sneezed. "That's the best you got?" He broke off a thick fennel stem and held it like a sword. The impact was diminished by the fact that the tip was a bunch of yellow flowers. Brixton snapped off a stem of cabbage left behind after I'd harvested the edible portion. As faux weapons went, Brixton's was a much better selection.

"So, um, Ms. Faust?" Veronica sat on a countertop with her cell phone in her hand. "Can I talk to you about something else?"

"Of course." With the grim look on her face, I wondered what could be on her mind. Was she worried about how Brixton would react if she started spending more solo time with Ethan? I'd seen how things were headed with the trio of friends.

"It's your website," she said somberly. "It isn't mobile friendly. Like, at all."

"My *website*?" Was it really that bad? "There was no such thing as a smartphone when I built the site," I said for the second time that day.

She gaped at me. "But how do you expect to sell anything?"

"I don't think my buyers are shopping on their cell phones."

Her confused expression deepened. "Um, I could help you with it. You know, if you wanted. I'm kind of good at stuff like this."

"I couldn't ask you to —"

"It's fun, so I'd be happy to. You don't have to use it if you don't like it, but I could play around and see if you like what I come up with. You at least need to fix your SEO."

"My what?"

"I think you'd like something like this." Veronica moved so we could both see the screen, and showed me an assortment of mobile-friendly websites for merchandise like mine. "Since you've got a bunch of items from China, I could draw Chinese characters that could go next to the English descriptions. And I'll ask my mom to check my work, to make sure I got them right. I think that would look really cool."

I smiled. I'd probably spent more time in China than Veronica's Chinese-American mother, and I could have checked the Chinese myself, but I didn't like to advertise the fact that I knew as many languages as I did; it invited too many questions. And I was pleased it would give Veronica something to do with her mom. Brixton had told me she was closer with her Italian dad, because of their shared love of soccer. "That sounds great, Veronica. You should pick out something from Elixir to let me thank you."

I wrote down the login information to get into my website. When I looked up and glanced out the window, instead of seeing Max at the grill and the boys fencing with plants, I saw the three of them gathered around something else: *Dorian's alchemy book.* The dangerous, secret book I could have sworn I'd locked up in the basement that morning before leaving the house. I'd been ambushed.

That was the real motivation for Brixton coming over. He wanted Dorian's book.

FOURTEEN

FRANCE, 1855

The young doctor did not think of himself as anything special. He knew himself to be a competent doctor, a fair man, and a mediocre alchemist.

He had not discovered The Philosopher's Stone, yet his modest laboratory contained herbs he used to heal his wife and son when they were sick. He was not above feeling jealous of the men who had lived in previous centuries, when alchemy was in its heyday. He fantasized that, had he lived then, he might have been honored with a spot in Rudolph II's court in Prague, where men from across the world were said to have been given a stipend to practice alchemy. But the doctor had been born centuries too late for that. Here in the nineteenth century, he had to live out his fantasies through books.

It was this hobby that led to the most

improbable day of his life.

Though the doctor and his family lived in Paris, the doctor's wife was originally from the town of Blois. He and his family frequently traveled there to visit her infirm mother. His love for books was well-known to his family, so they thought nothing of it when he spent the afternoon at a local bookshop. In truth, it was his desire to avoid the company of his mother-in-law at least as much as the pull of books that led him to the bookshop that afternoon.

He had learned not to openly express his obsession with alchemy. Even in the modern times in which he lived, alchemy was greeted with suspicion. Therefore he feigned an interest in a wide range of scientific subjects. Once he told the bookseller the range of topics that interested him, the stooped man without a hair on his head nodded and retreated to the back of his shop.

The doctor looked over the books selected for him, then politely asked if the man had anything that was perhaps . . . older.

The bookseller nodded with understanding. The doctor watched the small, elderly man climb to the top of a ladder, wondering if he should assist the bookseller, lest he fall from the high rungs as he clutched a large book in one hand. Before the doctor could make up his mind, the bookseller was back on the ground, pressing the book into the medical man's hands.

"This is more to your liking, sir?"

It was. The doctor paid more than a fair price for *Non Degenera Alchemia,* an amount that had the bookseller drinking fine wine for months to come. The bookseller was quite pleased, for he had not even purchased the book to begin with. It had been left on the stoop of his shop some years before. At first he thought the anonymous donor must not have realized its value, but when he turned the pages of the book, he guessed the donor's true motivation. A foul odor emanated from the book. When certain pages were opened, the stench grew stronger. But the bookseller was also a book-lover. He could not abandon such a carefully made book. Even after cleaning the book failed to remove the smell, he was unable to part with it. Instead, he climbed to the top rung of his ladder and set the book on top of his highest bookshelf, where the scent would not reach his nose. The scent would fade over time, he imagined. With the book far from his gaze, he promptly forgot all about it — until the day the young man with an interest in alchemy walked into his shop.

The doctor didn't notice anything odd about the scent of the book until he and his family returned to Paris. Was it his imagination, or did the book smell of more than dusty leather and mold? Perhaps one of the items in his medical bag had spilled onto it. He wasn't usually so careless, but with a young son, he was neither as methodical nor as well rested as he once had been.

He had a small collection of alchemy books, which he kept in the midst of a much larger collection of literature and scientific volumes. *Non Degenera Alchemia* was unlike any other alchemy book he'd seen. The transformations pictured were all wrong. Indeed, once he was back home in Paris, the doctor was no longer sure it *was* a real alchemy book. The tiny bookshop had appealed to his romantic tendencies. Perhaps he'd spent his money more on an idea than the book itself.

Now, it looked as if he wouldn't have a chance to find out. His wife insisted he remove the book that smelled like it had been stored in a stable of animals. He couldn't argue with her, and not only because she won every argument. In this case, he believed she was right.

He no longer knew any alchemists who might want to buy the book. He had once tried to join a secret society of alchemists in Paris, but he found them to be a very silly group of men. None of them had discovered alchemy's secrets, but all of them delighted in deciphering riddles.

Thus, with a heavy heart, he tucked the book under his arm and set out to find a bookseller who might pay him a few francs for it. Before leaving, he sprinkled a few drops of his wife's perfume onto the spine, hoping to mask the other odors. He hated to damage the book, but who would buy it in its current state?

His actions were for naught. A few steps out the door, the odor of the book returned. The perfume must have dispersed quickly in the dry air. Perhaps he could find a bookseller with a stuffed-up nose.

The doctor followed the path of the Seine River, the pleasant day balancing out his feeling of foolishness for his hasty purchase. As the spires of Notre Dame Cathedral came into view, the smell of farm animals dissipated, replaced with scents of the forest. So shocked was the doctor that he tripped. The book flew out of his hands, landing a few feet in front of him. He dusted off his trousers, which thankfully had not ripped, then lifted the book. Memories of childhood Christmases flooded through his mind as fragrances filled his nostrils.

Was he going crazy? Or could this be true alchemy?

Fifteen

"What's the big deal?" Brixton said. "I was just showing the alchemy book to Ethan because he took Latin in private school before he moved here. I thought he could help translate some of the crazy stuff in there."

"It's a valuable antique," I snapped. "It shouldn't be outside. The spores from the garden will ruin it." It was true, though that's not what I cared about.

"Is that why it smells so weird?" Ethan asked.

"Mold?" Max chimed in. "I met a book restorer a couple of years ago, on a case. He might be able to help."

"Thanks," I said, taking the book from Ethan's hands. "I'll keep that in mind."

"I'm the reason you got the book back, you know," Ethan said.

My shoulders tensed, but I kept the book firmly in my hands. I'd never asked Ethan to buy the book from the innocent rare books dealer, but I was thankful *Non Degenera Alchemia* hadn't gotten caught in police red tape as I fought to have it returned to me after it was stolen in a break-in a few months ago. Ethan's family was wealthy enough that the charge on his father's credit card hadn't been a problem. I wondered if he'd even noticed.

"You know I'm grateful, Ethan. And I'm working on paying you back —"

"Whatever. I just thought it would be cool to see what all the fuss was about. After all, this is the book Brix made up all those stories about. Like how it's what brought your shy French friend to life. Nice one, Brix."

Brixton became suddenly interested in a wild maze of mint leaves that were snaking their way up the fence. He knew why he couldn't tell them the real reason I needed to decipher the book, but I hadn't realized just how much he'd told his friends shortly after meeting me.

"Are we going to eat or what?" Ethan said.

I took the book inside, not trusting myself to speak to Brixton while the others were around. I knew what he was doing, and he meant well. He saw that Dorian was dying and knew that my own efforts weren't working to save him. Since Ethan read Latin, it was a natural leap for Brixton to think Ethan might be able to help.

I trusted Brixton's intentions, but he was fourteen. In my youth, that age was considered nearly an adult. But a teenager today wasn't an adult. I couldn't assume that Brixton was. I'd become too careless in what I shared with him.

He would never *purposefully* reveal my secret and Dorian's, but his actions could still lead to dangerous situations. I wasn't worried about Brixton slipping up, or even purposefully telling anyone about me and Dorian. When he did so shortly after we first met, nobody believed him. People see only what their worldview enables them to see. It's like we're all walking around with x-ray glasses set to different frequencies. When most people are told about a living "French gargoyle," their imagination conjures the image of a disfigured Frenchman who was self-conscious about being seen, not a stone gargoyle who'd accidentally been imbued with a life force when an unsuspecting stage magician had read from the pages of a book he never suspected contained actual magic. The few people who'd seen Dorian move when he was hiding in plain sight assumed it was a trick of the light or that they'd had one too many pints of Portland's exquisite beer.

True, my life would have been easier if I didn't have to pretend I had a shy friend from France, but I didn't fault Brixton for trying to be understood. The problem was when he acted recklessly by taking matters into his own hands. When he did so, I couldn't anticipate all the unintended consequences.

After taking the book to the basement bookshelf, I carried statue-Dorian to the basement. Between gardening and taking long walks, I've never been a gym person. Honestly, the whole concept of a gym that doesn't involve competitive sparring baffles me. Doing unproductive physical work within the confines of a dark building, as opposed to working up a sweat in nature? But as I hefted Dorian into my arms, I realized that perhaps lifting weights wasn't such a bad idea.

I set him down at the bottom of the basement stairs, feeling a twinge in my lower back. After locking us into the basement, I told him it was safe to wake up.

"I can see that." He stretched his neck, flapped his wings, and flexed his fingers. Moving his hips as if he was playing with an invisible hoola hoop, he frowned at his legs.

They were taking longer to regain movement than the rest of him.

"You heard what happened?" I asked. He hated it when I fussed over his condition.

"Of course." He shook his head sadly. "I can see and hear very well when I am trapped in stone. I saw the food preparations being made. Such poor cooking technique! You did not wait nearly long enough for the coals to heat properly to grill the vegetables."

"Dorian —"

"And I have the perfect recipe for a tarragon sauce to accompany asparagus, but I cannot show myself to prepare it —"

"Dorian!"

"Yes?"

"I was talking about whether or not you heard that Brixton showed Ethan your book."

Dorian narrowed his eyes. "You are trying to change the subject because you have never liked tarragon."

"I like tarragon just fine, as you know full well. I don't grow it myself because it doesn't have as many healing properties as other herbs."

"It is the King of Herbs, Zoe. The King of Herbs."

"Would you please focus? I need to go

back upstairs in a minute."

"Yes, yes. I heard you confront the boys. I was confused as to why you stopped Ethan from looking at my book."

"He's a *kid,* Dorian."

"Yet he is the one who enabled us to get it back."

"I remember, Dorian. I remember." When all this was over, I needed to work on creating enough gold to pay Ethan back. "But knowing how to type your wealthy father's credit card number is completely different from knowing how to comprehend an ancient and dangerous text."

"Fresh eyes. Is that not the expression?"

"Yes. He's a fresh set of eyes. But he's fourteen. And he doesn't know about alchemy. And did I mention he's fourteen! Look, I really need to get back. Lock yourself in here. Don't let anyone in. Don't let anyone besides the two of us look at the book."

"You show Ivan —"

"That's different. He's a scholar —"

The gargoyle threw his arms into the air in exasperation. "No *ham,*" he muttered. "No *butter.* No showing my *own personal possession* to whomever I wish."

I sighed. "Do you really miss ham?"

He scowled at me. "No, I do not. But that

is not the point."

"I give up. Stay here, Dorian. I'll make sure everyone leaves before too long."

Getting rid of my guests proved more difficult than expected. It was such a gorgeous afternoon for a barbeque that my outburst hadn't dampened the fun. When I stepped into the backyard five minutes after I'd left to deposit Dorian and his book in the basement, Max, Brixton, and Ethan were sitting in folding wood chairs in a semicircle around the grill while Veronica flipped pieces of asparagus.

None of them seemed to notice my foul mood. Dorian was right that I was failing in my own attempts to decipher his book, so it was no wonder he agreed with Brixton that any help was welcome. A kid who'd studied a little bit of Latin wasn't going to help. But an old alchemist was another story. Now that I knew Prometheus's true identity, I was eager to attend the *Phantasmagoria* magic show that night.

Since none of my guests were picking up on my impatient mood and suggesting they depart, it was time for another approach. I picked a stalk of ragweed to force myself to sneeze repeatedly. With a red nose and eyes, it was much easier to wrap up the barbeque.

With my overzealous inhalation of ragweed, I was certain I didn't look like someone Max would want to spend the evening with, leaving me free to get ready for the magic show. I hated the continued deception. It never got easier.

I counteracted the effects of the pollen by taking a bath with chamomile bath salts, then dressed in an oversize black blouse far too long for my arms, and black leggings that left nothing to the imagination. In simple black, I hoped I'd blend into the background.

I arrived early and got myself a glass of red wine at the lobby bar. At least two dozen attendees were there ahead of me, holding drinks and chatting with friends. I smiled but didn't strike up any conversations. I was there to see what else I could discover.

While I looked around the wood-paneled lobby, I sipped the wine. The spicy and sweet flavors of cloves, pepper, and black currants danced on my tongue. I've never been a big drinker, since my alchemically-trained body experiences heightened effects of everything I put into it. But I enjoy the complex characteristics in wine. And unlike coffee, which can keep me up for days, too much wine puts me to sleep. After one more sip, I abandoned the half-full wine glass on the edge of the bar.

The lobby was filling up, providing the cover I needed. Mirroring the authority of the magicians in the illustrated *Persephone & Prometheus's Phantasmagoria* poster next to me, I walked purposefully to the closed doors that led to the seating area. Unfortunately, they were locked. That wasn't uncommon, and I should have expected it. Stage magicians wouldn't want anyone seeing their setup. I wished I knew how to pick locks as deftly as Dorian did with his claws. I had to wait until the audience was let in, which happened a few minutes later. I lingered next to the doors, so I was one of the first members of the audience ushered inside. I spotted two staff members dressed in black. One was in the sound booth, and one stood at the side of the stage, guarding the curtains from curious patrons who might be tempted to peek. To me, neither of them looked much older than Brixton.

Instead of finding my seat, I walked to the front row and caught the eye of the staffer hovering in the wings.

"This is a wonderful old theater," I said. "Have you worked here for long?"

He grinned. "Two years this May, when I graduated with a degree in theater."

"What about the guy in the sound booth?"

His grin faltered. "He's been here a little longer, but I know a lot about this place. Listen, I've got to finish setting up, but do you want to grab a beer after the show? I can tell you all about it."

The revealing leggings had definitely been a bad idea. I politely declined his offer. He'd told me what I needed to know. Peter and Penelope hadn't brought their own crew with them. They were working with locals.

At this Saturday evening performance, there were a few empty seats in the theater, but not many. I was heartened to see that people were still interested in attending a classic magic show. I wished I could enjoy it.

The lights flickered, signaling that the performance would begin shortly. I was seated in the back row, and I watched the stage carefully.

The curtains opened slowly, revealing a dark stage. A glimmer of light bounced off a piece of glass. I was surprised at the sloppy setup. The night before, it hadn't been immediately obvious that the fire was an illusion.

The magicians must have realized something was wrong too. Instead of the swell of music that had kicked off the previous night's show, the curtains began to close again.

But at the same time, something was happening on the stage. As my eyes adjusted, I made out the form of a tall cabinet at the side of the stage. It had been there the previous night, I remembered, but it hadn't been used. At least not in a way the audience could see. This time, though, the door of the cabinet was slowly opening. There was someone inside. He held himself stiffly, almost as if he was playing the part of a dead body.

This was definitely in keeping with the *Phantasmagoria*'s theme of death and resurrection, but I was surprised that the magicians would change their act so drastically between performances.

The curtains continued to close, but the heavy fabric moved slowly. I could still see the middle of the stage. And I recognized the man inside the coffinlike cabinet.

It was the Floating Lady volunteer I'd seen at the theater earlier that day. What was he doing there? Had he stayed at the theater to spy on the magicians and hidden in this cabinet, not knowing it would be used on stage? He was a little late to be sneaking out unnoticed.

Right before the curtains closed, my

breath caught. Wallace Mason *wasn't* trying to hide. A dark patch of red stretched across his chest.

He tumbled out of the box just as the two sides of the curtains came together with a crash. Of course it wasn't the curtains making the noise. It was the sound of his dead body hitting the stage floor.

A murmur of voices echoed through the theater, as audience members turned to one another, presumably wondering about the strange opening of the show. Though magicians love morbid imagery, the scene on the stage had none of the previous night's dramatic flare. This was no act.

The magician had killed again.

And without revealing who I was, there was nothing I could do about it.

Sixteen

Looking at my face in the mirror the following morning, I barely recognized myself. My skin was drawn like it had been before I began taking care of myself, and the dark circles under my eyes were even darker than the day before. A large chunk of hair fell off in my hairbrush. Even my teeth had a faint gray cast to them.

Dorian was right. Helping him was killing me.

Each time I made the Tea of Ashes, the effects lasted longer and were more severe. Still, I was in better shape than Wallace Mason. I couldn't get the image of his body out of my mind. I hadn't realized he was dead until he hit the stage floor.

Though I've seen my share of death over the years, seeing two murder victims within three months was unsettling, to say the least.

Had Wallace Mason seen too much when he was at the theater earlier that day? If it was the magician-alchemist who had killed him to protect his secret, how could I ignore the murder? I was entangled, whether I liked it or not.

I doubted the two young crew members had anything to do with the murder. The elderly usher who took our tickets didn't seem especially likely, either. I expected the police would dismiss them from suspicion, making the magicians the most likely suspects. Would the police figure out Peter Silverman's true identity? It would be like the Salem Witch Trials all over again — only this time, the accusations against me would be true.

As an innocent sixteen-year-old I'd been accused of witchcraft, because of my affinity to plants. I could work with plants in ways that most people couldn't, both in coaxing them to grow and in extracting their mysterious properties. People are frightened of what they don't understand. It was their fear that had driven me away from them and into the arms of alchemists. Now I had become something that people might truly have reason to fear, not because I would harm anyone — I had spent my life trying to do the opposite — but because I had unlocked powerful secrets that could be used for both good and evil.

Breathe, Zoe.

Now that I'd gotten a few hours of sleep, I began to wonder about my hasty assumptions. Had I jumped to the right conclusion? Was the magician involved? I was looking at only half of the picture — the magician-alchemist, not the man who'd been killed. The dead man's life would be examined by the police. The police would look into Wallace Mason's life and follow the trail wherever it led.

Pushing thoughts of murder from my mind, I fixed myself a cup of turmeric tea and a green smoothie for breakfast, then I tended to my window box and backyard gardens. Three mint varieties — lemon balm, chocolate, and peppermint — were getting a little carried away, stretching their roots and tendrils too close to the parsley. That wouldn't make any of the plants happy. My garden choices had been made in part so I could harvest fast-growing plants for Dorian's Tea of Ashes. If it hadn't been for that, I would have planted the mint in containers.

The familiar routine of touching the plants and giving them the amount of water they needed served to calm me, but my mind was still restless. I dressed in my ill-fitting jeans and a sweatshirt and set out on a walk to clear my head. But the scents of springtime Portland only served to remind me of the strange scents I'd imagined coming from Dorian's book, and the scent of ether the magicians had used in their performance.

Back at the house, I went straight to the kitchen with the intention of having another cup of tea. Before the mug reached my lips, a knock sounded on the front door.

I'd already given a brief statement to a police officer the previous night, when I was questioned along with the rest of the audience. I'd said I didn't know anything, so I couldn't imagine they were following up already. I knew I should have told them about seeing the two men sneaking around the theater earlier in the day, but I couldn't do so without incriminating myself. Doing the right thing was always a delicate balance for an alchemist. Telling the complete truth could easily lead to greater confusion and injustices. If I knew anything that could help, I would have spoken up. But in spite of my initial reaction, I didn't know what had transpired.

I took a deep breath and opened the door.

"You were *there* last night?"

"Nice to see you, too, Max."

He pushed past me into the house. "You

didn't say anything about going back to the magic show."

"It was a last-minute decision. I wanted to see if I could figure out how some of the tricks were done. I told you I love old-fashioned magic shows."

Max stared at me. I suddenly felt very self-conscious about my hair and skin. "What are you keeping from me, Zoe?"

"Are you here officially?"

"No. I'm here as your . . . whatever the hell I am to you. But I suppose your answer shows me where I stand."

"Max —"

"A man is *dead,* Zoe."

"Why do you think it has something to do with me?"

"I didn't say that! I'm worried about you. That's why I came by. You were in the same place as a killer."

"Oh."

"You find it so surprising that I'd be worried about you?"

"No, it's just —"

"What?"

"Nobody has been worried about me in a long —"

A crash from the house interrupted us. I gave a start, and saw Max's shoulders tense.

"You attract burglars like anise hyssop attracts bees," Max whispered, then raised a finger to his lips.

Only Max would have thought up a simile that included anise hyssop instead of something simple like sunflowers. I put my hand on his and stopped him from heading to the house. "It's not a burglar. I was cataloguing my inventory and left a stack of books that wasn't very stable. I didn't anticipate being pulled away for so long."

"You sure?"

Another crash sounded.

"I'd better check it out."

"Max, really —"

I feared what he'd find inside. With solid stone covering a larger portion of Dorian's body each day, he might not be able to transform himself into the proper shape people had seen. I was already thought to be "quirky" for carrying my large gargoyle sculpture to different rooms of my house on a regular basis. That was fine. But how would I explain a strangely contorted gargoyle sculpture?

Ignoring Max's pleas for me to wait outside, I followed him up the stairs. Max cringed as each successive step groaned under our feet. Stealth was impossible in this old house.

The attic was crammed full of artifacts for

my business, but empty of life. There wasn't even a stone gargoyle anywhere in sight. However, there *was* a pile of books scattered across the floor, even though I'd lied about a precarious stack. Was my *house* alive now? That was all I needed.

My attic was the exact opposite of Max's house. Instead of his sparse decor, in which an iron tea kettle, a white couch, two scenic paintings, and two personal photographs gave the house its personality, my attic was an involved mess of relics I'd accumulated over the centuries. For the decades in which I traveled across the United States in my truck and trailer, these books, artwork, and alchemical artifacts had resided in a storage facility in Paris.

The hardwood floor was pockmarked with water damage from the winter rains. You'd think that after all these years I'd be good enough at home repair that I could fix the damage quickly and resume my alchemical work on saving Dorian's life. But in my defense, I'd rarely lived in my own home. Most of the time I hadn't even lived in a proper house. This Craftsman house in Portland was a luxury.

"Wow," Max said, taking in the room.

I couldn't tell if he meant that in a good way or a bad way.

"These are all real antiques?"

"They're not exactly antiques. At least I don't think of them like that. They're all related to the science of healing. That's why the store is called Elixir."

"I didn't realize you were still working at your business." He shook his head. "I guess we don't know each other as well as I thought."

"Max —"

"I thought you were working as the chef at Blue Sky Teas."

"Part-time. Why did you think I wasn't running Elixir? You knew I shipped the storage crates to the house when I moved here. I wasn't hiding anything." Well, I wasn't hiding *that.* "Is it because I haven't invited you up to the attic before? As you can see, it's not the kind of room where I'd invite a guest. I haven't gotten properly settled in yet."

"That's not it."

"No?"

"I checked out your website."

I groaned.

"It looked like you hadn't updated it in the last decade," Max said sheepishly.

Three comments on my website in as many days? I was definitely going to take Veronica up on her offer to update the site.

But I couldn't seem to care much at the moment. Dorian was dying an unnatural death. I was getting sicker by the day as I tried to save him. A murderous alchemist was in town, seeking his stash of loot, a stash which had led to the death of a guard and which had now washed up on the banks of the nearby Willamette River. And a man spying on the alchemist had been murdered, the body found in front of my eyes.

So yes, updating my website so I could make enough money to fix my house and pay Ethan back wasn't my top priority. I gave an involuntary shiver as I thought back to that damned theater, with Dorian's foot caught on the catwalk and the volunteer's dead body tumbling out onto the stage.

"You're thinking about the dead man, aren't you?" Max said. "I can see it on your face. I'm sorry you had to see that."

I nodded, but didn't trust myself to speak. I'd seen more death than I wanted to in my lifetime. It doesn't get easier. But that's a good thing.

"Is there something you want to tell me, Zoe?"

My throat tightened and anger flushed my face. Why was Max simultaneously the easiest and most difficult person to communicate with? "You really think I had something to do with his —"

"I didn't mean it like that! Of course I didn't mean that. Sometimes I feel like you understand me better than anyone, but sometimes . . . I can tell you're keeping something from me." He frowned as something in the corner caught his eye. He set down the cookbook of herbal remedies he'd picked up, and walked up to a whitewashed hutch that held glass jars with original vintage labels. "Imported herbal supplements? Really? After everything that happened last winter, how can you —"

"God, Max!" I snapped. "I don't know the man who was murdered, and these are vintage *jars.* With nothing inside. Nothing. These glass vessels were once used by famous scientists. That's why they're worth a lot of money."

"Really? People will believe Louis Pasteur used one of these *vessels*? Are his fingerprints on them?"

"Isaac Newton, actually, but yes. I don't have fingerprints, but I have documents that show —"

"You actually believe papers have survived that long and aren't faked? Jesus, Zoe. You do." He pinched the bridge of his nose. "I'm sorry. Look, can we change the subject?"

"Back to the dead man you think I have

something to do with? I told you, I don't know the man. He has nothing to do with me."

"Are we fighting? How did that happen? I came over here because I wanted to make sure you were okay, that you hadn't gotten mixed up in —"

A cough sounded from the closet behind me. I knew that cough. I quickly coughed, hoping Max would think the first one was mine.

"I could use some tea for my allergies," I said. "They're affecting my throat. Why don't we go downstairs?"

"I can see myself out."

"That's not what I meant."

"We don't seem to be communicating very well today. I'll leave you to clean up this mess." He paused, a veiled look I couldn't place passing over his face. "Where's that gargoyle statue of yours? I didn't see it when I came through the house."

"Why?" My intuition kicked into high gear. Max knew I "moved" my statue around, but he'd never seen Dorian move on his own.

"Never mind. It's nothing." He paused. "I hope it's nothing."

"What's that supposed to mean?"

"I have to go, Zoe."

And with that, he left. *Why did he want to know about Dorian?*

Seventeen

I rested my back against the closet door for a moment, allowing time for Max to drive away and for me to compose my thoughts.

When I was certain he was gone, I yanked open the attic closet door. "It's safe."

"I hope the boy did not ruin any of your books," Dorian said. His gray arm was wrapped around Brixton's shoulder. The two stood, and Brixton helped Dorian step out of the closet.

"He lost his balance," Brixton said. "That's why there was a crashing noise. We didn't know you were back until we heard you and Max raise your voices. So when Dorian fell down, I thought I'd better make this place look like you said it did."

"Max knows that *you* exist. Why didn't you just say you came over to raid the fridge or something?"

Brixton and Dorian stared at each other, both frowning.

"She is a smart one, this alchemist," Dorian said.

I pressed my fingers to my temples. I didn't remember signing up to take care of two adolescents.

"Don't be bummed, Zoe," Brixton said. "I'm sure Max'll come around." He made sure Dorian could stand without toppling over, then put his hand on my shoulder. Okay, sometimes he could be a thoughtful kid.

I looked at the two of them. "Why are you here, anyway? I didn't know you were coming over. I thought you'd be at Blue Sky to help your mom with the Sunday brunch crowds."

"Yeah, that was the plan, but then I heard about the guy who was killed by the alchemist —"

"We don't know for sure that's what happened."

"Alchemists," Dorian said, "are known to have gone to drastic measures to protect their secrets."

"You were the one who said we should give him the benefit of the doubt!" Brixton said, gaping at the gargoyle.

"My young friend," Dorian said to Brixton, "bring me the local newspaper, *s'il vous plaît.*"

Dorian didn't usually ask for help like that. His left foot hung at an unnatural angle. He saw me looking and tossed a small throw blanket over it.

He cleared his throat and opened the paper. "Wallace Mason was an important enough man to have a short obituary in the newspaper. He founded a wellness center in Portland in the 1960s, where he extolled the virtues of vegetarianism and herbalism, and he took in many troubled people. He's survived by a daughter who lives abroad."

"That's it?" I asked.

"Hey guys," Brixton said, "there's a lot more online." He scrolled on the screen of his phone. "He was quoted in the media after that sapphire necklace from the Lake Loot was found."

"Aha!" Dorian said.

"He was one of the treasure hunters?" I asked. His presence at the theater took on a new meaning. "What did he say?"

"That they should allow people to search," Brixton said, still reading his phone's screen, "because that's the best chance at recovering the loot for the family. Why didn't he want it for himself?"

"Use your *little grey cells,*" Dorian said, tapping his forehead and making me wish I hadn't checked out every single Poirot book from the library for him during the winter. "A 1960s wellness center. This means he is a *do-gooder.* Of course he would wish to find the *trésor* for the family."

"Unless he's lying," I pointed out.

Dorian scowled at me as he stretched his shoulders, his wings flapping gently as he did so. "We would know more if someone would confront the alchemist. Then we could learn if he might help us."

"We've already discussed all the reasons why that's a terrible idea."

"Yes, but this is a democracy," Dorian said. "The boy and I have outvoted you."

"This isn't a democracy."

"Of course it is," Brixton said. "I slept through a bunch of government classes, but even I know that."

"This *house* isn't a democracy," I said.

"But we will not confront him inside the house," Dorian said, his black eyes opened wide in a deceptively innocent expression.

I groaned. *A simple life, Zoe. You really believed you could have a simple life?* I wished I could say that if the magician was a murderer, the police would figure it out. But if he was an alchemist?

"Maybe Zoe has a point," Brixton said.

"Thank you," I said.

"I mean, Franklin Thorne is a really good

magician, with his Prometheus character. If you confront him directly, he might capture you before you knew what was happening."

I tried to stop Brixton to tell him that wasn't what I meant, but he kept going.

"You were there at the show," he said. "You saw him. Prometheus is, like, *Houdini* good."

Dorian made a squawking noise I'd never before heard escape his dignified gray lips. "Houdini! *Non!* Ehrich Weiss stole my father's name and dishonored him! Houdini is but a poor imitator of the great Robert-Houdin! Those illusions you witnessed at the stage show? These were not inspired by the crass, escapist acts of Houdini. *Non.* Many were created by the prodigious Robert-Houdin."

Brixton stumbled backward as Dorian's heavy wings flapped back and forth.

"He's a bit overly sensitive on this topic," I said to Brixton.

"Overly sensitive?" Dorian parroted back at me. "I am not the egotistical man who could not understand a family's wish to grieve for their relation in solitude. That was Houdini. Since the day he was turned away from visiting his idol's grave, Houdini set out to destroy Father's name."

"Wow," Brixton said, reading his phone

screen. "Son of a —"

"Language," I said automatically.

"Sorry, D," Brixton said, ignoring me and speaking to Dorian. "I didn't mean anything by it. I just meant that Prometheus is a wicked good magician who probably has lots of handcuffs and stuff, so Zoe should come up with another good cover story before she goes and talks to him."

"I'm right here," I said.

"Yeah," Brixton said, "but you look like you're resisting coming up with a plan. So Dorian and I should come up with one for you."

I sighed and tried to think of anything I could say that wouldn't result in them skewing the intent of my words and investigating for themselves.

"As long as you two stay out of it completely," I said, "and I do mean *completely,* I'll look into it."

"Bon," Dorian said. "In one hour I shall have lunch ready for you. That way you can keep up your energy for your investigation."

The scene outside the theater was much as I expected it would be. The building at the base of Mt. Tabor was roped off with crime scene tape, and officers milled around.

Peter and Penelope sat together on the

bumper of a powerful, late-model SUV that loomed over the tiny Portland cars surrounding it. With a hitch on the back, I presumed they used the SUV for hauling a trailer of the items for their magic act. They were no longer wearing their stage makeup or formal wear from the day before, though the sleek curls of Penelope's hair were ready for any stage. She puffed on a cigar and looked at the sky.

"If it isn't our friendly neighbor," Peter said in a voice even a toddler could tell was sarcastic. "Come to tell us our new gargoyle is ready? I'm so sorry, but as you can see, it's the world's worst time for a visit."

The man struck me as far too immature to have been alive for 100 years. He was immature even for 50. I've known alchemists who've lost sight of their humanity, but it tends to express itself in a different tenor. Aloofness and a lack of empathy, yes. But sarcasm? Not that I'd encountered. But then again, I'd never known any alchemists who practiced backward alchemy. And that's what he had to be, coming back from the dead.

"I'm so sorry for your loss," I said, though what I was really thinking was how murders followed Peter Silverman wherever he went.

"We didn't know him," Penelope said,

blowing smoke rings into the sky. She gave what appeared to be a heartfelt sigh, then extinguished the cigar. "But yes, it's a tragedy nonetheless."

"I assumed you knew him, since he was a volunteer."

"Everyone thinks they know how a show works," Peter said with a resigned smirk. "That's *cheating,* my dear."

Penelope turned her sharp gaze to meet mine. "Don't mind him. He's upset that the police are wrecking all of our earthly possessions as we speak."

"Looking for the murder weapon?"

"I don't know what they're doing," Peter said, "but that's certainly not what it looks like."

My phone buzzed in my pocket. "Excuse me," I said, scowling at the phone.

"Zoe, thank God you picked up," said the voice on the other end of the line. "There's an emergency. Listen —"

"You can't keep crying wolf, Brixton," I snapped.

"You don't understand! It's Ethan. I found out he took a photograph of a page in the alchemy book —"

"That's okay. It's not like the existence of the book is a secret —"

"You're not *listening* to me, Zoe! He read

it *out loud.* The Latin. He brought a stone garden gnome to life."

Eighteen

FRANCE, 1855

With trembling legs, the young doctor clutched *Non Degenera Alchemia* and walked to a nearby café, where he drank copious amounts of wine.

He had once read about a sect of alchemists from the sixteenth century who met in the crypt below Notre Dame de Paris. He had dismissed the notion as rumor, for even when he asked fellow alchemists about it, they had dismissed this "backward alchemy" as myth. But what if it was true? It was only when he returned to Paris that the book gave off a strong scent. And it was only when he came upon the cathedral that the odor changed.

Stumbling now, he made his way to the cathedral, unsure whether it was the wine or alchemy that made the book feel as light as a feather in his hands. He climbed the steps to the new Gallery of Chimeras and looked out over the city. So many great men had shaped Paris. He knew he would never be one of them. *Unless this book could turn him into a true alchemist.*

From high atop Notre Dame de Paris, the drunk doctor read from the pages of the strange alchemy book, hoping against reason that here in this sacred historical site, the knowledge would seep into his veins and make him more than the simple man he knew himself to be.

Directing his attention to the stone chimera in his path, he recited the Latin words. The stone began to shift. He must have been more intoxicated than he thought. He had only hallucinated once before, when given an incorrect dose of laudanum. The horned gargoyle stepped off of its pedestal and stood in front of him. What sorcery was this? He wasn't able to answer his own question, because he promptly fainted.

When he awoke, he was in a jail cell for drunkenness. He could no longer remember whether the events of the night before had been real or a dream. A sprained wrist was the only indication that something had taken place that night.

Had the book truly made it possible for him to bring a stone creature to life? It wasn't possible! Alchemical transformations could not be transferred in such a way. Yet he had seen it with his own eyes. He held his hands before him, half expecting his fingers to turn to stone.

When he was released from his jail cell, the book was returned to him. Ignoring the pain in his hand and wrist, he ran to Notre Dame, earnestly hoping that the events that had transpired there had only been a nightmare. When he reached the gallery, he found an empty pedestal where the gargoyle had once stood. Was he mistaken? Had there been a figure there at all?

For days, the doctor searched for the creature he was half convinced he'd imagined, but never found it. He read the newspapers each morning and evening, wondering if its presence would be reported. Nothing.

If this was what alchemy had driven him to, he had no right to try to be more than the unassuming man he was. That day, when his wife was in the park with their son, he tossed the book into the hearth.

It didn't burn.

He tossed more wood into the fire. Still, the book did not catch fire. He threw one of his most boring books into the flames. It popped and sizzled in the heat and was soon reduced to ash. *Non Degenera Alchemia* glowed in the fire, yet did not burn. Of this he was certain. Today he was completely sober. This was no hallucination.

The young doctor screamed with confusion as he pulled the book from the fire with a poker. He wrapped the book in a blanket, fearful to touch it once more. He wrote a note for his wife, then took his leave.

When he returned a week later, the young doctor no longer looked so young. But the book was safely hidden where he hoped nobody would find it ever again.

Nineteen

"What's the matter with your hand?" I asked.

"I took Ethan's phone from him," Brixton said, hiding his bloody knuckles. "He wasn't happy."

"You *hit him*?"

"What was I supposed to do? Anyway, he hasn't posted it online." Brixton swallowed hard. "Yet."

Dorian swore in French.

"We'll talk about your methods later," I said. "Play the video."

Brixton, Dorian, and I were huddled in my attic after I'd rushed home at Brixton's news.

The video image was bumpy and unstable. Ethan wasn't using a tripod. Someone was there with him, making the recording. It must have been Veronica.

On the screen, Ethan stood in a large garden of immaculate stone walkways and expensive potted plants, all ornamental rather than edible. Stone cherubs and garden gnomes poked out from behind three of the waist-high pots. In the distance, a high wooden fence enclosed the yard. This must have been Ethan's home.

"A book of ancient magic," the boy said to the cell phone camera, "has recently come into my possession. I'm going to conduct my first experiment for the world to see. I'm told that these Latin words are known to have brought monsters to life —"

Dorian huffed. I put my hand on his shoulder.

"Today," Ethan continued on the video, "I'm going to prove or disprove the 'magic' of this old book. I'm going to see if I can bring Harry here to life. He will be 'Harry, the garden gnome who lived.' "

He took a few steps down one of the well-tended stone paths. The screen went blurry for a moment as the person holding the cell phone camera zoomed in closer. It came to focus on both Ethan and a two-foot garden gnome wearing a pointed red hat and an evil grin. This was not good.

Ethan picked up a weathered antique book. It wasn't *Non Degenera Alchemia.*

"What's he doing?" I asked. "That's not Dorian's book."

"Look more closely," Brixton pointed. "I watched it five times while I was waiting for you. You can see a piece of paper sticking out of that old book. He's being dramatic, like he loves to do. He must've found that old book in his parents' library and put a printout of the picture he took of Dorian's book inside."

"To pretend he's reading from a real magic book . . ." I murmured as Ethan read the Latin words. He wasn't half bad. I hadn't expected his Latin to be good, but he was a smart kid. Brixton was friends with him, so it figured.

"What the —" Ethan abruptly broke off. His expression changed from a confident, smug smile to wide-eyed horror. The camera zoomed in on his face. "No!" he shouted. "Don't film *me,* Veronica. Get Harry!"

The camera swirled around from the sky to the ground, its focus landing in the spot where the garden gnome, apparently named Harry, had stood. The figure was gone.

The video went black.

"Ethan called me," Brixton said, his voice shaking. "He's totally freaked out. What do we do?"

"You didn't have anything to do with this?" I asked.

"Of course not! Ethan was making a joke

about what I told him right after I met you guys, when I wanted him and V to believe me about Dorian. Only it didn't turn out to be a joke. So, what do we do?"

"We find Harry," I said. My heart thumped in my throat, but I had to remain calm for Brixton's sake. I turned to Dorian. I hadn't known him to ever be at a loss for words, but the gargoyle stood dumbstruck. "Dorian, think. When you had been brought to life, what did you do? Where did you go?"

He ruffled his wings and blinked at me, as if coming out of a trance. "Where did I go? It was a confusing time, at first. Since the words that brought me to life were Latin, I was born speaking and understanding Latin. But no other languages. Not until Father taught me French."

"The library?" Brixton suggested. "That's where Latin books would be."

"Or a Latin professor at a university," I said.

Dorian waved his hand to dismiss both ideas. "This garden gnome will not know any of these things. He is a child right now. He needs guidance and tutelage. He will not have gone far."

"Maybe you could lure it here to Zoe's house with your cooking," Brixton said.

"I wish I shared your enthusiasm for this

idea, my young friend. It would provide an excuse to ask Zoe to buy the expensive ingredients she does not think are important for my gourmet cook —"

"Hey!" I cut in. "We need to focus."

Brixton paced back and forth, his thumb rhythmically flicking his phone screen like it was a security blanket. "Yeah, there's a little baby monster —"

"I am not a monster!"

The phone dropped from Brixton's hand and clattered to the attic floor. None of us made a sound. The only one moving at all was Dorian, whose chest was heaving. His snout flared and his black eyes narrowed. If I had any doubts about Dorian, I would have feared for Brixton's safety. As it was, I wasn't entirely comfortable with how quickly his moods changed these days.

After a few seconds, Brixton scooped his phone from the floor. "I didn't mean anything by it," he mumbled.

"There's power in words," I said softly. "Always remember that. Brix, why don't you take your bike and see if you see anything weird out there. Start at Ethan's house, and circle the streets."

"What are you two going to do?"

"I'll do the same thing, but in my truck. Since we can't ask anyone else for help, we need to split up —"

"What about the alchemist?" Brixton asked.

"You're staying away from that man, Brix. I mean it."

"Whatever."

"What are Ethan and Veronica doing?"

Brixton rolled his eyes. "I think Ethan is 'comforting' Veronica. He said she was totally freaked out."

"You didn't see her?"

"Only for a second. She wouldn't look at me. I thought this was urgent. That's why I took his phone . . ."

"Good work, my young friend," Dorian said.

Now was not the time to explain that punching a friend was anything but good work, especially for a kid who had a juvenile record. "Call me if you see Harry," I said. "Don't approach the gnome on your own."

Brixton blinked at me. "He's a little tiny garden gnome."

"Still."

"When we find him," Dorian said, his earlier anger apparently forgotten, "I could tutor him. He could become my apprentice."

"A garden gnome junior chef," Brixton mumbled. "My life is so weird."

"Once the sun sets," Dorian said, "I will begin the search. For now, I will remain here. I shall compose a list of ideas of where he might go."

"Good," I said. "We'll meet back at the house at sunset."

Brixton and I left Dorian in the attic. I took a last look at his gray face. It now bore a wistful, almost happy, expression.

I drove to rose gardens, cemeteries, and parks looking for any evidence of a rogue gnome. I stopped frequently to check the news on my phone, hoping I wouldn't see news reports of a living garden gnome.

My heart sank along with the sun. This was hopeless. I checked my phone for the hundredth time for sightings in the news or a message from Brixton. Nothing.

Brixton was already in the attic with Dorian when I returned. His knuckles were still bloody and his hand had swelled up in the intervening hours. I admonished myself for not tending to it right away. I retrieved a healing salve, applied it, and wrapped his hand in a clean bandage.

"Ethan called me," Brixton said. "He's pissed off. He wants me to come over and give his phone back. Should we do it? I already downloaded the video and then deleted it from his phone."

"We're going to have to tell him something . . ."

Not knowing what else to do, I drove us to Ethan's house in silence. Even though people believe only what they're ready to believe, seeing an inanimate object come to life would be difficult to explain away.

Ethan opened the door with a stoic expression. His cheek was red, as was half his nose.

"Look," Brixton said, "I'm really sorry —"

"For what? I fell off my bike while doing a trick. No way did I let anyone sucker punch me."

"About why I had to —"

"My parents are out at some fundraiser tonight, so we can talk inside." Ethan invited us into an opulent living room with high ceilings, a grand piano, and ultramodern black-and-white furniture that looked like it belonged in a cosmetic surgeon's waiting room, not a home.

Brixton handed the phone back to him.

"Took you long enough. What have you been doing all afternoon?"

"Looking for Harry, of course!"

Ethan gaped at us. "You guys took me seriously?"

Brixton gaped right back at him. "The video —"

"It was a joke! God, you really believed it?" Ethan laughed so hard his injured nose started bleeding again. He dabbed it with a tissue from a porcelain container next to the couch I didn't dare sit on.

"You got Veronica to go along with it?" Brixton said, his face red with fury and embarrassment.

"Yeah, that was tough," Ethan said in between fits of laughter. "I'm not sure if she's more pissed off at you for hitting me, or at me for making her play a joke on you."

"It wasn't funny," Brixton said. His face flushed bright purple with either anger or embarrassment. Probably both.

"Yeah, you're right," Ethan said with a straight face before again bursting into laughter. "It's not *funny.* It's *hilarious*! Can't you take a joke, Brix?"

"You're quite a moviemaker, Ethan," I said. I didn't dare speak too much. My own emotions were far from under control. A combination of relief, anger, and confusion swept through me.

"I didn't think it would work," Ethan said. "No offense, Zoe, but I thought you'd set Brix straight."

Brixton flung open the front door and stormed out.

"Hang on!" Ethan ran to the open doorway. "You guys should stay for dinner! I'm going to order takeout from that Vietnamese place you like but say is too fancy. My parents are at a stupid charity event all night. I've got my dad's credit card. Anything on the menu you want. Come on, Brix. Brix?"

Ethan's shoulders slumped. I walked over to stand with him in the entryway. From where we stood, I could see Brixton standing at my truck with his arms crossed, looking into the distance.

"We'd better go," I said. "But thanks for the invitation."

When Ethan turned toward me, nodding half heartedly, there was no mistaking the loneliness on his face. "Tell him it was just a joke, okay?"

"He'll get over it, Ethan," I said. I hoped I was right. In spite of his shortcomings, Ethan was a good kid. He thought of himself as a rebel, but in his world that meant buying designer clothes to mimic the style of James Dean and refusing to participate in the numerous extracurricular school activities his parents pressured him to join. Brixton and Veronica had been best friends since childhood, and Ethan found his first true friends in the two of them.

I walked through the excessively pruned

front yard that could have been featured in a modern landscape magazine, and glanced back at the house as I unlocked my truck. The oversized front door was closed, but I thought I saw someone peeking out from behind the heavy white curtains.

"I'm going to kill him," Brixton said, slamming the door of my old truck.

"You know," I said, sitting still for a moment before starting the engine, "his joke tells us something important."

"That Ethan is the biggest jerk — and Veronica too. She's why I never doubted it was true!" He sank down into the seat.

"Brixton, he read the words. He read the real Latin that Dorian knows brought him to life."

"Yeah, I know."

"It didn't work."

"You mean that's not how Dorian came to life?"

"There must be something *else* that has to trigger the Latin words," I said. "There's more going on." The book, I now realized, was far more dangerous and enigmatic than I'd suspected.

Twenty

"The answer," Dorian said, pacing across the creaking attic floor, "must be that the boy was not reading directly from my book."

"Maybe," I said. "Or maybe it's because the gnome was made of plaster, not stone." I thought back on the backward alchemy illustration Ivan had shown me, with the angel turning to stone. But even as I spoke the words, I wasn't convinced.

"There is one way," Dorian said, "to find out."

"We talked about this already. It's too dangerous." I didn't want to mess with implementing the dark forces of backward alchemy, only combatting them. That's why in all of my research into rejuvenating Dorian, I had never tried to bring an inanimate object to life. But desperate times call for desperate measures.

"Your face betrays you, Alchemist. You are as curious as I."

"It's not about curiosity," I snapped. "I never wanted to be an alchemist in the first place. I was happy as an herbalist. Spagyric alchemy was a way to understand more about the properties of plants. But this?" I flipped my white hair, my daily reminder that alchemy had saved the rest of my body from the ravages of time, while my hair and the rest of the world aged around me. "Sometimes I wish Nicolas and Perenelle had never seen my potential and taken me in. Then I might have been able to cure my brother the way I'd always done before I met the alchemists, because I wouldn't have wasted time chasing the false hope that I could find the Elixir of Life for him."

Dorian blinked at me. "But then you would not be here with me. And where would I be without you?"

"You would have found a more competent alchemist to help you." I picked up the object closest to me, a puzzle box missing the key that told how to open it. I threw it across the room as forcefully as I could. It bounced off the wall and landed on the Persian rug that covered the hole in the floor. It didn't break. I was even a failure at expressing angst. The thick wood pieces were linked in such a manner that I doubted anything besides a sledgehammer, or fire, could break it open.

Dorian limped over to me and rested his head on my elbow, then wrapped a wing around my shoulder. "If smashing objects helps you feel better, I can scavenge many things that would make the world a better place if they were broken."

I laughed, and a tear escaped to roll down my cheek. I extricated myself from Dorian's wing to pick up the puzzle box on the other side of the room. I didn't want him to see how upset I was. Was I so desperate for answers that I was seriously considering purposefully bringing a stone object to life? Would it tell me something that I couldn't hope to otherwise understand?

True alchemy is a focused, heightened state of natural processes, but backward alchemy turns nature on its head. I didn't understand nearly enough about the "death rotation" illustrated in *Non Degenera Alchemia.* In spite of my lack of understanding, I was certain with all my heart that although Dorian had been brought to life by the book, he wasn't evil like the backward alchemists who had created *Non Degenera Alchemia.*

"Intent," I said aloud, feeling hope rise within me.

"Pardon?"

"I was thinking through what we do know." I placed the carved box back on the shelf and looked at the articulated pelican skeleton. Pelicans are an important symbol in alchemy because of the sacrifice they make for their young. "*Intent* is important for an alchemist's work. Since alchemy is about transforming the impure into the pure, the alchemist's intent is as important to a transformation as are the ingredients."

"Intent," Dorian murmured.

"You weren't corrupted by this book, even though the backward alchemy inside shows so much death along with power and resurrection. I wonder if Ethan's incantation didn't work because of his intent. He *knew* he was playing a joke."

"Non," Dorian said, shaking his head. "My father was not an alchemist. He did not know the words he read would bring me to life."

"But he read the words with purpose. He was planning on building a gargoyle automaton that would 'come to life.' "

Dorian gasped. "*C'est vrai!* This was his intention. And this will be your intention when you read the words."

"I still don't know if we should mess with the dark forces of backward alchemy."

"If you are not willing, I can enlist the

boy's help."

"No. That's not going to happen." I'd taken Brixton home after our enlightening visit with Ethan, so it was just me and the gargoyle in the house. I'd already involved Brixton more than I should have.

"He would be happy to help."

I rubbed my temples. Sometimes there was no arguing with a desperate gargoyle. If I didn't help him, I had no doubt he would try it on his own or with Brixton. My unwillingness to take risks was causing us to spin our wheels. There were too many unanswered questions. Compared to approaching a murderous backward alchemist, bringing a baby Dorian to life seemed like the safer choice.

"If we do this," I said, "you follow my lead. Whatever happens, you do as I say."

Dorian mumbled something under his breath in French about narcissistic alchemists who think they know best. I ignored him and closed the attic door, locking us in, then set a foot-high stone carving of Buddha on the floor.

I opened *Non Degenera Alchemia* to the page Jean Eugène Robert-Houdin had read from all those years ago. The disturbing woodcut illustration showed a dead basilisk perched atop the ruins of a crumbling building, and bees circling overhead in a counter-clockwise rotation. In stark contrast to the desolate image, the sweet scent of flowers wafted up from the faded page. Underneath the stronger aroma of cloves and honey I detected the scent of roses.

Dorian frowned. "Buddha is a bad choice."

"He's got a full body, just like you. He's made of a similar stone. This statue is a perfect choice."

"But it is *Buddha.*"

I considered. "You think it's blasphemous?" I asked.

"Non," Dorian said. "Boring. If I am to have a companion, he should be someone who enjoys great food. The Buddha would insist on eating simple meals. The words 'simple' and 'meal' should never be used in the same sentence. *Non.* That will not do."

"I'm not bringing to life the spirit of the Buddha, you know. We don't yet know where the power comes from, but surely you see you're not the devil you look like."

Dorian touched his horns with his stone hands, his eyes opening wide. "You think I am a devil?"

I sighed. "Of course not. I don't know what Viollet-le-Duc had in mind when he carved you, but I'm certain it wasn't the soul of a gourmet chef. You've become your own person, Dorian. Just as this little Buddha will be. If this works."

"*D'accord.* You may try it." He scowled at Buddha, then retreated into the corner.

I held the book in trembling hands and read the Latin. I'd studied this page to such an extent over the past months that I knew the words by heart. But I was careful to read the words from the page, with my energy and intent directed at the stone Buddha statue.

I finished the incantation and looked to the stone Buddha.

Twenty-One

"He does not move," Dorian said, poking the Buddha statue with a clawed fingertip.

"No," I agreed. "I read the words perfectly. You're sure that's all Robert-Houdin did?"

"That is what he said. And yes, he was a man of details. This is how he was such a successful stage magician. He would not have left out any details when he told me what happened. Perhaps it is my presence?"

Over the next hour, we tried everything I could think of. Different figurines of different materials and sizes, different locations in the house, and with Dorian both present and absent from the room.

Nothing worked.

"Perhaps it is your clothing," Dorian suggested. "The forces of nature must not believe you are an alchemist. Before the flooding, your clothes were much nicer."

I looked down at my frumpy jeans, remembering the torn dress that had been the only thing I owned for the first year after my brother and I fled Salem Village. "It's not my clothes."

"*Alors,* I am truly a freak of nature."

"Dorian —"

"You are exhausted. It is nearly ten o'clock, and we have not yet eaten dinner. I will cook."

"I'm going to bed."

"Zoe, you have not eaten for half the day. Your skin is drawn. Your eyes are bloodshot. Your hair scatters the floor. You *must* eat."

He was right. There was a time when I didn't take care of myself at all, and it was surprisingly easily to let those bad habits take hold again while under pressure. We descended the steep stairs from the attic. Dorian moved slowly, no longer the agile creature I'd met three months ago.

"Ah!" he cried out.

I saw what was happening but couldn't reach his flailing arms in time.

He tumbled down the steep attic stairs, living stone crashing into each thick wood step. I cringed as I watched his gray body contort and land with a crash on the hardwood floor in front of my bedroom.

"My left wing!"

I hurried down the steps and knelt next to his prostrate body. "It didn't break off."

“I cannot move it.” His lower lip trembled.

“You need to let me give you another infusion of alchemy.”

The gargoyle struggled to sit up, yet he brushed off my attempts to help him. His left leg was now fully stone, and he was unable to bend it to balance. After pushing himself up with his working wing, he grudgingly accepted my help to limp down the flight of stairs that led to the living room.

“If you let me cook you a hearty dinner tonight,” he said without meeting my gaze, “I will consent to your assistance with another batch of the Teas of Ashes.”

I awoke the next morning with the sun, unsure if I felt optimistic or defeated. I knew both more *and* less about Dorian’s book.

Ethan’s prank had forced my hand into making the discovery that invoking the power of the words in the book wasn’t enough to bring a piece of stone to life. I now had more information. Yet at the same time, I felt as though I was further from unlocking the secrets of the book. And even if I could, unlocking the coded messages of the book still might not be enough to save my friend.

I needed help. I again came back to the question of whether it was worth the risk to ask Peter Silverman, the murderous magician alchemist, for help. Should I make a deal with the Devil to save an innocent?

That was a question I first grappled with 300 years ago. That time, I waited too long to make my own decision. It wasn't literally a deal with the Devil, but it felt like it all the same. My brother had suffered and died because of it. I'd gone on a fool's errand that took me from my brother during his last days on earth and cursed me to live on.

My little brother, Thomas, died of the plague in 1704, when he was just twenty-six years old. At the time, I didn't believe my shattered heart would ever heal. I already knew heartbreak, of course. Between disease, distrust, and death, life in the "Age of Enlightenment" was brutal. I watched three of my siblings die in infancy, watched my mother and father stand mutely by as I was accused of witchcraft for my connection to plants, and heard the whispers as my former friends abandoned me one by one.

It wasn't Thomas's death *itself* that broke my heart; it was the cause of it. It was Thomas who helped me escape being burned as a witch. At age sixteen, I fled from Salem Village, Massachusetts, to London, England, with the help of fourteen-year-old Thomas. He was the only person to stand with me through the next twelve years. And I let him down. I might have been able to save him if I'd been there for him instead of abandoning him to study alchemy.

I spent his last weeks on earth trying to find the Elixir of Life. I ignored the advice of Nicolas Flamel, refusing to believe I wouldn't be able to transfer an alchemical protection to another person. Nicolas had advised me to enjoy Thomas's company for his last days on earth, making him as comfortable as possible. Instead, I discovered the Elixir of Life for myself without realizing it, and Thomas died alone.

It was my deal with the Devil. Asking for immortality so I could save my brother, but being granted it only for myself, cursed to live out my endless days alone. I've never forgiven myself for that youthful mistake. I spent the next hundred years trying to atone for my sins, helping everyone except myself. I didn't feel worthy of receiving my gift of immortality. An accidental alchemist, I atoned for my sins by healing others. Sometimes it was enough; and sometimes it wasn't.

I didn't want to repeat the same mistake again.

I pulled on the thick wool socks I kept at

the side of my bed and put on a robe. Even though it was spring, the house was cold from the drafts that had crept in during the night, a result of not having properly fixed up the place. One day.

In the kitchen, I got myself a glass of water with fresh lemon slices. I was still full from the late dinner Dorian had cooked of roasted asparagus with a tarragon and avocado sauce, a French lentil salad, and cashew cheesecake, but I knew I needed to eat breakfast if I was going to have the energy to make Dorian's backward alchemy tea.

I took a mug of steaming green tea to the back porch along with a pen and notebook, and one of Dorian's oat cakes. I watched the sun begin to cast light over my incongruous garden: half of the backyard filled with thriving greenery, the other half barren dirt where I'd pulled plants from their roots to mix into the backward alchemy that began rather than ended with fire.

With the Venetian fountain pen, I started a list of what I knew: One, I needed help with Dorian's book. Two, Peter Silverman was an alchemist who was most likely in town to retrieve his lost hoard before someone else took it.

As for what I didn't know, that list was

much longer:

Was it safe to approach Peter openly? Would Peter admit what he was, or get defensive and attempt to silence me, as he might have done to Wallace Mason? Was Wallace's friend in danger, too? I paused in my scribbles. If that was the case, didn't I have a moral obligation to warn him? If it was indeed the magician-alchemist who had killed Wallace, the police would never be able to unlock the motive. I could only hope they had enough physical evidence to lock him up. But, as evidenced by his presence here, the police hadn't stopped him before.

Speaking of the police, why had Max expressed an interest in my gargoyle statue right before he left? I hadn't had time to think about it while worrying about Ethan's garden gnome, but anything that drew attention to Dorian filled me with unease.

I wished I had someone else I could confide in besides a teenager and a gargoyle. But alchemists were so few and far between. A bad feeling tickled my cold fingertips and spread through me. Since finding the Elixir of Life is personal, it was rare for both members of a couple to find it. True, both Nicolas and Perenelle Flamel had managed this, as had Ambrose and I. But we were the exceptions. Could Penelope be an alchemist as well? If so, knowing now what I knew about backward alchemy and how I suspected Peter's involvement with it to fake his death, he could have used it to help Penelope achieve the same degree of unnatural immortality. At the very least, she must know Peter's secret.

I couldn't trust the magician-alchemists. Nor could I get the help I needed from my teenage ally or the dying gargoyle. Ivan's theoretical knowledge of alchemy was helping, and though I couldn't trust him with my secret, I knew he was on my side. But his help was coming too slowly.

I finished my tea and oat cake, got dressed, then gathered enough plants from the garden to fill a copper bucket. The plants that looked most energetic this morning were stinging nettles and sunflowers. I avoided my thriving lemon balm. Paracelsus, the sixteenth-century doctor and alchemist, called lemon balm the Elixir of Life. Lemon balm tea worked wonders for me, but when I'd tried to work it into Dorian's Tea of Ashes, it resisted the unnatural process. Now I stuck to weedier plants.

I descended the stairs to the basement. For half the morning, I transformed the healthy plants into ashes that I dissolved with sulfurous fire and mercury. Like Paracelsus and other alchemists before me, I focused on the *tria prima* of mercury, sulfur, and salt.

I knew firsthand how dangerous mercury was. Many an alchemist had been poisoned by it. It was a dual-faced rebus, capable of both healing and hurting. I kept mercury on hand for true alchemy, but it was also an ingredient of backward alchemy.

As I stirred the mixture counterclockwise and performed the steps of alchemy in the hastened, backward way explained in the book, the energy from the plants and my own body transferred to the ashes. The plant leaves wilted. My lips and the tips of my fingertips shriveled in a way I now recognized — a cross between soaking in a bathtub for too long and being stuck under the desert sun. I blinked to combat my aching eyes that felt as dry as the ashes I'd created.

Success. I held up the unnatural ashes in my weakened hand.

A normal alchemical operation of this importance would have taken months, even years, to perfect. But because this was backward alchemy, the Tea of Ashes took only a small fraction of that time. The problem was its effects. They were severe and long-lasting. The first time I made the unnatural tea for Dorian, I hadn't realized the sacrifice it involved — or how much it could hurt me.

My "success" was a disingenuous one. Each time I went through the process, I felt it pull more of my own life force out of me.

After steeping the ashes in hot water, I found Dorian in the attic. He sat on the floor reading another science fiction novel that he'd requested I pick up at the library for him. His left leg was askew.

He shifted under my gaze. "I was extra careful on my way to and from Blue Sky Teas during the night. The baking is done, and nobody saw me." He set the book aside and looked up at me with concern.

"You've been reading a lot of science fiction lately." I handed him the Tea of Ashes. Before I'd discovered this quick fix of the Tea of Ashes, Dorian had to keep moving to avoid turning to stone. The movements could be small, so he'd had me check out dozens of classic mystery novels from the library to stay awake through reading. Before he met me he'd been a literary snob, but I'd expanded his horizons. Most recently he'd been giving me lists of science fiction novels, like the one he had in his hand.

"There are more beings like me in science

fiction than in detective novels." He accepted the sour-smelling concoction. "Though I'm not sure I enjoy the ambiguous endings. Next time, I will ask you to bring me more cookbooks as well."

"The last time I did that, you scribbled notes in the margins throughout the books. You can't do that to library books."

"They should thank me!" he replied indignantly.

Dorian's snout scrunched as he drank the thick, grainy tea. As soon as he handed the mug back to me, with only sediment remaining, the near-black color of his left leg and wing lightened. A moment later, his wing flapped, and he was able to bend his knee.

"Merci, mon amie."

He bounded down the stairs. I was glad his newfound energy had given him the speed to depart quickly. That way he didn't see me falter. My legs no longer had the strength to hold me upright. I tried to push myself up from the floor, but my shriveled fingertips felt as if they were still clutching the leather binding of Dorian's book. I tried to breathe, but I imagined I was still smelling the confusing scents from *Not Untrue Alchemy.* My vision clouded and I collapsed onto the dusty floor.

Twenty-Two

SAINT-GERVAIS, FRANCE, 1860

The retired magician lifted the book from the dusty shelf. A jolt of electricity caused his fingertips to tingle as the leather spine touched his skin.

The scent of the volume pushed its way through the still air of the old magician's study, seeming stronger than anything that could possibly emanate from the leather binding and onion skin pages. He identified cloves, honey, and dung, accompanied by an imprecise hint of decay. It was as if the book was greater than the sum of its parts.

The magician shook his head. He knew that wasn't possible. He was becoming fanciful in his old age. Yet there was something mysterious about the antique book. He hoped others would sense its power.

Though officially retired, Jean Eugène

Robert-Houdin wanted to keep his mind sharp. The Father of Modern Magic had moved to Saint-Gervais to write his memoirs. When the French government had taken him away from his writing, calling upon him to serve his country by intervening in Algeria to help divert a military crisis, he had been skeptical. True, he was arguably the most famous stage magician in the world, but his sleight of hand wasn't magic. Nobody was more surprised than Robert-Houdin when his new way to perform the bullet-catch illusion convinced Algerian tribal leaders of France's power. They believed he was performing real magic.

Perhaps most unexpected was his own reaction to his assignment. Instead of discomfort at the dangers he encountered, Robert-Houdin found himself craving further adventure. No longer content to sit in his study and write his memoirs, he wished for a continued audience. Not necessarily on the stage in Paris where he once performed, but creating new illusions he could show to his family and friends.

It was for this end that he selected the curious book with a Latin title. It would be the perfect prop for an automaton he was building.

Robert-Houdin carried the hefty volume to the drawing room, where a meter-high stone carving rested in the corner, underneath a sheet. He chuckled to himself. His wife hated the gargoyle given to him by his friend Eugène Viollet-le-Duc, and tossed a covering over it whenever her husband wasn't looking.

The carving was unlike other gargoyles Robert-Houdin had seen in his travels across Europe. First, it was not technically a gargoyle, in the original meaning of the word, for it did not function as a waterspout. This stone carving was purely ornamental. Viollet-le-Duc had been commissioned to renovate the great cathedral of Notre Dame de Paris, and he had the fanciful idea of creating a gallery of monsters looking over the saints below. The stone creature sitting in Robert-Houdin's drawing room was an early prototype of Viollet-le-Duc's that the architect realized was too small to sit aloft the cathedral's high walkway.

Robert-Houdin pulled the sheet away from the stone carving. Folded wings curled around the stone beast. The little gargoyle looked remarkably like *Le Styrge,* the carving of Viollet-le-Duc's that held a prominent spot next to the stairway entrance to the cathedral's gallery of monsters. An impish grin adorned the creature's face. Yes, this gargoyle would be perfect for what the great Robert-Houdin had in mind.

The magician was known for his ingenious engineering as much as for sleight of hand. His most well regarded invention was an automaton that could both write and draw, a creation which he had shown to King Philippe before it was sold to P.T. Barnum. His favorite, though, was his orange tree. Symbolizing spring renewal and rebirth, the mechanical tree "grew" from a withered stump into a lush patchwork of leafy branches that sprouted real oranges. Mechanical birds appeared in the tree, which was impressive enough, but these birds would then perform yet another feat for the audience. They flew above the tree and revealed a ring "borrowed" from an audience member. The mechanical tree was his crowning achievement — until now.

Robert-Houdin had given a metal plant life. Now, he would bring a stone chimera to life. His own personal golem. He allowed himself a sly smile nobody was there to see. The feat wasn't real, of course. Merely an illusion. He would craft a metal automaton and cover the moving parts with a dummy made in the mold of Viollet-le-Duc's stone creation. Then, on stage, he would recite a few words of "magic" from an ancient book, bringing the creature to life.

He stroked his chin. He would have to time it perfectly, by adding a winding mechanism to the automaton so it could be wound up several minutes before springing to life. But for a former clock-maker, this was a trifling task — far easier than lifting an assistant above the stage with ether.

First, however, it was time to practice. The most important part of any illusion was the drama surrounding it. Without expectation, an illusion was a simple trick, easily forgotten. And Jean Eugène Robert-Houdin did not wish his work to be forgotten.

Sitting in an armchair in front of the creature, he leafed through the book. The intermingling scents were stronger now, as if the book had been dropped in a farmer's field. But no damage showed upon the pages. Odd, that.

No matter. The book was almost twenty centimeters by fifteen, large enough to be easily seen from a stage, especially in a small theater with only a dozen people in the audience.

The book was written mostly in Latin, but many pages were filled with woodcut illustrations rather than text. Robert-Houdin had seen many things in his life, both horrible and wondrous, but the illustrations in this book sent a shiver from his head of gray hair down to the bunions of his feet in his patent leather shoes.

An admirer had given Robert-Houdin the book as a gift, and now Robert-Houdin would put it to good use. Yes, this antique book plus his new gargoyle automaton would create the performance of a lifetime.

Non Degenera Alchemia, the title read.

Twenty-Three

I wasn't unconscious for long, but it was longer than I would have liked. The taxing act of creating the Tea of Ashes caused me to have disturbingly vivid dreams. In my unnatural sleep, the pages of *Non Degenera Alchemia — Not Untrue Alchemy* — came to life before my eyes and transformed into Jean Eugène Robert-Houdin's stage magic performance I'd seen in 1845. The bees rose from the dead and circled sluggishly around me, as if by the magical ether that raised sleeping people above the stage in the theater. When I woke up, I was shivering. I half expected to see a dead bee next to me.

My legs and arms shook as I climbed down the attic stairs. I drew a bath, the most comfortable option in a house with pipes that insisted on alternating between scalding hot and freezing cold water. I applied a poultice of plantain and salt to my skin to suck out any toxins from my alchemy. The wild plantain weed was from the equally wild yard in front of Blue's cottage.

My skills were only one of the reasons I made my own remedies. I'd lived through times when supposed medicines were filled with poison. The "blue pills" dubbed as cure-alls during Victorian times were full of mercury, and many medicines for babies had contained opium. Though I was born in New England during Colonial times, I think of myself as a Victorian more than anything else. I left home at sixteen, and it was during the Victorian era that I settled down for a time after a long period of travel. Therefore the fears and mores from that era were etched into my mind more firmly than the culture of other places where I lived for shorter periods of time.

Right now, I wished there was a cure-all that would be as easy as swallowing a pill. I knew I should fix myself a healing tea or tincture, but I couldn't fathom doing anything besides sleeping after my bath, so I dressed in flannel pajamas and crawled into bed. I was planning on taking a nap, but as soon as I lay down I detected the fragrant scents of berries and cream.

I opened my eyes. Dorian stood at the foot of the bed, carrying a tray of food.

"Is it lunchtime already?"

"Brunch. You had a taxing morning, so I have made crepes for you. One is filled with chocolate, the other coconut cream and wild strawberries. The English cannot compete with the French when it comes to any food invention — besides Vindaloo, of course — yet their idea for this extra meal of brunch is quite a good one."

I smiled with my cracked lips, happy to see Dorian back to his old self. "I don't think it's supposed to be an *extra* meal, but I'll take the crepes. I'm famished."

He set the tray on the side table and hopped up on the edge of the bed. "This is my fault," he said, his gray legs dangling without touching the floor.

"You're apologizing for the food? That's a first." My throat was so dry that I barely recognized my voice.

He clicked his tongue. "You are sick. I was unsure which herbal remedy you would like, so I brought food. I will return with tea, once you tell me which one you would like."

"There's a glass jar in the backyard labeled Lemon Balm Infusion. Would you bring it to me?"

When he returned a few minutes later with the sun-infused tea, I had nearly finished the first crepe. That morning's transformation had expended a lot of my energy.

"Are you are strong enough to hold the mug yourself?" Dorian asked.

I nodded, unable to conceal a smile, and accepted the giant porcelain serving carafe in which he'd warmed several servings of tea.

"*Bon.* Then I will read you the news we have missed." He jumped up onto the bed and spread *Le Monde* in front of him.

"What's the matter?" I asked as his wings drooped.

"For the past month, I have not found any more news of gold statues crumbling in Europe."

"I noticed that too."

"Does this mean the false gold is already . . . dead?"

I knew what he meant. Just as Dorian's life force was reversing for a reason I had yet to identify, false gold in Europe had begun to crumble into dust at the same time. The newspapers had reported the missing gold as thefts, but we knew better. Whatever was happening to both Dorian and the crumbling gold, the gold had already wasted away. Or as Dorian had put it, the gold was dead. I shivered. My Tea of Ashes alchemy might be the only thing keeping Dorian alive.

At that moment, with the scared look on Dorian's face, I abhorred the backward alchemists with the strongest conviction I'd felt this century.

There have always been rogue alchemists. I'd learned from Nicolas Flamel, who was my mentor for a brief time, that the core group of men who'd practiced backward alchemy in Europe were long-since dead. It was an inevitable outcome, since backward alchemy is dangerous and unsustainable. But a break-off sect of alchemists from the heyday of Western alchemy had set forces into motion that were coming to a head half a millennium later.

What I didn't know was why this was happening *now.* The backward alchemists were dead. *What was it they had done?*

I'd failed miserably when I tried to find true alchemists, some of whom should still be alive. But I was out of my depth. I had to try again.

I wasn't well enough to leave my bed, so I asked Dorian to bring me my laptop. From the bed, I searched for any leads I might have overlooked before. I'd searched before, but the Internet rabbit hole had many winding paths. I decided to join a chat group of alchemy enthusiasts. What can I say? I was desperate.

After joining the online group, I was allowed to look through the discussion archives. An hour later, I was certain these alchemists were an assortment of well-meaning amateurs across the spectrum of alchemical interests.

All alchemy is about transformation, but it's approached in different ways. The three core elements of alchemy are sulfur, mercury, and salt. Sulfur is the soul, mercury is the spirit, and salt is the body. Over the centuries, alchemy has involved transformations of base metals into gold, of the mortal body into an immortal one, and of the corrupted spirit into something pure.

In the past, the first two were primarily what alchemists studied, thus acting as a precursor to modern chemistry and medicine. More recently, spiritual alchemy had become more prominent. That's what the members of this listserv were mostly concerned with. The few new members who asked about making gold were met with derision, and they quickly left. Interesting how times had changed.

Though I didn't learn anything on that website, it showed me that perhaps expanding my search would lead me somewhere. I wondered if any of the few real alchemists

I'd once known had gotten involved with spiritual alchemy to ease their discontent with outliving everyone they cared about.

With renewed hope, I felt a surge of energy. I scoured the Internet for spiritual alchemy gatherings. I felt my stomach rumbling and was about to give up, when my hands froze above the keyboard.

I knew the light hazel eyes of the spiritual alchemy speaker in the photograph on the screen. I knew the man not from my many travels throughout the United States since 1942, but from long before.

Or at least, that was my first impression. It couldn't be true, though. Toby was a man I'd known in the late 1850s, during the time I spent with the Underground Railroad. He'd been a sickly man when I first encountered him and nursed him back to health. Nothing like the vibrant man in the photograph named Tobias Freeman. Toby had known nothing of alchemy, and I hadn't taught him. I was heartened, though. This strong resemblance must have meant that Toby had survived and had children.

Because I was good with herbal remedies, my role in the Underground Railroad was to help slaves who were too weak to make the journey north, nursing them back to health to give them a fighting chance to make it. Tobias was one of the weakest men I'd cared for. He was close to six feet tall, and I doubt he'd weighed much more than 100 pounds when he was brought to my doorstep.

But there was no mistaking those light hazel eyes, so light they shone like gold.

The online conference program listed an email address for Tobias Freeman. Nothing ventured . . .

My friend Levi Coffin recommended I get in touch, I wrote in an email from my Elixir email account, signing my name simply as *Zoe.* Levi had been involved in the Underground Railroad, so if this was the same man I'd known, I hoped he'd pick up on the reference. If not, I'd simply get a polite message telling me I was mistaken.

Not five minutes later, an email reply pinged on my phone.

Zoe Faust. I never thought I'd see you again, my friend.

Twenty-Four

I hadn't yet decided how much would be prudent to tell my old friend — that a living gargoyle was living with me, that a murderous alchemist had recently come to town, or perhaps that a book of dangerous backward alchemy was in my possession — when he sent me a second email.

Too much to say over email, he wrote. *Checked my schedule and I've got a couple of days off work this week. As long as you're in the U.S., I can catch a flight to see you.*

I agreed there was too much to say over email. In person, I would also be able to confirm that he was still the same good man I'd known over a century before. Some things about people change over time, but some don't. I hoped Tobias was still the pure-souled Toby I'd once known.

We made plans for him to fly to Portland in two days. I also had an email from Veronica, apologizing for the joke she and Ethan had played and saying she'd started work on my website. I sent quick email replies, then practically flew down the stairs in search of Dorian, my sickness nearly forgotten.

"Salut!" the gargoyle said as I came through the kitchen's swinging door. He hopped down from his stepping stool and wiped his hands on his flour-covered apron. His balance was a little off, with two missing stone toes, but he quickly recovered. "You are well enough to venture to the market! I have made a shopping list."

"Dorian, I found someone who can help us." I didn't even care that flour and some sort of red paste covered a swath of the kitchen walls, including the curtains that prevented curious onlookers from spotting Dorian. I took the list and set it on the countertop.

"You are feeling braver about the magician?"

"No, I found a man I *trust.*" I accepted a miniature red velvet cupcake from Dorian's outstretched hand, and told him about Tobias.

"And he will be here in two days?" Dorian asked once I concluded.

"He's flying in on Wednesday. Can I have another cupcake?"

"Non."

"No?" That was a first.

"You have not yet eaten lunch." He gave a sniff. "Have I taught you nothing about being a civilized person in these months we have known each other?"

I threw my arms around the gargoyle.

"Nor have I taught you enough about being dignified," he mumbled, though he hugged me back. "Your fidgeting is making me nervous, Zoe. I can see you do not wish to be cooped up in the house with me today. I will pack your lunch as a picnic basket to take with you."

"Take with me?"

He gave a Gallic shrug. "Your friend is not arriving for two days. Plenty of time for exploring more leads that might help us, *n'est pas*?"

With a heavy picnic basket loaded into the passenger seat of the truck, I drove to the theater. I didn't know what I hoped to find, but Dorian was right. There was so much going on that if I was well enough to leave the house, I should be doing something productive.

As I approached the theater, I caught a glimpse of Penelope's distinctive hair. She was driving the SUV I remembered, with

Peter in the passenger seat. They were pulling away from the theater.

Should I?

I followed them for several minutes, careful not to get too close in my distinctive 1940s truck. It turned out I was *too* careful. In a city of narrow bridges with hidden entrances, it was impossible to hang back and still see where they turned. I lost them.

I pulled off the road and realized I was next to River View Cemetery. Could that be where they'd gone? The cemetery land was on a hillside overlooking the Willamette River, near where the sapphire necklace from the Lake Loot had been discovered by the young boys. I put the truck into gear and eased up the winding hillside drive that lead through the cemetery.

I could see why Dorian liked this graveyard, one of the forested areas he frequented under the cover of night. River View Cemetery cultivated a peaceful beauty, from its welcoming walkways and weeping cherry trees to its personalized headstones and mausoleums, each in its own style rather than dictated by the cemetery board. It didn't have as many ornately carved statues as some, such as Highgate Cemetery in London, but it was calm and hospitable.

I felt myself fading, so I was glad Dorian

had insisted on packing me a picnic lunch. My body was too exhausted to carry the picnic basket far, so I found a sunny spot on a patch of cut grass with views of the river, a small grouping of ornate mausoleums, and headstones with loving memorials from families. I spread out a blanket and opened the basket from Dorian. The heaping picnic basket contained enough food for at least four people. I found two homemade baguettes with vegetables flavored with olive and walnut tapenades, an assortment of fruit, a thermos of chai tea, and a large mason jar of homemade green juice made with apple, celery, parsley, spinach, and ginger. I knew what was in the juice because of a handmade label with Dorian's distinctive French handwriting that adorned the outside of the jar. While he'd taught me many things about transforming food through cooking, I'd taught him the importance of labeling all of one's transformations.

Though picnicking in cemeteries has fallen out of fashion, the Victorians loved it. Society wasn't always death-phobic in the way it is today. Death used to be much more integrated into life. It was difficult to dismiss it so easily when it was more common, but it also wasn't hidden from sight when it did happen. Though sorrow was involved, it was a natural part of life, and therefore it was celebrated as such, in part through beautifully constructed cemeteries.

I wondered how I would one day die. Through violence while helping someone? An incurable sickness? Or simply a car accident I never saw coming? I thought of it often. Though I had achieved a degree of immortality in a more natural way than alchemists who practiced the "death rotation" of backward alchemy, I hadn't purposefully sought out this aspect of alchemy. Yet I would never end my own life as my old love Ambrose had, when he took his own life after he outlived his son. My life wasn't easy, but it brought many joys, including many new ones I'd found here in Portland.

The reason most true alchemists seek out the Elixir of Life is so they may live long enough to achieve a greater understanding of life. Especially in past times when life spans were so much shorter, there was so much unfinished business. Therefore a longer life goes hand in hand with alchemy's quest to turn the impure into the pure. The Flamels used their longer lives and alchemical skills to transmute gold that they gave to charities. I and others I had once known used our herbal healing skills to help others, such as what I'd done for Toby. We couldn't purify all of the world's evils, but maybe one day the world would be ready.

I sipped Dorian's chai tea and wondered what it would be like to see Tobias (as I should now call him, apparently) again, until I was startled out of my thoughts.

I was under the impression that the treasure hunters had packed up and left the area, but that didn't appear to be the case. Not completely. A fence was in place in an attempt to keep people out of the unstable areas where a minor landslide had occurred due to the winter flooding, but I spotted two men with metal detectors. They were cutting through the cemetery on their way to the steep public lands beyond that had suffered the brunt of the landslide. That was the area where experts speculated the sapphire necklace had come from before it washed down the hillside.

I froze when I spotted a third man with a metal detector. This man stood out. *I knew him.* A thick head of gray hair that fell to his shoulders and hearty black eyebrows gave him a distinctive look. This wasn't someone who could be easily forgotten. He was one of the two men I'd seen sneaking around the theater. The friend of the dead man, Wallace Mason.

TWENTY-FIVE

"Hello there!" the dead man's friend called to me.

Dammit. I'd been staring.

"I couldn't help notice you looking at my metal detector." He walked over to my picnic blanket, eyeing it suspiciously. "You here for the same thing? Got one concealed in that gargantuan picnic basket of yours?"

"I read about the treasure hunting in the paper." I stood and extended my hand. "I'm Zoe. And I'm not here searching for the missing loot. Only enjoying the view."

"Earl Rasputin." He took my hand. His hand was rough, calloused. It matched his gritty, deep voice.

I also noticed his eyes were rimmed with red. Of course. His friend had been murdered.

He scratched his stubbly cheek. "You look familiar. Have we met?"

Had he seen me inside the theater with

Dorian? Had he and Wallace still been there when I spoke with Peter and Penelope? I would have seen him if he'd been in my line of sight, but perhaps he'd heard my voice. That could have been why he thought I was familiar.

"You look familiar to me too," I said. "I've got it. You were with the man who volunteered for the *Phantasmagoria* magic show."

"You were there?"

"I love a good magic show." I cringed inwardly at my inept response. Clearly it wasn't just my body that was lacking at the moment; my mental faculties weren't at 100 percent either. Plus, his bushy black eyebrows were distracting.

He sighed. "You haven't seen the news."

"Oh, how stupid of me. Yes, of course." I fiddled with my hands, trying to appear flustered as if I'd only just now remembered that Wallace was dead. It wasn't difficult, since I was flustered for another reason. I tried to think of a good segue to warn him about the magician without sounding crazy. I also needed to find out what he knew about the loot that had led him to spy on the magicians, when nobody else seemed to have made the connection. But all I came up with was, "I'm so sorry. I did hear about the man who was killed. He was your friend?"

"You get to be my age, and you lose a lotta friends," he said. "It's not an enjoyable experience, but you learn to live with it. But this one's different. I'm not used to losing friends through violent death — if you don't count war." He paused and his dark eyes bore into me. "In the face of death, what you learn most is that you've gotta keep on living. That's why I'm out here today."

I looked around. A lot of trees and birds, but not a lot of people. "His funeral?"

"Nah, the police still have him."

"That's awful." I shivered, and I wasn't acting for Earl's benefit. When I thought of Wallace Mason's dead body falling onto the stage floor, the image replayed itself in slow motion in my mind, as if I could have done something to prevent it. "Do you know what happened?"

"He went and got himself stabbed to death." Earl shook his head. "He always had a temper, so who the hell knows who he pissed off this time. Stupid bastard. Gets himself killed just when we're so close!"

"So close?" *What did he know about Franklin Thorne, aka Peter Silverman, and his loot?*

"Wallace and I are treasure hunters. Been doing it for close to a decade now. Instead of sitting at home alone drinking the bottle of rye he bought me for my last birthday, I thought I'd honor his memory by coming out here today. See if I can find the treasure."

"You're talking about the Lake Loot? I thought everyone had given up on it."

He looked from me to the picnic basket, his eyes narrowing as he did so. "You know a lot about it for someone who says they're not here for the treasure. You having a party here? Where are the rest of your friends hiding?"

"It's just me. Would you like to sit down and have something to eat? I was hungry, so I overdid it."

"You got that right." He set down the metal detector and a fanny pack, then hitched up his jeans and sat down on the plaid picnic blanket. Apparently he'd decided I was harmless. I wasn't so sure about him, though, when I caught a glimpse of what was in the fanny pack. Flyers about Bigfoot sightings. *Bigfoot.*

Yes, I'd just invited a conspiracy theorist to join me for a late lunch in a cemetery.

Well, since he was already sitting down, I might as well sit back down, too, and give him a sandwich. After all, I needed to warn him to stay away from the magician-alchemist.

"What's a pretty little lady doing all alone in a cemetery?" Earl asked, taking a bite of the olive tapenade and vegetable sandwich.

"It's peaceful here." I pressed my locket to my chest, my daily cemetery reminder. "I'm surprised they allow metal detectors in here. Seems like that's an open invitation for grave robbing."

"Some poor sap was arrested for that very reason. Nah, they run a tight ship here. You stick a shovel in the ground and they'll stop you before you toss the first pile of dirt over your shoulder. But I know what I'm doing. I was just passing through to the landslide area." He waved his hand over to where I'd seen the other treasure hunters headed.

"The landslide area that's blocked off —"

"You work for the police, missy?"

"No, but —"

"Then maybe you should mind your own business."

I contemplated skipping the warning to stay away from the alchemist's hoard, but my conscience got the better of me. "I was only trying to help. It seems awfully dangerous. It seems like you'd be doing a disservice to your friend to get arrested or die trying to find the loot."

"Neither is gonna happen."

"Do you know something more than the

others about the Lake Loot?"

Earl narrowed his eyes at me.

"Don't you think it's suspicious," I said, "that your friend was killed right when you two were so close to finding it? I don't mean to be nosey, but I'd hate to see the same thing happen to someone else."

"Like I said, Wallace had a temper. He was a good man, and helped me out years ago when I was going through a rough time, but lots of people would say he had it coming. I already told the police. Don't you worry about it. *Damn.*"

My skin prickled. Had he remembered something? "What is it?"

"This is the best sandwich I've eaten in years. You a chef?"

I sighed. "I cook pastries for a café part-time. But you've got me curious. What do you know about the loot?"

"I used to work as a chef."

"You did?"

He nodded. "I was born at the wrong time. I owned a food truck twenty years before they became popular."

"What did you cook?"

"Chocolate fondue. Now, I can tell what you're thinking. That's pretty dang messy for a food truck. But that was the genius of it. I've got a knack at tempering chocolate, bringing it to the right temperature so it doesn't melt when you don't want it to. Each morning dip an assortment of sweet and savory foods in chocolate, then pop 'em into the truck's fridge. Voilà. I'd have fresh chocolate-covered fruit, scones, bacon, you name it. I'd take custom orders. Those were the most popular. I never understood grilled cheese sandwiches dipped in chocolate, but to each his own." Earl shook his head. "I'm a man ahead of my time. When I was ready to retire I sold my truck to a young punk for a song, and now the kid's got lines down the street for some sort of curried chick pea burrito. Baffles the mind."

"And now you look for lost Oregon treasures?"

"You've got talent, young lady." He tucked the last piece of a sandwich into his mouth and closed his eyes as he chewed, giving me a chance to study his face. As he ate in blissful silence, his weathered skin accentuated the lines around his mouth and eyes. He gave a contented sigh, then his dark eyes popped open and startled me with the intensity of his gaze. "I don't give out praise willy-nilly. You mind?" He indicated the basket.

"Help yourself. And thanks. But you never answered my question. What's your secret information about the Lake Loot? You've got me intrigued."

He squinted his eyes at me. "If I told you, how do I know you wouldn't take it for yourself?"

"Why would I do that? I don't understand why *anyone* is after it. Whoever finds it can't keep it. It belongs to the Lake family."

"You're forgetting about the reward."

"You're in it for the small reward?"

He picked up a second sandwich and stood up. "You wouldn't understand. It's the thrill of the hunt, honey. The thrill of the hunt. And now that Wallace is gone, I'm going to find it to honor his memory."

After Earl left, I again felt like I knew less rather than more. Earl was a strange fellow. Bigfoot sightings? An inside track on the treasure? He knew a lot more than he was telling me, but what? It couldn't be a coincidence that he'd been sneaking around the theater. What had he discovered about Peter Silverman's connection to the Lake Loot? If he believed in Bigfoot, did he believe in alchemy? Or could it all be an act? Could he have killed his friend once they were close to finding the treasure?

I was tired of thinking. At least Earl had saved me from lugging a heavy picnic basket back to the car. He'd eaten almost everything.

I was still tired from the effort I'd expended that morning, but a walk would do me good. I was cold despite the warm spring air and my thick sweater, another indication that my energy was depleted in ways that food couldn't heal. Either that or this polyester sweater wasn't nearly as warm as my favorite wool sweater that had been impaled by a sharp piece of ceiling.

I followed a winding path past a set of mausoleums. Either by accident or design, the plants circling several of the raised crypts mirrored the family names. I imagined that in late summer, giant sunflowers shadowed the Sun family mausoleum. The Thorne mausoleum was surrounded by thorny rose bushes, destined to bloom vibrant and fragrant. And a skilled gardener had somewhat successfully coaxed blackberry bushes into growing up the outer stone walls of the Blackstone crypt.

There weren't any funerals taking place that Monday afternoon, so I had the place mostly to myself. Until a figure caught my eye. Though he was on a path below me on the hillside, it was impossible to miss him. He was juggling three pine cones in his left hand. In his other hand, he held the hand of a woman who stood a head taller than him.

Peter and Penelope Silverman. The magician-alchemists.

TWENTY-SIX

It wasn't a fortuitous coincidence, after all, that had led me to the cemetery that afternoon. When I'd lost Peter and Penelope two hours before, I wasn't far from the entrance to the cemetery. They must have seen me following them and waited to come to the cemetery.

"Good afternoon," I called down to the path below me on the hill.

"Hello!" Penelope said. If I hadn't known she was so successful at acting the part of her role of Persephone on the stage, I would have believed she was genuinely happy to see me. Peter, on the other hand, dropped the pine cones he was juggling.

They cut across the grass, walking briskly up the steep incline to meet me. Peter's hair was no longer red and spiky, but medium brown and combed back. And in place of his bright-red suit he wore a sedate combination of khakis, polo shirt, and loafers. The difference was so striking that if I'd seen him in the street I would have assumed he was a banker or an accountant on his day off, but never a magician or an alchemist.

"We're here visiting family," Penelope said. Unlike Peter, she looked much the same as her stage persona with her perfectly rolled sleek curls. She was dressed in a flowing black dress that wrapped elegantly around her tall frame.

"I didn't realize you were from Portland," I said. "The show is a homecoming of sorts."

"Something like that," Peter murmured, studying my face. "Are you feeling all right?"

"I'm fine. It's just spring allergies. I've been wandering the grounds. I didn't see any Silverman headstones."

"Distant relatives with a different name," Penelope said without missing a beat.

The family connection clicked. One of the mausoleums I'd passed was for the Thorne family. *Franklin Thorne.* They'd postponed their visit when they thought I was following them. Why didn't they want me to see them visiting the cemetery? Did they think I'd connect Peter to Franklin Thorne and the loot?

"It was *you,*" Penelope said, staring at me with a horrific recognition on her face. The Goddess of Spring Growth had turned on me, becoming Queen of the Underworld.

My throat constricted. Penelope had to have known Peter was an alchemist. Could they tell that my sickness was brought on by practicing backward alchemy? By letting them see me in my weakened state, had they figured out I was a fellow alchemist, despite my lie about having bad allergies?

"Zoe Faust," she continued, ignoring the confused look on Peter's face, "who is the reason the police searched through every inch of our possessions."

"I don't know what you're —"

"Your cheap knock-off statue, Zoe. The gargoyle you brought to the theater was such a shoddy piece of work that a piece of him must have broken off."

I froze.

"That," Penelope said, "was what the police were looking for."

"My statue?" I croaked.

"Wallace Mason," she said. "That poor man someone murdered and planted in our set piece — the police found a fragment of a stone statue clutched in his dead hand."

Dorian's toe. That's where it had gone. The dead man had it.

I drove like a madwoman on my way back to the house. I couldn't reach him any other way. Dorian didn't have a cell phone. Not because it would be ridiculous for a gargoyle to have a cell phone — even though we both agreed that would be true as well — but because he had trouble using small keyboards, and touchscreen phones didn't respond well to his touch. I had a land line so he could make outgoing calls. But because he wasn't supposed to exist and live with me, he didn't answer the phone.

Max was waiting for me on the rickety front porch.

"I'm so sorry, Zoe," he said.

"For what? What's going on?"

"I really hoped the piece of evidence would match something found at the theater, but it didn't. They'll be here any minute. I had to tell them."

"Tell *who, what?*"

"About your gargoyle statue. The crime scene guys were looking for a piece of evidence relating to something the investigating officer found. They didn't find a match in the magicians' props. But that gargoyle of yours . . . The magicians said you brought him to the theater. Zoe, it may have been used in the commission of the crime."

The world around me spun in and out of focus. Stars flashed in my eyes. I couldn't let myself faint. I focused on Max's deep brown eyes, trying to steady my breathing.

"You don't understand," I said, raising my voice. I hoped Dorian would hear me inside the house and hide, rather than turning to stone as soon as a guest appeared, as he usually did.

"Then why don't you tell me?"

I opened my mouth but couldn't speak.

"What's going on with you, Zoe?"

"I need to go inside."

Max stepped in front of me. "I can't let you do that."

"What are you talking about? This is my house."

"There's a search warrant on its way."

I clutched his arm. "You have to let me inside, Max. My statue isn't simply a statue."

Max frowned, but at the same time he took my hand in his and squeezed it gently. "Our guys know how to be careful. They won't break it. But really, Zoe, I didn't know you were so attached to physical objects."

I'd respected Dorian's wishes that we not share his existence with anyone else, and I agreed with him about the need for secrecy. But this was an emergency. I had to trust Max.

"You're not listening to me. He's not a

statue." I took a deep breath. And another. "He's my French friend."

"Oh, you mean you borrowed him from that shy friend of yours? Don't worry, he'll be able to get his statue back after the investigation."

"Listen to me, Max. The things you saw your grandmother do when you were a child, when she helped people as an apothecary — there were parts of what she did that you thought were magic, before you decided you didn't believe in it. *You were wrong.* It's not a supernatural magic that apothecaries and alchemists perform, but their work is real. Alchemy brought the statue to life."

I held my breath and waited for him to respond.

"Zoe," Max whispered. "I know you've been under a lot of stress lately, moving to a new place, buying a house that was a bigger fixer-upper project than you thought, and getting up in the middle of the night to bake for the teashop. I've seen how tired and ill you'vc been. And between my trip and work I haven't been around this month —"

"I'm not going crazy, Max! I'm trying to open up to you and tell you what I've been holding back. Come inside with me. I'll show you."

I took a frantic step toward the door, but Max's gentle hold on my hand turned into a firm grip. He held me in place and shook his head as a police car drove up and parked in the driveway.

I stared mutely at the duo who walked up to us.

"It'll be easier," Max said softly, "if you let them in and let them have the statue. I'll get you some help, Zoe. Fighting us right now will only make things worse."

I closed my eyes and breathed. This couldn't be happening. It was daytime, so Dorian would be somewhere in the house. I couldn't warn him. As soon as he heard voices in the house, he'd turn to stone. A defenseless stone statue that the police could take in as evidence. And the longer he stayed in stone, the harder it would be to awaken him.

I nodded numbly and unlocked the door.

The police found a three-and-a-half-foot gargoyle statue standing in the kitchen, next to the fridge. It was missing a pinky toe that matched the piece of stone clutched in Wallace Mason's hand. But he was very much a stone statue, not the living creature I'd tried to tell Max about moments earlier. I watched helplessly as they carried Dorian from the house.

Twenty-Seven

SAINT-GERVAIS, FRANCE, 1860

"Non Degenera Alchemia," the retired magician read aloud. Something to do with alchemy. Robert-Houdin knew basic Latin, and he knew of alchemists. He, in fact, had many books on the subject. Not one but two rooms of his home had been designated as libraries, filled with over a thousand volumes both accumulated by himself and given to him by friends. He devoured books the way some men devoured bottles of wine. It had been an obsession of his ever since he was a young man. While studying to be a clockmaker, he ordered a set of books on the subject. After the books arrived, he unwrapped the paper packaging and found there had been a mistake. Not truly a mistake, though. It was *fate.* Instead of books on the craft of clockmaking, he had been sent books on the mechanics of magic.

Instead of returning the books, he read them. To the curious boy, the idea of true magic opened up a world of possibilities. But where the books explained the technical structure of magic tricks, it seemed to Robert-Houdin that they failed to elevate the conjuring tricks into a true art form. Why was magic lower-class entertainment of the streets? Would French society not appreciate skillfully enacted illusions in the comfort of the theater?

From that moment on, the clockmaker was no more. The formally dressed stage magician who became the Father of Modern Magic was born.

He performed on stages across Europe, honing his craft. He spoke often of the fated books that showed him the path to his true destiny. He wasn't sure he actually believed in fate, yet it made for a good story. Because of it, friends and well-wishers often gave him strange books on a wide range of subjects. Alchemy was as strange a subject as one could find, and therefore several dozen acquaintances had brought him alchemy books over the years.

But *Non Degenera Alchemia* enticed him more than the others.

He ran his weathered fingers over a

woodcut of a globe encircled by flames. He hadn't noticed before that the globe was also a face. It screamed in agony.

A knock on the drawing room door startled him. He'd been so caught up in the wonderful and horrible illustrations that he'd lost all track of time.

"Well, *mon ami,*" he whispered to the stone beast, "our illusion will have to wait." He closed the book. Was it his imagination, or did the scent of decay permeating the room disappear as soon as the book snapped shut?

When Robert-Houdin returned to the drawing room the following day, the strange alchemy book lay open on the side table. He narrowed his eyes. His wife knew he hated it when she fussed with his books. At least she hadn't covered up the carving again.

He glanced at the clocks in the room, all of which kept perfect time, from the grandfather clock next to the window to the glass clock on the mantel. Three hours until dinner. He would not let himself get distracted by the illustrations again. He wished to find a passage to read that would sound mysterious to his audience, providing the drama to elevate his illusion to the perfection he demanded.

Ah! There it was! He took back what he was thinking about his wife. She'd selected — accidentally, almost certainly — a page with a perfect section of text. It was almost as if it was calling to him . . .

He shook his head, feeling the aches of old age as he did so. As he lifted the book into his hands, the pain in his joints lightened, as if the book itself were affecting his body. *"Bof!"* He was definitely growing fanciful in his old age. It wasn't the book itself. It was the anticipation of creating a new illusion that made him feel young again.

He mouthed the Latin words on the page. Three lines of text. A strange combination of words, he could tell, even though he didn't speak Latin well. He'd studied Latin in school, of course, but the method of study was so rote that he'd memorized written passages without understanding their meaning. He formed the words of the first sentence. In spite of his incomprehension, the first line rolled off his tongue. He practiced it again. Yes, he liked the sound of it. Very theatrical. The first two were easy, the last more difficult. He decided he would try again later.

That night after dinner, he moved the

statue onto the small stage he'd erected at the house. The automaton would take much more work to complete, but in the meantime he could practice timing with the stone beast.

Alone in the miniature theater, Jean Eugène Robert-Houdin licked his dry lips, looked out over the empty chairs, and read the incantation. His shoulders drooped. The words fell flat, and not because of the lack of an audience. The words were incomplete. The first two lines screamed to be read with the next. He licked his dry lips and read the last line of text. His tongue stumbled over the foreign words.

Squaring his shoulders, he tried again. The words again came haltingly, as if he were trying to speak backward. He knew an English magician who read backward to pretend he was conjuring the Devil. This Latin evoked a feeling at least as dangerous.

He read the words again. Better. They became easier each time he tried. Having practiced, he turned at a right angle to the empty seats, facing the stone carving, and read the three lines together.

The heavy book became light in his hands, as if an illusion using ether were in play. He glanced upward, annoyed. Someone was surely playing a joke on him, using fishing wire hanging from the ceiling to lift the book without him seeing the mechanism. Yet he saw no wires. His eyesight was not as good as it once was. To be sure he wasn't missing anything, Robert-Houdin held the newly light book in one hand and swiped his other hand above the book. His fingers did not find any wires. What type of illusion was this?

He looked back to the stone gargoyle — but the creature was gone.

Twenty-Eight

Dorian was gone, taken into police custody as evidence.

I didn't know how my life could get any worse. My closest friend had been forcibly removed. The longer he stayed in police custody, the more likely it was that he'd remain trapped in unmoving stone forever. The first man I'd been interested in in years thought I was insane. I was a failed alchemist, unable to create enough gold to make any of my other problems go away. My hair was falling out. And now, after decades of not drawing attention to myself, I was being questioned by the police for the second time since moving to Portland.

Max hovered nearby while the investigating officer asked me a few questions. The pitying look on his face made it easy for me to ignore him. I kept my focus on the other officer as I explained how I brought the statue to the theater to tell the magicians about my business, because I thought they might like some of my wares as props. The magicians would back up my story. I had no connection to Wallace Mason, and I had no idea why he would be interested in a stone toe that rolled away. He was a treasure hunter, so had he thought it was a treasure?

I again neglected to mention that I'd seen Wallace Mason and Earl Rasputin sneaking around the theater. That admission would bring further scrutiny. Scrutiny I couldn't afford. All it would do was lead the police down a path they would never believe.

"You have a roommate?" the detective asked.

I looked at him closely for the first time. As tall and thin as Ichabod Crane, his drawn face and dark craters under his eyes completed the look.

"No," I said. "I started cooking earlier and haven't yet cleaned up." Luckily Dorian hadn't started the oven, or I would have had more explaining to do. The detective raised an eyebrow at my messy housekeeping, but seemed to accept my explanation.

I didn't have to go to the police station to answer further questions, but I had the distinct impression they'd be looking into any possible connections I had to the victim.

Max stayed behind after the other officers

left. The look of concern on his face was too much.

"Maybe you could take a few days off," he said softly. "The teashop can survive a few days without your cooking."

"Sorry for my emotional outburst." I couldn't look him in the eye. "I just need to get some sleep."

"Maybe you could talk to someone. I hated when the department made me talk to a psychologist, but —"

My gaze snapped to his. "I'm *not* crazy."

Memories flooded my mind of what different societies have done to "crazy" people over the years. Doctors had explained and treated mental illness in many different ways. What was called "hysteria" in the 1800s became known as "nervous complaints" in the early 1900s, then a "mental breakdown" in the 1940s, followed by what we currently categorize as depression. Many of the poisonous drugs and physical traumas inflicted upon patients did more harm than good.

But many of us who institutionalized our loved ones did it because we truly wanted to help them. When Ambrose snapped after his son died, psychiatrists were still called "alienists," and I believed they could help him get better, or at least prevent him from harming himself while he took the time he needed to recover on his own. One of the ailments Ambrose was diagnosed with was "dementia praecox," a condition later re-characterized as schizophrenia. I was able to find him one of the most humane asylums that existed in early-twentieth-century France. Charenton was located only a few miles outside of Paris, so I was able to visit Ambrose regularly — until he took his own life.

I steadied my breathing enough that I could continue speaking. "I was simply trying to explain my emotional attachment to my statue. I got a little carried away."

"But you said —"

"I want to be alone, Max."

What I *really* wanted was to try telling Max the truth again. But with how he'd reacted by not even giving me a chance to explain, how could I? It pained me that no matter how much we had in common and how much we were drawn to each other, his worldview was so different from mine in so many important ways.

Even if Max would listen to me, I didn't know the whole truth of what was going on. Why was Wallace Mason clutching Dorian's stone toe?

■ ■ ■ ■

Without Dorian, the house felt strangely empty. After all these years, I was surprised by how quickly I'd become accustomed to living with someone. Though Dorian left the house during the darkest and quietest part of the night, he was always here for breakfast, lunch, and dinner. Not to mention tea, appetizers, desserts, and snacks.

A tear slid down my cheek when I noticed what Dorian had been cooking in the kitchen. The thoughtful gargoyle had been fixing me an extravagant dinner with my new favorite dish — a smoked paprika macaroni and "cheese" made of creamed nuts. Soaking raw nuts ahead of time, then blending them with water and a little salt and lemon juice created a thick cream more decadent than the heavy cream Dorian used to cook with before he came to live with me. My old blender was far more versatile in the gargoyle's hands.

I called Heather and told her I was sick and that I'd be unable to bake pastries for Blue Sky Teas the next morning, or for the foreseeable future until I was better.

Brixton would wonder what was wrong with Dorian, since the gargoyle was the real chef, but I didn't have the heart to tell him. Maybe I could figure out what was going on and get Dorian back before Brixton knew he was gone.

But how could I get Dorian back? After cleaning the kitchen and fixing some of the healing lemon balm tea I'd been drinking regularly to combat the effects of backward alchemy, I tried to sleep. I failed miserably.

There was no point in lying in bed not sleeping while Dorian was trapped in a police evidence locker, slowly dying. His capture was only obscuring the real motivation and clues surrounding Wallace Mason's death.

I dragged my tired body out of bed, unlocked the door to the basement, and lit every candle. I didn't know what I could do to get Dorian back, but once he was returned to me, I needed to have a real cure figured out. It was my best hope for being able to awaken him from stone after having to hold still for so long.

I pushed all thoughts of Max out of my mind. Intent is essential in alchemy, and focus is key. I couldn't let myself be distracted with regrets about Max. Maybe it was for the best that he hadn't believed me. If Max had seen Dorian in living form, how would he have processed the information?

With his attachment to the rule of law, would he have let Dorian escape, or would he have captured Dorian as a suspect? I didn't want to know the answer.

I brought *Non Degenera Alchemia* to the best viewing table in the lab, a slanted wooden desk once used by monks painting illuminated manuscripts. The desk was one of the high-end items for sale on my website, but until it sold, it was a great book stand. Standing in front of the old pages that had weathered the years so well, I willed my mind to understand the morbid woodcut illustrations. My vision blurred as I stared at the counterclockwise circle of bees. Through my unfocused eyes, the black ink of the dead animals underneath blended into a smoky haze.

My focus snapped to attention.

Why did the image trigger a disturbing memory as soon as my vision blurred? I stared at the bees, as if the intensity of my gaze could capture the animals through sheer will. The memory slipped from my grasp.

I needed to get away from the book for just a moment. I stepped back and sat down in front of the table containing the glass vessels and the mortar and pestle I'd used to make Dorian's Tea of Ashes. Though I'd cleaned it well, I could still smell the ashes. Backward alchemy called for using fire too early in the transformation, burning too hot.

Fire and ash.

My eyelids felt heavy.

The next thing I knew, a faint glow of light was coming through the narrow frosted glass window high on one of the basement walls. It must have been shortly after sunrise. While I'd accidentally slept, the candles had extinguished themselves and the dim sunlight was the only light in the room.

A lurch in my stomach reminded me that Dorian was gone, and a kink in my neck told me I'd slept all night with my head resting on a table. Damn. I'd tried so hard to stay awake! But it's not my nature to be awake in darkness. Ever since I was a small child, the perceptiveness that made me understand plants affected my body the same way. When plants slept, my eyelids drooped. I was called a "simpler" at the time. The people in Salem Village thought of it as magic. But being observant of the natural world isn't magic. If I'd been born in the late twentieth century and was the age I looked, I would probably have been a botanist. As it was, I became a plant alchemist.

The planetary cycles and light and darkness don't affect all alchemists equally. Living with Ambrose in early-twentieth-century Paris, I begged him to go out to the *bal-musettes* without me, since I needed to sleep and renew my energy. There was no need for my weakness to prevent him from enjoying himself. He wouldn't hear of it. He argued I was the best herbalist around and could make myself an energizing tonic so I could go out dancing with him all night. It usually got me through to midnight.

I unlatched my locket chain and looked at the images inside — a black-and-white photograph of Ambrose and a miniature portrait of my brother. I had a larger photograph of Ambrose somewhere. I'd kept it hidden from sight for so long because it was too painful to have a daily reminder of my loss. But the more I thought about it, that was backward. Suddenly, I desperately wanted to find that larger photograph.

Aside from my journal of alchemical notes, I've never kept a proper diary. But my notebooks serve much the same purpose, holding pressings of flowers, ticket stubs, sketches, and photographs. The photograph wasn't in my notebook that encompassed 1935, the year of Ambrose's death. I ransacked the attic in search of the photograph. It wouldn't be in an articulated bird skeleton, an apothecary jar, or any glass vessel. It must have been inside one of my notebooks. Half an hour later, I found it tucked inside a palm-sized sketchbook from the 1950s, the book I'd carried with me for the first few years I traveled around the country in my brand-new Airstream trailer that was now six decades old.

Ambrose's kind eyes smiled up at me. For many years after his death, his image had caused me pain. But looking at him now, I felt hope. Ambrose would have told me he had faith in me.

I thought back on what I'd been working on before falling asleep. My eyes had glazed over while staring at the pages of Dorian's book. No, that wasn't quite right. They hadn't glazed over. My tired eyes had made the illustrations blur together. Much like the blurry image of the German book Ivan had showed me. I'd gotten sidetracked by too many other things to research that academic book. I hadn't prioritized it because the scholar who wrote it clearly didn't have an understanding of the backward alchemy illustration he'd included.

But what about the backward alchemy image *itself* . . . an angel turning to stone? Or was it a stone angel that had been brought to life? Death and resurrection. Mercury and sulfur. *Fire and ash.*

I needed to talk to Ivan. It was too early to talk to him now, but after watering my garden and fixing myself two cups of tea, I called him.

I brought Dorian's book to his house, along with the printout from the art of alchemy book he'd given me with the disturbing image of the stone angel, dead jesters, and bees.

"This substance," I said, pointing to the sooty markings on the edge of the page. "Do you have any thoughts on what it might be?"

"No," Ivan said with a shake of his head, "but I take good notes about where I find all of my reference materials." With unsteady hands, he searched through an electronic document on his computer.

A few minutes later, he found the location of the German book that had been written by a nineteenth-century scholar of alchemy. Ivan had found it digitally archived by a Czech university. Not much was known about it, but the cataloguing librarian's notes indicated that the book had been damaged by a fire, and some soot remained on the pages.

Fire and ash.

"You have a working fireplace, don't you?" I said to Ivan.

"Is it cold today? I hadn't noticed, since I'm always cold these days. I rarely use the fireplace. Would you like me to turn up the central heat?"

"That's not what I meant. Can I see your fireplace?"

Ivan gave me a strange look, but motioned me through to the living room.

I scooped up a handful of ashes from Ivan's fireplace and brought them back to his study. There, I smeared the ashes onto the page of *Non Degenera Alchemia* that the book always opened to, the one with the Latin that had brought Dorian to life.

"What are you doing?" Ivan cried. "You will ruin the book!"

"I don't think so." I spread the cold gray ashes across the paper. "If I'm right, I'm revealing its true meaning."

I had assumed that the ruined stone buildings illustrated in *Not Untrue Alchemy* were what they appeared to be: fragmentary ruins that symbolized death. But that was only half of the story. Death *and* resurrection. That's what we were missing.

Before our eyes, the ashes turned the opaque pages translucent. Remaining on the transparent paper was the black ink of the illustrated plates. The individual woodcuts that showed desolate landscapes with crumbling ruins weren't what they had seemed. They weren't barren landscapes at all. Five illustrations were lined up, and their individual pieces made up a coherent whole.

The backgrounds of crumbling remains weren't ruins at all. Together, they revealed one intact building.

A cathedral.

TWENTY-NINE

There was even more to *Not Untrue Alchemy* than I had imagined. Alchemists love codes, using them out of necessity from a time when they were persecuted, but also, I suspected, because they like to feel clever. This was a deeper level of hidden meaning than I'd ever encountered. The woodcut illustrations weren't only coded images themselves, but worked with a trigger.

But even with my breakthrough in the book, I didn't know enough to save Dorian. The cathedral had no identifying features. It could have been one of a hundred cathedrals. Even if I could identify which one, what did that tell me?

It was mid-afternoon when I returned home, but I'd been too sick with worry to eat anything. I was falling into old patterns. I forced myself to drink the last of my healing lemon balm–infused tea, and I found lentil and cucumber salad leftovers. I brought the late lunch to the back porch overlooking my half-thriving, half-depleted garden, and forced myself to eat. Before I'd finished, I heard the sound of someone approaching. A moment later, Brixton dropped his bike next to the porch.

"Aren't you supposed to be helping your mom at the teashop after school?"

"Since there aren't any pastries today, there's hardly anyone there. My mom's teas aren't nearly as good as Blue's."

"Come inside, Brix. There's something I need to tell you."

"Mom said you were too sick to cook today, so I already know it's Dorian who's sick. What's wrong with him? I thought you were going to heal him. I brought over some Stumptown coffee for him."

"That was thoughtful. But he's not here."

Brixton gave me a look that suggested I'd sprouted a second head. "It's daytime. He has to be here."

"That's the problem," I said.

"His mind is going, too, and he wandered off? That sucks. Why aren't you out looking for him?"

"He's not outside. The police took him into custody. My stone gargoyle statue is a piece of evidence."

"How can they do that?" Brixton sputtered. "Did he get caught somewhere he wasn't supposed to be and turned to stone to save himself?"

I forced myself to keep my voice calm in front of Brixton. "You've seen how his left leg has been turning back to stone more quickly than the rest of him. His toe broke off at the theater. The man who was killed was found clutching it in his hand."

"That doesn't make any sense! Why would he care about a piece of stone?"

"I don't know. But Dorian is now evidence in the investigation."

"Prison break," Brixton said. "That's your plan, right? We can't leave him in there."

"I don't have magical powers that allow me to walk into a secured evidence facility."

Brixton balled his fingers into fists. "Then what are we supposed to do?"

I hesitated. Though Brixton was the one person I could talk to about Dorian, he was still a kid. He was on the verge of becoming a man, but his actions continued to remind me that the transformation wasn't yet complete. I couldn't tell him that I'd had a breakthrough with Dorian's book but that it wasn't enough. That I needed the help of a backward alchemist — both to unlock the secrets of *Not Untrue Alchemy* and to wrap up the murder investigation so I could get

Dorian back.

"I'm thinking about what to do," I said. "Right now, I need to do a few things around the house. You can raid the last of Dorian's cooking from the fridge before you go."

"You have a plan you're not telling me, don't you? That's why you want me to leave."

"I have a friend coming to visit. I need to get ready —"

"A *friend* is coming to visit? Don't you care about Dorian at all?"

"Of course I care!" I snapped. I was surprised by how much his words hurt. "That's why Tobias is coming for a visit. He's an alchemist. I thought he could help."

"I thought you didn't know any alchemists anymore. Or are you lying to me about everything? After what happened earlier this year, and after Ethan and Veronica's *joke,* I thought you were the one person I could trust."

I'd hurt Brixton too. He'd been let down by so many people. Not only had a trusted authority figure betrayed his trust earlier that year, but his stepdad's absence must have weighed heavily on him. He refused to talk about his mom's absentee husband, Abel, so I didn't know the whole story. But because of Brixton's refusal to speak of him, I suspected it wasn't good.

"I only just found Tobias. I knew him a long time ago, but we lost touch and until yesterday I didn't even know he was alive."

Brixton squinted his eyes with confusion. To someone raised in the modern world, it's pretty unbelievable to not have instant access to anyone you wanted to find.

"He's flying to Portland tomorrow," I continued. "Only . . ."

"What?"

What I wanted to say was that since Dorian was gone, I didn't know what good Tobias's visit would do. Instead, I said, "I wish I didn't have to wait until tomorrow for Tobias to arrive."

As soon as Brixton left, I climbed to the attic and rooted through a box until I found the object I was after. I held it up. The copper hadn't even rusted. *Perfect.*

I waited five minutes, then slipped out of the house. I put "Accidental Life" on the cassette player to give me courage, and drove to the theater.

The police tape had been removed, and the magicians' SUV was parked in front of the theater. I banged on the back door until Peter opened it.

"I told you not to open the doors," Penelope's muted voice could be heard behind him.

"I know what you are," I said, pushing my way past Peter into the dark backstage area, and onward to the stage where I could see them clearly. "And I know what you're doing here. I'm not interested in exposing you. I don't care that you're after the Lake Loot —"

"Call the police, Pen," Peter said. "Zoe Faust is unwell. Delusional, I'd say."

"Hear me out," I said. "If you help me, I won't tell the police that I know the real reason you're in town —"

A cell phone materialized in Peter's fingers. His sleight of hand was good.

Penelope put her hand on top of Peter's. Her red lacquered nails caught the light and for a moment it looked as if her fingertips had been dipped in blood. "We're not calling the police."

"But —" Peter protested.

"Didn't you hear what she said? She *knows,* Peter. I could tell she knew. That ruse with the gargoyle . . ."

"How?" The muscles on Peter's neck looked like they were ready to pop out. I only hoped he didn't have an aneurism before he could help me. "How did you know? I took steps so no one would piece it together."

"Never allowing your photo to be taken was a good try," I said, "but there's a photo in a book from the 1970s on Portland murders."

"Damn. I went to all the trouble of taking down that website, but a real book . . ." He shook his head and pursed his lips.

"How did you do it?" I asked. "It was backward alchemy, wasn't it? I'm not judging you. It's why I think you can help me —"

"Help you?" His eyes widened and then narrowed. His mouth followed suit, as if he was struggling for words.

"Don't lie to me!" I said. "I have nothing more to lose."

For the next few moments, the three of us stood staring at each other, sizing each other up.

Penelope cleared her throat. The sound echoed through the empty theater. "Are you wearing *chain mail* under your blouse?"

Chain mail was the object from my boxes that I'd taken as a precautionary measure. I may have been acting somewhat recklessly by venturing to the theater alone, but when confronting a man who had killed before and his knife-throwing wife, I wasn't going to be *completely* defenseless.

"Are we on *Candid Camera*?" Peter asked. "As you know, I *hate* cameras. I'll never consent to being featured on television."

"I don't care what you've done," I said. "I'm not going to turn you in. Going to the police is against my interests as well."

"We didn't kill that man," Penelope said. "That hasn't got anything to do with the loot. We're not doing anything illegal."

"Even better," I said, playing along. "Then you won't mind helping me with this." I pulled two photographs of Dorian's book from my bag. "Please. It's important. It's a matter of life and death, or I wouldn't be asking."

Peter's expression was even more perplexed than before. "What does this have to do with the riches my father was accused of stealing?"

"Your *father*?"

"Franklin Thorne. You said you'd figured out my secret and that we're back in Portland to find his hidden treasures. But you've only got half the story. I don't care about the money. I'm back because he was innocent. I'm here to clear his name."

Thirty

"You're not Franklin Thorne?" I said.

"What are you talking about?" Peter said. "He was killed in 1969. I know theater makeup can do wonders, but you really think I'm ninety-five?"

Peter Silverman *wasn't* an alchemist who'd used backward alchemy to recover from a shootout with the police after he killed a man. I had the same biases as everyone else. I saw what I expected to see. What I *wanted* to see.

Before I could think of how to respond, someone else spoke up.

"No way!" a young voice said from the shadows.

Brixton? It couldn't be. He stepped onto the stage, the squeaking of his sneakers' rubber soles the only sound in the nearly deserted theater.

"I don't know how you're here," I said, "but we're leaving." I put my hands on his shoulders to steer him back outside. "Sorry to have intruded," I called over my shoulder.

Brixton shrugged free. "You should be better at checking the back of your truck before you drive off," he said. "I could have been an axe murderer! Anyway, I knew you were up to something. Hi guys, I'm —"

"*Not* telling them your name," I said sharply.

"How very maternal of you," Penelope said. "He's too old to be your son. Younger brother?"

"Neighbor," Brixton said.

"I can read your mind," Peter said casually, slowly circling the two of us, "so there's no need for you to voluntarily tell me your name."

"Very funny," Brixton said.

"I thought so, Brixton Taylor," Peter said.

Brixton's voice caught.

"Stop joking around," Penelope said. "Zoe thinks we're cold-blooded killers. That's why she doesn't want us to know her young friend's name."

"How did you —" Brixton began.

"Check your pocket, Brix," I said. "I bet he lifted your school ID card."

"If I were to have done such a thing," Peter said, "it would already be back in his pocket." His graceful steps carried him across the stage in a flash, and he sat down at the very front of the stage, dangling his feet over the edge. "I can see how curious you both are. I can assure you, we're not murderers."

"We're supposed to just, like, take your word for that?" Brixton asked.

Peter exchanged a look with Penelope. "Since you know the truth about why I'm here, you might as well know everything." He pointed at the front row of seats a few feet in front of him. "Why don't you get comfortable?"

Brixton jumped down from the stage and sat in front of Peter. Short of tossing him over my shoulder, I wouldn't be able to get him out of the theater. But now that I knew Peter Silverman wasn't a reckless backward alchemist, the immediate danger went up in smoke along with the motive I'd theorized. I sat down next to Brixton.

"What are you wearing?" Brixton whispered. "This outfit is even worse than those jeans."

"Never mind." I tugged at the heavy chain mail.

"I changed my name because of my father's infamy," Peter explained. He twirled three tennis balls in one hand, his fingers deftly looping the balls around one another.

"I spent my childhood under the dark shadow cast by being the son of a murderer." In the space of a heartbeat, the three tennis balls became two. In another beat, one ball became half the size of the other — father and son.

"That wasn't the worst part," Penelope added from the other side of the stage. "It was knowing that Peter's father was framed. Franklin Thorne is innocent."

"How'd you do it?" Brixton asked, his wide-eyed gaze fixated on Peter. "How'd you erase your identity so completely? I mean, I really thought you were like a Doppelganger or something." Brixton glanced briefly at me, making sure I realized he was keeping my alchemy secret. "A *library book* says he didn't have kids. My friend Ethan changes stuff on Wikipedia all the time, just for fun. But a *library book*?"

Of course Ethan, the bored and entitled rich kid, would alter history for fun. But even more reliable books weren't the absolute truth. I should have known better than to take the book at face value. Recorded history isn't objective. Everyone has an agenda. Most of the time historians get much of the story right, but I've lived through plenty of events with history book descriptions that diverged from reality.

"You two both really thought *I* was the man in this photograph?" Peter's eyes darted from me to Brixton. It must have been a trick of the light, but his eyes glowed red for a fraction of a second. "You thought I could help you with cheating death? You mentioned . . . What was the phrase? *Backward alchemy?*"

"I was trying to act crazy," I said with a nervous laugh, "to get you off-guard so you'd open up. The police confiscated my gargoyle statue, so they think I'm involved somehow. I was hoping I could get you to confess. Dumb idea, I know."

"Dumb, indeed," Penelope murmured. She strode across the stage, watching me closely, and stopped next to where Peter was sitting at the front of the stage.

"It's really disturbing to be under suspicion," I said. "I'm sure you can imagine."

"I can imagine a lot more than a nosy girl who dyes her hair white for attention," Penelope said. She sighed and sat down next to Peter, letting her long legs dangle next to his. "Peter has spent his whole life running from a past that he had no choice in creating."

"How'd you run?" Brixton asked.

"I had a skip-tracer help me write myself out of Franklin Thorne's story," Peter said.

"That's how I learned about deception and illusion, and that led me to become a magician. Being ridiculed as a boy caused me to retreat into magic. It made me simultaneously invisible and powerful. I guess you could say I'm an accidental magician."

I groaned. Along every step of the way, I'd seen only what I wanted to believe. People dismiss anything that suggests I'm older than twenty-eight because it doesn't fit their worldview, and I was just as guilty. Because *my* worldview involves alchemy, that's how I'd interpreted the clues. But Peter Silverman wasn't a centuries-old alchemist who hung onto old-fashioned ideas; he was a lonely boy who'd latched onto ideas from the past because they were more comforting than his present-day reality.

Even the theme of death and resurrection in the *Phantasmagoria* stage show didn't necessarily suggest Peter was a backward alchemist. The macabre theme is common across cultures and eras, and just because it wasn't popular in this form at the moment, I'd jumped to my own erroneous conclusion. The little things he did that I took as clues were simply the actions of a skilled performer playing the role of Prometheus.

"It's not about big changes," Peter said, "it's the *small* changes that count. Feeding tiny errors to different sources — a different error each time. That obscures everything."

I'd known other children who had to grow up too fast, my brother and myself included. Years after growing up, it's easy to forget how much young people are capable of when they're thrown into adverse circumstances. Especially when they're shunned by their peers.

"So you just erased yourself from history?" Brixton asked.

"Not exactly. Pieces of me are there. First, one agency was informed that there was a mistake in their records. Franklin Thorne didn't have a son; he had a daughter. Another agency was given a different birth date. And another a note about a foreign adoption, with no biological children at all. When my mother had a breakdown, she moved us across the country to live with her sister, my aunt, providing another opportunity. She started using her maiden name, Oakley, to distance herself from the Thorne scandal. I registered for school with a different surname. For the first time, I was my own man."

"Wicked," Brixton whispered.

"As for my first name, I wasn't born Peter. But I played Peter Pan in high school. I was smaller and had more muscle strength than all the women, so they cast me. The nickname 'Peter' stuck. And when I turned eighteen, I took my aunt's married name, Silverman. Of course if anyone *really* looked into my past, they'd be able to figure it out. But I was more concerned with getting through my life each day. In time, people forgot about me. But they never forgot about him. *A murderer.*"

"But even the press reported Franklin Thorne had no family aside from an older, childless sister," I said.

Peter nodded. "Those first few days, sure. I remember it well. My aunt on my father's side was fiercely protective. She took over and answered all the calls from the press." He laughed sardonically. "As a kid, I thought she was protecting us — my mom and me. But she was only protecting herself. She talked about him being a loner and having no family. She wanted to distance herself from him, and not make him seem sympathetic by having a family. She needn't have worried. As soon as reporters did a little digging, they found us. It took ages to undo what they put me through."

If only I'd read more newspaper accounts, I would have discovered Franklin Thorne had a son! It was the same problem I was having with Dorian's book. I was pulled in far too many directions. The necessity of studying the "quick fix" to prevent Dorian's immediate death had kept me from delving deeply enough into my alchemy practice to find real answers.

"My aunt had it all wrong, though," Peter continued. "He was *innocent.* You thought we killed that man to keep the secret that we're here to find the Lake Loot and keep it for ourselves?"

"He and his friend were treasure hunters," I said, "so I figured they were on to you."

"If they were," Peter said with a shrug, "I had no idea."

"Why do you think your dad is innocent?" Brixton asked.

"And how do you think you can clear him?" I added.

"As *lovely* as this evening interlude has been," Penelope said, "now that your big mystery is resolved and you know why we're here and that we had no reason to kill anyone, why do you two care?"

"The police confiscated my statue," I said through clenched teeth, "and they think it might have been involved in the murder. I'm involved whether I like it or not."

"The murder," Penelope said, "has nothing to do with us." She paused, then shook her head and swore. "You think that poor man found out that Peter was Franklin's son, and thought Peter could tell him more information that would lead him to the loot?"

Peter began to juggle three oranges. I wasn't sure where they came from, and I wasn't entirely certain Peter did either. The look on his face made me wonder if juggling was such an unconscious action that he didn't realize he was doing it.

"If that's true," Peter said, "I suppose you think that gives me a motive. But I didn't kill him. I didn't even know he was here before the show that night."

"Zoe," Brixton whispered to me as Peter ranted. "Look at your phone."

Brixton had texted me, presumably as a more secretive way of passing along a message: WALLACE WAS IN THE NEWSPAPER AS TREASURE HUNTER, REMEMBER? P & P MUST HAVE KNOWN. THEY'RE LYING.

Thirty-One

I finished reading the text message and looked up at Brixton. His eyes were wide and he was trying to raise a pointed eyebrow, but both were raised. In the half-lit theater, the effect made him look like a demented clown.

I gave my head a subtle shake. Brixton was jumping to unfounded conclusions in thinking the magicians were lying to us. People who weren't conducting their own investigation wouldn't necessarily read up on the history of a murder victim. An equally rational — or, it could be argued, *more* rational — approach would be to let the police handle things.

"You asked how I know my father is innocent," Peter said. He continued to juggle, but his eyes were locked on Brixton's. "You read that book, so you know the thief is supposed to have pulled off countless heists throughout the 1960s. But they never identified the culprit until this last heist. There's *no evidence* it was my father. Only the fact that he was killed by the police that day."

"But the media —" Brixton began.

"I lived with him," Peter snapped. The juggled oranges swooped higher into the air, nearly reaching to the catwalk. "Don't you think I would have noticed? He was a woodworker who made children's toys. We didn't have much money. My father's family once had money, generations before I was born, but that's not how we lived. He was a simple man who made an honest living. He didn't deserve this."

"Franklin Thorne was accused of killing the guard, Arnold Burke, in cold blood," Penelope said. "But really, Franklin was a hero. It was Burke who was the thief."

"How did everyone get it wrong?" Brixton asked.

"Franklin Thorne and Arnold Burke looked similar," she said. "Nothing like how much Peter resembles his father. But both men had mustaches, brown hair, and were close to fifty years old. *Witnesses mixed them up.*"

"Eyewitness accounts are *always* unreliable," Peter said. "It's the same principle that makes magic shows successful. People see what they want to see — and what they're led to seeing. Nobody wanted to believe a trusted guard who'd once been a policeman was actually a master thief, so they didn't see it. But the truth is that my father was the guard's hostage, not the other way around."

It was an all-too-common story. I'd seen it play out across the world through the centuries. In many ways the world progressed toward more just societies, but this wasn't one of those areas. But it's a noble failing. Nobody wants to believe that a dependable member of society would betray their trust. That's why our minds fill in the blanks with unreliable, yet well-meaning, eyewitness accounts.

"The story the police tell," Penelope added, "is that Franklin held up the train car, and when confronted by the guard, Franklin took him hostage. But really, the guard was the thief. That's how he'd gotten away with so many robberies. When Franklin stepped up to stop the corrupt Burke, he was himself taken hostage."

"They escaped," Peter said, "but the police caught up with them later that day. That's when the shoot-out took place. Both men were killed, and my father was blamed for the whole thing, instead of being hailed as the hero he was for trying to stop the jewel heist."

"But you *are* here because of the sapphire necklace that was found," I said.

"In a sense," Peter said. "But not for the money. I'm hoping there will be evidence that shows it was found in Arnold Burke's hiding spot. That will prove Burke was the thief all along."

"We were performing in Reno when we heard about the discovery of the sapphire necklace," Penelope said. "We were booked through the end of last month, but we made plans to perform a run of shows here as soon as we could."

"You look skeptical," Peter said. For a change, the sarcastic edge from his voice was gone, replaced with a flat, resigned tone. "It's a look I know well. But let me ask you this: The jewels are identifiable. Utterly unique. How could I profit from selling them? I'd only get the reward money, which isn't much. Those treasure hunters were in for the fun of it. Maybe some of them came for the trivial reward. But nobody besides the Lake family cares as much as I do. Nobody."

"What've you found out so far?" Brixton asked. "You going to be able to clear your dad's name?"

Penelope took Peter's hand in hers. The three oranges he'd been juggling fell to the floor at my feet. She sighed. "Our first lead was a bust. We thought the guard's old house must have been in the area affected by the winter flooding. On a map it looked like it was. But the flooding didn't affect that area much. I was wrong. We've also tried to talk to Julian Lake, but he's quite elderly and a notorious recluse, so he wouldn't see us."

"We got so busy with the stage show that we haven't had time to think of next steps," Peter said. "But nobody is more motivated to find the truth. I'll get there."

I was filled with a combination of relief and disappointment. There wasn't a dangerous alchemist in town, so no one was going to expose my secret. But at the same time, I could no longer hope there was a backward alchemist I could turn to for help with Dorian's book.

If it hadn't been for Dorian becoming entangled, at that moment I could have walked away from Peter and Penelope Silverman. I didn't know how serious a suspect I was, but I did know that Dorian was now central to the investigation. The magicians' motive had gone up in smoke, and Dorian's stone toe in Wallace Mason's hand was confusing the line of inquiry. With the focus on Dorian obscuring the facts, I had little faith the investigation would be resolved quickly. I feared for my friend, trapped in both stone and police custody.

THIRTY-TWO

The following morning, I drove to the airport to pick up Tobias Freeman.

A practicing alchemist was my best hope for saving Dorian. However, the more I'd seen of backward alchemy, the less sure I was that a true alchemist could help. Also dampening my optimism was the fact that Dorian was still in police custody. Now, even if Tobias had insights about *Not Untrue Alchemy,* it might be too late for him to help.

Yet I still found myself looking forward to seeing an old friend who would understand. Especially after Max's rejection of the very idea that alchemy could be real.

I spotted Tobias as he walked slowly through the secured section of the airport. He was no longer the sickly man I'd known as an escaped slave, but a muscular man standing tall as he helped an elderly couple with their bags. He winked at me from afar, his brown skin crinkling around his golden-flecked hazel eyes in a manner that told me he often smiled. He waited to greet me until he'd left the couple with their grown grandson.

"Zoe Faust," he said, shaking his head, "as I live and breathe." He swallowed me in a bear hug.

"I never thought I'd see you again, Toby," I said into his shoulder, feeling my eyes well with tears.

"Hey," Tobias said as he let me go. "No need to cry. But why do I think those tears have more to do with the reason you reached out to me than me being here?"

I wiped the tears from my cheeks. "Let's get out of here first."

He grinned. "All those years ago, I *knew* I was right about you being an alchemist."

I took his elbow and led us toward the parking garage. "I can't say the same about you. I thought of you often for many years. I hoped you'd made it to Chicago and were growing old in peace, sitting on a rocking chair on your own front porch, as you said you dreamed of doing." Was this man who looked like he could star in an action movie really the same man I'd nursed back to health so many years ago? If it wasn't for his unusual eyes and his familiar voice, I wouldn't have believed it.

"You didn't notice that I was paying attention to what you were doing all those weeks you looked after me."

"You were barely conscious."

"You were single-mindedly focused on what you were doing, I doubt you would have noticed if the livestock from the farm next door had run through the house."

"Nice try. I remember when that happened. I seem to remember the pig — Charlene? — took a liking to you."

"Charlene was a nice pig! They're smart, you know. I think she sensed I was sick and was trying to keep me warm."

I stopped at the edge of the parking garage and turned to face Tobias. "If it wasn't for that voice, I'd swear I was only imagining you were the same man."

"This voice of mine nearly got me into a whole world of trouble."

I raised a questioning eyebrow.

"You're right that we should get away from here before we talk," Tobias said, glancing around the gray and confining cinderblock-like structure.

"This way."

Tobias took my elbow and held me back. "Let me pick."

"Pick what?"

"I bet I can guess which car."

"Cars didn't exist when we knew each other."

"But cars have personalities. Take me to the right floor, and I'll guess yours."

"You're on. And this is the right floor."

"I get three tries, right?"

"Something tells me you won't need it."

Tobias walked directly up to my green Chevy truck. It was certainly one of the oldest cars in the parking garage. I saw a couple of others from the 1960s, but nothing besides my pickup was from the forties.

"That obvious?"

"I may have cheated. You've got myrrh in here. Who has myrrh these days? I can smell it. I still could have guessed right in three tries, even without the scent of myrrh." He pointed at a black Mustang. "That would have been my first guess. You hated bicycles. I figured you'd be a car person. But myrrh?"

"It's a good air freshener. And you really were a lot more observant than I gave you credit for."

"When you're in servitude," he said, leaning against the truck with a confidence I would have expected in a man who grew up with servants of his own, "you learn how to speak little but see everything."

I unlocked the truck. Tobias gave a low whistle as he climbed inside.

"You fix this up yourself?" he asked.

"I did. Like you said, I'm a car person. Fixing the interior and the engine has a similar energy and rhythm to working in an alchemy lab."

He picked up the cassette sticking out of the tape player. A flash of anger — or was it confusion? — crossed his face. "If you *knew* what I was, why didn't you ever try to find me?"

I frowned. "I was about to ask you the same thing. But I didn't know what you were until I saw your photograph online yesterday —"

"This *tape,* Zoe. This is my song. 'Accidental Life.' "

I stared at him. The reason for my love of the song clicked into place. "*You're* the Philosopher?"

He returned my shocked stare with a grin. "You really didn't know?"

That's why his voice had felt so familiar. Like home. A man I'd once cared for who'd become an alchemist. I shook my head and laughed, feeling tears escape my eyes again. "I was always drawn to this song, but I never knew why."

"Truly?"

"By the time that song came out, you

should have been about a hundred years old."

"It was my hundredth birthday. That's why I wrote the song. I realized I couldn't give this 'gift,' if that's what it is, to anyone else, and I needed an outlet to deal with that. I never dreamed it would take off. When you're on the way to being famous, everyone wants a piece of you. You can't have any privacy."

"And you can't have any secrets — not ones you want to remain secret, anyway. Which is no way to be invisible, like we have to be."

He nodded.

"I always wondered why The Philosopher never recorded another song."

"Now you know why. It was reported that he moved to Mexico to find himself. He was a philosopher, after all."

I shook my head as I started the car. We drove in silence for a few minutes as I exited the parking garage.

"Even though I didn't know you'd become an alchemist," I said slowly, "you knew about me. Why didn't you contact me? You didn't think I'd help you again? I understand you'd want to put those times behind you —"

"Shoot, Zoe. That wasn't it. You know

those were different times. I did try to find you once. I heard that you'd moved to Europe. I never got involved with the society of alchemists — mostly a bunch of traditional white men, especially at the time. Are they hassling you? Is that why you're so upset and why you tried to find a friendly face from your past?"

"Not exactly. It's complicated —"

"You're preaching to the choir."

"My story will make more sense if I can show you something I've got at my house. An alchemy book that's unlike any other. We've got a few minutes until we get home. Why don't you tell me how you became an alchemist? And are you in touch with other true alchemists?"

Tobias ran his long fingers from the dashboard to the eight-track and shook his head. "I don't know any true alchemists, in the way that you mean it. The spiritual alchemists are kindred spirits in many ways, but they're interested in perfecting their own souls, not seeking out the Elixir of Life. I've watched them age."

"But you saw through me in such a short time."

"I saw much of what you did with herbs to heal me, so the next time I fell ill, I sought out herbalists. It was then that I realized nobody else was doing what you did."

"Lots of herbalists use family Bibles and put their own energy into the tinctures they create to heal people," I said. "What made you think what I did was anything more? I was careful —"

"That you were. But not everyone's favorite book is in a strange code, and not everyone works only when they think nobody else is looking. I doubt anyone else noticed."

"But you did."

"I didn't think much of it for years. Then once I learned to read, I read everything. It was about ten years after you knew me that I found a word for what I saw you doing: alchemy. I was intrigued, because you were unlike anyone else I'd ever known. I was lucky to know many kind people in my life — conductors, other abolitionists, and just plain old folks who didn't like to see another human being suffer. Alchemy had been pretty much discredited by then, so books were cheap to come by. I liked so much of the philosophy — transforming one's life. Taking the impure and making it pure. Plus" — he paused and laughed his deep laugh — "I enjoyed the puzzles of the coded pictures."

"And you always liked puzzles."

"You remember that?"

"I'd forgotten until this very moment."

"About fifteen years after I started toying with alchemy, I had my breakthrough."

"The Philosopher's Stone and the Elixir of Life."

He nodded. "I transformed myself from that scrawny, scared pile of bones into a spiritually and physically healthy man."

"You look great, Tobias."

"You look pretty damn good, too, Zoe. You used to be skin and bones yourself. I hardly ever saw you eat, and you always had dark circles under your eyes. But even though you look healthier than when I knew you, there's something . . ."

"When you knew me, I didn't feel I deserved to be taken care of." I felt for my locket. "I healed others, but never myself. I didn't take care of myself until decades later. A fellow alchemist helped me realize that if I wanted to heal others, I first needed to heal myself." I smiled at the memory. "That's when I transformed myself by eating to take care of my body. Cooking with the plants I used in my laboratory."

"But . . ."

"But what?"

"I can see there's something wrong with you, Zoe. *You're sick.*"

I stole a glance at Tobias as I shifted gears

and turned off of Hawthorne. Was it still that obvious? I thought I was doing better that day. "You can tell?"

He shrugged. "I help acutely sick people every day. You're not at that stage yet, but it looks like you're on your way. It's not only your sallow skin, but your jeans are at least two sizes too big. That can't be good."

I sighed. If I survived the week, I was going shopping. "I'm getting over the effects of a taxing transformation."

"Whatever type of transformation it is that you're messing with," Tobias said, "you're in dangerous waters. You need to stop before it kills you."

Thirty-Three

"I shouldn't judge," Tobias said. It was clear he regretted his directive from a moment before. "I haven't seen you in two lifetimes. I don't know what's going on with you."

"You're right that I'm sick," I said. "But don't worry. It won't last much longer." I spoke the truth. Either I'd figure out how to get Dorian back and cure him, or I'd die trying.

"I always wondered something," Tobias said. "I feel bad even asking, since you gave so much of yourself to the cause . . ."

"You can ask me anything. You're probably the oldest friend I've got." I reached for my locket. I'd lost so many people I cared about. It was nice, for once, to find someone.

When he spoke, his voice was almost a whisper, so soft I could barely hear him over the hum of traffic around us. "We were all so poor."

"You're wondering," I said, "why I didn't simply make gold?"

"Knowing what I know now, it's a fair question."

"I'm great at spagyrics —"

"Plant alchemy, sure."

"The thing is . . ." I paused as I pulled into the driveway. "I never got the hang of making gold."

"Truly?"

I sighed as I turned off the engine. "Why does everyone think making gold is easy?"

"Damn, woman, *nothing* worthwhile is easy to come by."

"Did you forget you're talking to the woman who saved your life?"

He laughed heartily. "I wish I had some gold left to say thanks. It looks like this house could use a top-notch repairman." He stepped out of the truck and eyed the tarp that covered a sizable chunk of the roof. As he reached back inside to lift his overnight bag, I was again struck by his physique. Tobias was at once the same good man I'd known 150 years before, and also a completely different person.

I pointed at the roof. "That's why I'm wearing ill-fitted clothing. A winter storm did in a section of the house and ruined most of my clothes. I haven't had time to shop for anything that fits properly."

I led him into the house. Tobias dropped his bag next to the green velvet couch and followed me to the kitchen. Out of habit, I looked around for Dorian, even though I knew he was across town in police custody. The gargoyle was either in an evidence locker or in a lab being examined for trace evidence. If I ever saw him again, I'd never hear the end of it.

"You looking for someone?" Tobias asked. "You live here with someone?"

"That," I said, "is a more complicated question than you realize. Let me get us some sustenance first. Coffee or tea?"

"I've never met an alchemist who could stomach coffee."

"Come to think of it, I believe you're right." I opened the curtains, lit a burner, and set a kettle on the stove. "But that espresso maker isn't mine."

"Oh, the mysterious roommate." Tobias stood in front of the espresso machine and breathed deeply.

"You said you didn't like coffee."

"I didn't say I don't *like* coffee. I said I can't drink it. The scent of coffee is one of my favorite things on earth. Sometimes I'll brew a pot to act as potpourri. But the last time I fell off the wagon and drank a double espresso, I was awake for days."

"The trace amounts of caffeine in chocolate is all I can take," I agreed. "I didn't realize that metalurgic alchemists were sensitive to plant compounds."

"I'm primarily a spiritual alchemist. Couldn't you tell from the lyrics of 'Accidental Life'?"

"But you mentioned you've been making gold."

"I've become somewhat of a generalist — by necessity. You been to Detroit lately? They need all the help they can get."

"Your email didn't mention what you're doing there. You said you help acutely sick people, and I noticed you wear a bloodstone on a necklace chain. Let me guess. ER doctor?"

"EMT. An emergency medical tech. The paperwork is easier than if I were a doctor, but I still get to heal people. Some of the guys who ride with me in the ambulance were wary that I keep a bag of herbal remedies with me, but ever since I saved a man from bleeding to death using cayenne pepper, they don't give me grief."

"Ouch. You didn't learn that one from me. I prefer less painful ways to slow bleeding."

Tobias moved away from the espresso maker and looked past the glass window box above the sink into the backyard garden. "Your backyard is both a medicine cabinet and a chef's dream garden."

"Speaking of which, have you eaten breakfast?" I lifted a domed copper lid from a platter of misshapen blueberry scones, oatmeal nut cakes, and whole grain three-seed muffins. Dorian always brought home the less aesthetically pleasing baked goods from Blue Sky Teas. He was convinced that only the most perfectly shaped creations were worthy of being sold to customers at the teashop. Personally I preferred the misfit pastries. "They're all vegan. And none of them have coffee in them." At my insistence, Dorian had ceased making espresso ginger cookies that looked identical to chocolate cookies. The ginger masked the smell of coffee, and I'd accidentally nibbled on them more than once.

But Tobias wasn't paying attention to the platter. He was still staring out the window. "What happened to that corner of the garden?" He tilted his head toward the section I'd pulled to make Dorian's life-saving tea.

"That's what I wanted to talk to you about. It's —" The kettle gave a high-pitched scream. "Why don't you pick a tea, then I'll get the book I wanted to show you and explain everything." I opened the cabinet that held an assortment of loose-leaf teas. They were hand-dried herbs stored in glass jars.

Tobias selected a flower blend of goldenseal, calendula, and chamomile. The kitchen was bursting with fresh and preserved foods and had no room left for a kitchen table, so Tobias carried the platter of breakfast pastries to the dining table in the large living/dining room. I brought a steeping teapot along with two mugs looped around my fingers to the solid oak dining table, then went to retrieve Dorian's book.

Tobias was already biting into a second deformed pastry when I sat down at the table.

"Ignoring their odd shape, these oat cakes are heaven on earth, Zoe. Heaven on earth." He gave a contented sigh as he ran his calloused fingertips along the edge of the table. "And this table is older than I am."

"Not quite. I bought it from the man who carved it in France shortly after the Railroad wrapped up and I was no longer needed."

"You were still needed, Zoe. I wished I'd had you around so many times . . . Now —" He clapped his hands together. "Is this old book what's making you look so sick and sad today?"

With a dangerous backward alchemy book, a dead man, a dying gargoyle, and missing loot . . . "I don't know where to start," I said.

"I do," a deep French voice cut in. "She needs help because of me."

THIRTY-FOUR

SAINT-GERVAIS, FRANCE, 1860

Under the moonlit sky, the shadow creeping slowly across the roof might have been mistaken for a man. But this man was smaller than most — and had wings.

Jean Eugène Robert-Houdin wondered if his years of creating illusions had played with his mind. Was the belief that he had brought a stone gargoyle to life some form of insanity? The creature seemed so real! But perhaps it was an illusion. He, of all people, knew the power of illusions. They convinced the mind that the impossible was true. This could be an elaborate hoax constructed to fool him. Yes! That must have been what was going on, for what other explanation could there be?

It took him several days to revise his opinion. There was no illusion on earth that could explain the living, breathing creature who looked to him for answers he didn't have. Nothing except for the possibility that the alchemy book he'd read from contained *real* magic.

His wife had a strong constitution, so Robert-Houdin considered sharing the secret with her. But he knew what she would do. She would say it was the work of the Devil and send the gargoyle away. But Robert-Houdin knew the creature was no devil. He was as innocent as his own children upon their birth.

The creature did not cry like a baby, but in other ways he was much like a child. He craved food and attention, as all newborns did.

However, unlike a newborn, the gargoyle spoke some Latin and possessed an acute intelligence; though Robert-Houdin's Latin was poor, that much was clear. It was impossible to deny the creature's existence, nor would he relegate him to a freak show. He would raise the creature as his own flesh and blood. Was it not his own work that had brought the gargoyle to life?

But calling him "creature" wouldn't do.

"Dorian," Robert-Houdin said. "I will call you Dorian."

To his family, it appeared that Jean Eugène Robert-Houdin isolated himself as he worked in secrecy on the greatest illusion of his career. Nobody was allowed to enter his studio. No one. Under any circumstances. If anyone dared defy him, they would be written out of his will.

Needless to say, they all obeyed.

In the solitude of his studio, the old magician taught Dorian, whom he came to think of as Dorian Robert-Houdin. Dorian quickly picked up several additional languages, and also excelled at stage magic.

Unlike most men who worked in seclusion, Jean Eugène Robert-Houdin didn't forget to eat. If anything, his family observed that his appetite doubled, perhaps even tripled, in size. On top of that, he became a picky eater, insisting on the highest-quality foods.

In truth, Robert-Houdin's appetite lessened as he came to grips with the import of what he'd done, and he cared not what he ate. It was Dorian who had a voracious appetite and who craved superior meals. When not given the finest foods, he would sneak out at night to obtain them himself. It wouldn't do to have Dorian seen, so Robert-Houdin made sure to bring the gargoyle his favorite foods.

In this way, the gargoyle's unique personality became apparent, convincing

Robert-Houdin that Dorian was as much a man as any other. Robert-Houdin was happy that some of Dorian's preferences mimicked his own. Like his father — which is how Dorian came to think of the man who had given him life — Dorian devoured great books. Authors like Flaubert, Baudelaire, Molière, and Dumas opened up a whole new world to him. He grew into a proper French gentleman.

Thirty-Five

I jumped up. "Dorian!"

The gargoyle descended the stairs with a limp so pronounced it was painful to watch. He thought of himself as a self-reliant gentleman, so I knew how much it pained him emotionally to show such physical weakness. Staying still in stone must have sped up his progression back into stone.

As he reached the bottom of the stairs I threw my arms around him. "You escaped!"

Tobias handled the appearance of a living gargoyle better than I could have hoped. He broke only one mug as he pushed back from the table to stand defensively. The solid oak dining chair remained in one piece as it hit the floor with force.

"Don't be frightened," I said. "He's a friend."

"Ah." Tobias chuckled nervously. "Channeling Georges Méliès, are you?"

"Not exactly," I said. "He's not an automaton."

Tobias's face clouded. "Damn, Zoe. What are you messing with? You can't control a homunculus. Surely you know that. You need me to help you kill it? Why didn't you say so in the first place?"

Dorian's eyes opened wide with distress. "Zoe?"

"Nobody is killing anyone," I said.

"You sure?" Tobias said.

Dorian pinched the ridge of his snout and shook his head. "I am not a homunculus, nor am I a golem, a robot, or an automaton. I am a gargoyle."

Tobias stood in a fighting stance as he stared at Dorian.

"Tobias Freeman," I said, "meet Dorian Robert-Houdin."

"A man trapped in stone?" Tobias asked, his shoulders relaxing slightly.

"He's a good soul," I said. "The two of you are among the best men I've known in my life."

Tobias stepped forward hesitantly, then stuck out his hand for Dorian to shake.

"We are not sure *what* I am," Dorian said, "yet I appreciate and will accept your gesture of friendship."

The formerly stone gargoyle and the

former slave shook hands.

"Amazing," Tobias said, gripping Dorian's rough gray skin. "You didn't think this little man was worth mentioning until now, Zoe? I thought he'd be the first thing you told me about when we walked through your door."

"Speaking of which —" I ran through the house to make sure the curtains were drawn and returned a minute later, breathless. "It's no longer safe to stay here."

"What have you pulled me into, Zoe?"

"We should tell him," Dorian said to me, then looked up at Tobias. "I believe you are trustworthy, Monsieur Alchemist."

"You heard him praise your cooking, huh?" I said. If the gargoyle continued to use an endorsement of his cooking as a signal to trust people, we were in big trouble.

"*Mais oui.* From the bannister above, I spied his reaction."

Tobias looked from the half-empty platter to the gargoyle. "*This* little fellow cooked all this? You've gotta give me the recipe for the oat cakes. The muffins too."

Dorian puffed up his gray chest.

"Don't encourage him," I said.

"You're right. I don't know what came over me asking about food when there's a living gargoyle in front of me."

Dorian blinked at Tobias. "That makes more sense than anything that has befallen me, Monsieur Freeman. Food is the key to understanding the soul —"

"Dorian," I cut in.

"Oui?"

"Why don't you skip the philosophy and tell Tobias what's going on. You also need to tell me how you escaped. Did anyone see you? Do they know you're gone?"

The gargoyle sighed. "Americans. Always so impatient." He flexed his shoulders, causing his wings to partially unfurl.

Tobias's jaw dropped.

"Let's get upstairs into the attic," I said. "If the police raid the house in search of their missing statue, you can crawl out the hole in the roof to hide where they won't find you."

"But I wish to go to the kitchen," Dorian protested. "I am hungry. They did not feed me —"

"I'll bring food," I said. "Tobias, can you take Dorian and this book up to the attic?"

I joined the two of them five minutes later, carrying a platter of day-old bread along with curried hummus, sliced cucumbers, and olives. They had their heads together over the alchemy book, and Dorian was pointing at the disturbing woodcut illustration of bees swarming around dead animals.

"No fruit?" Dorian asked, looking up.

"He's a particular little fellow," Tobias said.

"One who's about to tell us how he escaped from police custody."

"The *police* in this town know about him?" Tobias asked.

"Not exactly." I briefly told Tobias how Dorian was brought to life with the backward alchemy book, then explained how he could shift back into stone at will, and that it was his stone statue form that was thought to have been used in a crime. "But what I don't know," I finished, "is how he found his way back here from police custody."

Tobias and I looked expectantly at the gargoyle as he finished eating a mouthful of bread slathered in hummus.

A small burp escaped Dorian's lips. *"Pardon."*

"Amazing," Tobias whispered.

"I do not wish to relive the humiliating ordeal," Dorian said, "but for the sake of our investigation, I will. The first indignity was a fine powder they dusted over my whole body."

"Looking for fingerprints?" I asked.

His eyes narrowed. "*Oui.* They did not

find any. This frustrated them. They were not very nice when they carted me to a storage facility. It was from this room that I escaped."

"You were careful?"

"Am I not always careful? I took care of myself long before I met you, Zoe. It took me quite some time to make all of my limbs move again after being still for so long. Once I was confident I would be able to walk, I took a blanket and covered myself, in case there were video cameras. This was shortly before sunrise —"

"That was hours ago!"

"Yes, I made it to my attic entrance before the sun rose."

"You've been here this whole time? Why didn't you come downstairs?"

"I could not get my legs to move," Dorian said slowly, his wings wilting at his sides. "You see, Monsieur Freeman, I am dying."

"I'm going to find a way to save you, Dorian," I said. "I'm getting closer."

"That's why you wanted my help," Tobias said.

I nodded. "But now a murder has gotten in the way —"

"A murder?" Tobias repeated. "What on earth is going on here, Zoe?"

"It's a long story," I said.

"Ah!" Dorian said. "I nearly forgot." He scampered, lopsided, to a corner of the attic. He retrieved a gallon-size plastic bag with a shiny object inside, which he then handed to me.

"A *knife*?" I said, a horrible realization dawning on me. "You took this knife from the evidence room?"

"*Oui.* This is the knife used to kill Monsieur Mason. You did not wish the police to learn the secret of the alchemist, and this is his knife —"

"He's not an alchemist, Dorian!"

"Pardon?"

"I was so worried about you that I went to confront him last night." I explained how Peter Silverman was the son of Franklin Thorne, and that although we were right that Peter and Penelope had returned to Portland because of the discovery of the sapphire necklace, the real reason they wanted to come back was to clear Peter's father's name.

"He's just a regular guy who can't help us with your book," I concluded.

Dorian's wings crumpled. His whole body seemed to deflate, from his horns down to the stone foot that was missing its toe.

"Why did you think this man in particular would be able to help you?" Tobias asked.

"I get that you thought he was an alchemist, but it sounds like you thought he was a special kind."

"You did not tell him what is peculiar about my book?" Dorian asked.

"Tell me what?" Tobias asked.

"Perhaps," Dorian said, "I should leave the two alchemists to discuss matters further."

"You're staying right here in the attic, Dorian. And keep the knife with you. If the police come and you have to flee, take it with you. You can't let the police find it — or you — here."

"So," Tobias said, "our only chance to save this little fellow is to keep him out of sight while the two of us figure out what's going on with his book. Shouldn't we get started?"

THIRTY-SIX

I led Tobias to my basement alchemy lab. The light switch at the top of the stairs turned on a solitary twenty-watt light bulb. It was one of my many failsafe's to make sure nobody looked too carefully at what I was working on in the basement. I'd removed bulbs from the other light fixtures in the basement and used a combination of kerosene lanterns and candles to light the laboratory for my work. They served the dual purpose of keeping prying eyes from easily seeing what was there, and providing the natural energy of fire that fueled my alchemy.

I found a match and began lighting lanterns and candles.

"How is it possible that Dorian is dying?" Tobias asked. "Isn't he made of stone?"

"Dorian was once a piece of stone. He was a gargoyle carved by the architect Eugène Viollet-le-Duc, as a prototype for a gargoyle on the cathedral of Notre Dame in Paris."

"Wait. Robert-Houdin. You said that was his surname. Like the French magician?"

"One and the same."

"You're telling me that magician was an alchemist who somehow transformed himself into a gargoyle during one of his experiments? It certainly gives a whole new meaning to his being the Father of Modern Magic."

"I didn't mean it like that. Jean Eugène Robert-Houdin was Dorian's father — in a way. He was reading from a book of 'magic' as a prop for an illusion he was creating. He didn't realize it was alchemy, or that it could bring a piece of stone to life."

"It can't."

"That's what I thought too. But you saw Dorian with your own eyes."

"There's got to be something else going on with him."

"I think there is." I finished lighting candles and swept my arm across the room. "That's why I've resumed practicing alchemy after decades. I was planning on setting it up properly and easing into it, but Dorian sped up my plans."

"None of this is very stable for laboratory experiments," Tobias commented, eying the folding tables serving as countertops. "It isn't very *secret* either."

"The best laid plans . . ." I murmured to myself in the flickering light.

"What was that?"

"When I bought this place at the beginning of the year, I did it with the intention of fixing up the whole house. It's so rundown that it was the perfect cover for doing extensive renovations. I hired a jack-of-all-trades contractor to fix the roof, patch up the house, and create a true alchemy lab in the basement."

"So what happened?"

"It didn't work out." I didn't need to distract Tobias by telling him about how the handyman ended up dead on my front porch.

"What you've got here is what you did yourself?" he asked.

I nodded.

"In that case, you've done a pretty decent job."

"Not the world's most ringing endorsement. I put a lot of effort into this."

"You know there's still a garage salc tag on that card table. And it smells like beer."

"Touché."

"And what's that on the ceiling?"

I sighed. "I couldn't get all the nettle spurs

off the ceiling, so I'm pretty sure it germinated."

Once Tobias stopped laughing hysterically, his mood shifted. His hazel eyes flecked with gold could show great warmth, but now their brightness turned fierce. The transformation was jarring. Tobias grew more serious than I'd seen him since picking him up at the airport that morning.

"This isn't like you, Zoe. The haphazard nature of this lab. It's not true to alchemy. It's not true to *you.* Why don't you tell me what's going on with that little gargoyle gourmet? What are you holding back? What's really going on?"

I hesitated. I couldn't bring myself to say the words *backward alchemy* out loud to another alchemist.

"*This* is why you're sick, isn't it?" His angry eyes flitted across the laboratory. "You're practicing alchemy, but you're not doing it right. Is he forcing you —"

"No, it's nothing like that."

"What's going on, Zoe?"

"This isn't what I wanted. I haven't practiced true alchemy in ages. You saw my trailer parked in the driveway. I was living out of it, for most of the time, since the fifties."

"Since we can never stay in one place for

too long . . ."

"When I came through Portland, I felt such a longing to put down some roots, at least for as long as I could. For a few years at least. I thought I could at least have that."

"As much as I'd love to get caught up properly and discuss all the things I can't talk about with anyone else, that's not why you asked me here. I've gotta tell you, you're even better at avoiding the subject than your stone friend. Why don't you tell me what's really going on with him?"

I looked up at the nettle hooks on the basement ceiling. "Whatever is killing him, it's only affecting his body. Not his mind. You saw his limp. He used to be able to turn from stone into flesh and back again with ease. Now it's getting harder and harder for him to do so. But when he's trapped in unmoving stone, he's perfectly conscious. If I don't figure out a way to save him, he'll be awake but trapped in a stone prison."

"Damn. Not dead, but trapped in a stone coffin. That's worse than death."

"I know, Tobias. I know."

"You two go way back?"

I gave a weak laugh. "I only met him three months ago. He hid out in my shipping crates when I had them sent from a storage facility in Paris. The only thing he had with him was an old book."

"The alchemy book the magician read from?"

"At first, I didn't think it was alchemy." I paused and lifted it from the bookshelf. *"Non Degenera Alchemia.* Which roughly translates to *Not Untrue Alchemy."*

But Tobias wasn't paying attention. Instead, he picked up the framed photograph of Ambrose.

"I wondered about him," Tobias said.

I froze. What was going on? Tobias couldn't have known Ambrose. I hadn't yet met Ambrose when I knew Tobias. A tickling sensation ran from my spine to my nose. "What do you mean? I know different alchemists are sensitive to different things, but I didn't realize any of us were capable of being psychic."

"What's my knowing him have to do with being psychic? We're scientists, Zoe. There ain't no such thing as a psychic."

"When I was helping the Underground Railroad, I hadn't yet *met* Ambrose. You couldn't have seen this photograph."

Tobias gave me a strange look, a cross between bewilderment and enlightenment. A look common to the faces of alchemists.

"I mean," he said, "I knew him in person."

"How wonderful! So you knew him in the

late 1800s, before I did? We didn't meet until 1895. I knew he'd spent some time in America, but I didn't realized he worked with other alchemists."

Tobias shook his head. "It had to have been the 1950s." He closed his eyes for a few seconds, then nodded slowly. He opened his eyes and snapped his fingers. "1955."

I felt myself shiver. "That can't be right. Ambrose killed himself in 1935."

Tobias gave a start, then looked intently at the photograph. "I didn't mean to shake you, Zoe. You know that over time, faces begin to blur together. I must be mistaken." But his words were too quick, stumbling over one another. Whatever Tobias really thought, he didn't think he was wrong.

Was it me who was mistaken? Was there any way that Ambrose could have survived? The asylum had shown me his body. *Unless it had been an illusion.* My stomach lurched. Why would they have lied? There was no reason for them to have done so.

There had to be another explanation. Ambrose had had a son, Percival, who hadn't taken to alchemy. But maybe Percy had fathered a child, unbeknownst to us. He had never married, but it was the kind of thing the cad would do. It must have been a family resemblance that Tobias had seen in the man he met in the 1950s. After all, that had been the case with Peter Silverman. It was the easiest explanation. Was it the right one?

Thirty-Seven

"Zoe, you with me?" Tobias's voice pierced through my confused thoughts.

"What? Sorry. I was distracted."

"I feel wretched that I rattled you so badly because I thought I recognized the man in the photo. I've seen so many faces over the years. I was wrong in this case."

"I know. It's just been a long time. I miss him." I set the frame down and turned it away. "Let's get back to work. With your interest in alchemical codes, you might be able to shed some light on this. I had the text translated by an expert, to make sure I had a good handle on it."

"I've gotta warn you," Tobias said, "I always hated Latin, so I'm not sure how much I'll be able to help you with this book. I learned alchemy from deciphering the riddles in the pictures, not from solving coded Latin."

"Even better. The text states that the

answers are *in the pictures.* And the illustrations inside aren't like any alchemy I've ever seen. I recently figured out that the woodcut illustrations showing cathedral ruins make up one coherent cathedral when ashes are spread onto the pages to make them blend together. But it's a generic cathedral, so I can't figure out what it means."

"I think you misspoke, Zoe. You mean acid, not ashes, right?"

I shook my head, then I spread the book open on the angled scriptorium desk and stood back and watched as Tobias slowly turned the faded pages. Only, the pages weren't quite as faded as I remembered them.

"I see what you mean," he said, startling me. "These illustrations. Are you sure this is truly old? It doesn't have the scent of an old book."

"It's the strangest thing," I said. "At first, I thought I was imagining it. But now I'm sure it's not my imagination. The scent of the book keeps getting *sweeter.*"

Tobias's breath caught.

"What is it?" I asked. "You've encountered something like that before?"

"I've read about codes that involve all of the senses, but I've never come across one."

"I think I know why you've never seen one

before." I hesitated, still feeling hesitant to speak the words aloud. "This book is backward alchemy."

Tobias gave a low whistle and quickly closed the book. "*That's* why you've been so evasive since I got here. That's what you didn't want to tell me."

"You know about it?"

"Only that you should steer clear of it." He stepped away from the book and crossed his arms. "The death rotation. You sure about Dorian?" He paused and ran an anxious hand across his face. "I mean, if this book is what gave him life —"

"I've never been more certain of anything. Whatever he is, he's a good soul. Unlike the intent of the backward alchemists who made this book, Robert-Houdin's intent was pure. Dorian is an innocent victim."

"His *intent,*" Tobias repeated. "You think that's what kept Dorian from being corrupted?"

"It's not working for his body, though, since it's reverting to stone."

"You know," Tobias said slowly, "you might not be able to save him."

I reached for my locket and steadied my breathing. "I have to try."

Tobias relaxed his arms and stepped slowly back toward the desk. "I'll do what I can to help you two, but . . ." He hesitated briefly, then opened the book again and shook his head. "I'm sorry, Zoe. Even though I enjoy codes, I'm primarily a spiritual alchemist. I only practice my own form of alchemy, and I don't know anyone who works with this type of whacked alchemy."

"Normally I'd say that was a good thing."

"Back up a sec." He looked at the book as if seeing it for the first time. "Why is this happening *now*? What changed?"

"That's what we can't figure out. We think it's happening to other things too. Several works of art made of gold have been crumbling in European museums."

"You mean the gold thefts in the papers earlier this year?"

"They *weren't* thefts. The culprits were reported to be cheeky thieves who left gold dust in place of the items they stole, but it happened at the same time Dorian began to return to stone. I think it's related."

"Damn. But you don't know why?"

I shook my head.

"Then we'd better get to work."

For the next several hours, Tobias and I went through the book's woodcut illustrations.

His interest in puzzle codes led us to a

coded reference I hadn't picked up on — the placement of the flying bees relative to the planets in the different illustrations.

"The bees," Tobias said. "If you take all the images together, looking at which planets are represented in each image, it's as if they're telling you to follow a path."

"The ladder of planets," I said. "I thought of that already, but it doesn't lead anywhere. The Tea of Ashes I'm creating for Dorian isn't like any other transformation I've done. Beginning the process under a certain planet doesn't increase its strength."

"You're looking at this too literally, Zoe."

"That's always been one of my problems with alchemy," I grumbled. "What did you have in mind?"

"The planets have forces that pull different metals to them. Codes convey ideas without being literal about the example."

"Right. Like how the Language of Birds only symbolically involves birds, and hundreds of different dragon symbols have nothing to do with finding a real dragon."

"Exactly. A planetary pull is a strong one, controlling massive oceans through the tides, even keeping us glued to the ground instead of flying off into the universe."

"But you just said this didn't have to do with planets." I forced myself not to tug at my hair in frustration.

Tobias heard the defeat in my voice. "Let go of literal thinking, Zoe," he said softly.

I closed my eyes and breathed deeply, visualizing the melded illustrations of death and resurrection, the ruined cathedral now whole. "The cathedral," I said, my eyes popping open.

Tobias grinned. "*That's* the planet."

"It's trying to pull the book toward it."

"You've gotta find this cathedral."

"I don't see any identifying markings," I said, "but the book dates back at least to the sixteenth century, so it's not a modern cathedral."

Tobias sighed. "Most of them aren't, so that doesn't narrow it down much."

"Thanks for your optimism."

Tobias held up his hands. "Don't shoot the messenger."

"Dorian was originally a carving meant for Notre Dame in Paris," I said, then shook my head. "But the book came into his possession in Blois."

"Is there a Blois cathedral?"

"I'm pretty sure there is. But there have got to be hundreds of cathedrals in France alone. There's got to be something else . . ."

My cell phone rang.

"You're not answering the door," Brixton

said on the other end of the line. "Dorian says you've got him held hostage in the attic and you're starving him to death. How come you didn't tell me he got out?"

I winced. "I'm so sorry, Brixton. So much is going on that I didn't stop and think. He's only been back for a few hours. How did you find out? Don't tell me it's on the news."

"Nah, Dorian emailed me. He's on your laptop in the attic."

Of course he was.

"I think your 'B' key is broken. He kept spelling Rixton."

"You can let yourself in. I'm in the basement and I'll meet you in the kitchen in a second." I hung up the phone.

"Who was that?" Tobias asked.

"The only other person who knows who I really am."

Dorian refused to stay in the attic. He claimed it was safe enough to be inside with the curtains drawn. With Tobias and Brixton at the house, he insisted on cooking all of us a celebratory welcome-home dinner.

"The police must show you a warrant if they wish to come inside, no?" he asked, his arms crossed and his snout flaring.

"Yes, but —"

"My legs are functioning well enough for me to make it upstairs before you let them in. If they come for me, I will be gone before they find me."

I gave up arguing with the gargoyle and let him cook a gourmet dinner for the four of us. I didn't have much food in the kitchen, having been preoccupied by other things, but Dorian created a feast out of the staples in the cabinet and the greens he sent Brixton to harvest from the backyard *potager.*

While Brixton was outside, I considered telling Dorian about the revelation Tobias and I had about the cathedral. But without a solution, I decided against it. I'd at least let him enjoy this evening.

Dorian had been giving Brixton cooking lessons, and he thought it would be a great lesson for Brixton to see how to create a feast when a pantry was nearly bare, so he invited us all to join him in "his" kitchen as he cooked.

"Now that Dorian is back," Brixton said when he returned to the kitchen with a basket full of assorted greens from the garden, "and you've got T helping you with the book, we can help Peter clear his father's name, right?"

There were so many things wrong with

that sentence that I didn't know where to start.

"Dorian is on the lam," Tobias said first. "That's not a fun place to be."

"You escaped from jail, too?" Brixton asked with wide eyes. "Wicked." Only after staring at Tobias with wide-eyed awe for a few seconds did it occur to him that this might not be cool. He cleared his throat and let his eyelids droop into a pose of indifference.

"A jail of sorts," was all Tobias said on the matter. "But he'll never be free until the police are no longer searching for him."

"We must point the police in a different direction," Dorian said. He drummed his clawed fingertips together.

"Here's a crazy idea," I said. "Now that you're safe at home, we should stay out of the investigation. It doesn't have to do with us."

"But Peter's whole life was ruined," Brixton protested. "And all because of what people thought of his dad."

"Helping the magician clear his father's name is a worthy goal," Dorian agreed, "but Zoe is correct. This is not our concern."

"How can you say that?" Brixton asked. "People think his dad is a murderer. It sucks when people don't understand what's really going on with your dad."

"I thought you did not know your father," Dorian said.

"I mean my stepdad."

"People do not understand him?" The gargoyle blinked at the boy. Dorian knew a lot about the local community, but he missed out on a lot too.

"He works out of town," I said gently.

"Doing what?" Dorian asked.

"It doesn't matter," Brixton mumbled. He looked away.

"Yet you said —"

"Drop it, okay?"

"How about I put on some music," Tobias suggested. "I think we've all had an exhausting day."

"I've got a better idea." I put on a recording of the *Adventures of Ellery Queen* radio show. We listened to the 1940s classic detective radio broadcast as Dorian and Brixton cooked.

"Why do their voices sound so pretentious?" Brixton asked.

"It's not pretentious," Tobias and I said simultaneously.

"It was the style at the time," I added.

"Why don't you talk like that, then?" Brixton said. He stopped stirring.

"Before the days of reality television," I

said, "there was more of a distinction between how actors spoke and how people spoke in real life. I was never an actor."

"I must insist," Dorian said, his snout flaring, "that if you remain in the kitchen, you do not distract my young assistant."

"Amazing," Tobias murmured as Dorian showed Brixton how to deglaze a pan containing a fragrantly charred mix of shallots and spices using a small amount of broth before adding the lentils and homemade vegetable broth to stew a red lentil curry. I wasn't entirely certain whether Tobias was amazed that a gargoyle was cooking, that Dorian was creating a gourmet feast from nearly barren shelves, or that a fourteen-year-old boy was enthusiastically helping.

To go with the curry, Dorian made a cashew cream sauce with the last of our raw cashews, speeding up the process of soaking the cashews by plumping them in boiling water. Dorian sautéed minced garlic in olive oil infused with chili peppers, added a splash of water to steam the heaping bunch of nettles Brixton had picked in the garden, and right before turning off the heat he added the arugula greens also from the garden. I normally ate the arugula raw in a salad or added to a smoothie as a zesty kick, but the brief sautéing brought out its peppery flavor.

Dorian gave Brixton the assignment of dipping freshly picked wild treasure blackberries in melted dark chocolate, giving him a coarse sea salt to sprinkle on top. Brixton was once skeptical of how Dorian added salt to just about everything, including desserts, but he'd come around once he tasted the results. A small amount of high quality salt could transform a dish into a heightened version of itself. The salt worked all too well with the chocolate-covered blackberries; Brixton ate more of them than were added to the parchment paper–covered plate that was supposed to go into the fridge to harden while we ate dinner.

I didn't grow up eating chocolate (I couldn't imagine what Brixton would think of that), but once I was first offered it in France, there was no going back. Many high-quality chocolates don't contain any dairy, such as the barely sweetened dark chocolate I preferred.

The sun was beginning to set when Dorian turned off the stove and declared dinner was served. We were eating an early dinner because Brixton had to help his mom clean up at Blue Sky Teas after it closed for the day. Before we sat down at the dining table, I triple-checked that the house was securely locked up and all the curtains drawn.

I was the last one to sit down at the table. I noticed Brixton had taken large helpings of everything except for the nettle mélange.

"You missed this one of the serving dishes," I said.

"They stung me when I picked them. You guys are crazy to eat those weeds."

I was reminded of a story about Frederick the Great, the King of Prussia in the mid-1700s. Many of the poor were starving, but they wouldn't eat a plentiful new food: the potato. Using reverse psychology, the king placed armed guards around the royal potato field. Sure enough, the peasants snuck into the field to steal the potatoes. The French had been similarly tricked into realizing the goodness of the potato by Antoine Parmentier earlier in the century, which is why potato dishes in France often contain the world "Parmentier" in the title.

"I'll fight you for the rest of the Parmentier nettles, Dorian," I said.

"There is no potat—ah! *Oui.* I mean *non.* This is my celebratory dinner, so I wish to eat all of the nettles. You understand, of course, *mon amie.*"

"Just a little bit. The curry won't be the same without them."

"Hmm," Dorian grumbled. He wasn't a

bad actor. "I am feeling magnanimous this evening. Please, take the nettles."

I served a scoop to both myself and Brixton. He didn't say a word, but he ate every bite.

When Brixton reached across the table to collect our empty plates at the end of the meal, Tobias noticed the callouses on his fingertips.

"You must play that guitar a lot." Tobias nodded toward the guitar case backpack Brixton had left in the corner.

Brixton shrugged.

"It looks like you've got some time before you've gotta get back to help your mom. How about we make some music?"

As Tobias sang "Accidental Life" and taught Brixton how to play it on the guitar I almost started to feel optimistic. Dorian clapped along until the claw of his left pinky finger broke off.

"Merde," he whispered. He scampered after the claw.

Brixton ceased his strumming and Tobias stopped singing. The sound of Dorian's claws on the hardwood floors echoed through the house.

"You said you were doing better," Brixton said.

"I am," Dorian said, holding the broken

claw in his hand.

"I'm old enough you don't all have to lie to me," Brixton said.

"We're not —" I began.

A brisk knock sounded at the front door.

"Dorian," I whispered, "go up to the attic. If you hear *anyone* coming up besides me, crawl onto the roof. And don't forget to take the knife with you."

THIRTY-EIGHT

As Dorian limped up the stairs, I caught snatches of the words he mumbled under his breath, but chose to ignore them.

After I heard the attic door squeak shut, I opened the front door to a familiar face.

"Yo, Max," Brixton said. He gave the detective a fist bump.

"Sorry to interrupt your . . . dinner party?" Max said, his gaze floating to the dining table in the open living/dining area.

"This is my old friend, Tobias," I said. The two men silently appraised each other and shook hands.

"Can I talk to you in private?" Max asked. He was speaking to me, but he kept glancing at Tobias. Was he *jealous*?

I already had a good idea that Max was here to tell me that my gargoyle statue had been stolen from the evidence lock-up. But I hated how we'd left things, so I invited him in rather than stepping outside for a brief chat. I left Brixton and Tobias playing music in the living room, and took Max through to the kitchen.

"What's up?" I asked. I crossed my arms and leaned against the counter.

"I wanted to give you the bad news in person." Max stood awkwardly, unsure of what to do with his hands and equally unsure how close to stand to me. He shook his head. "It'll keep. I shouldn't have come in person. I didn't think you'd be entertaining. Stupid of me. I'm intruding —"

"You're not intruding, Max."

"It's not a date?"

"With Tobias?" I laughed. He *was* jealous. "Brixton is here, too, in case you've already forgotten."

"Right. So you and Tobias —"

"He's a dear old friend. Just like I said. And he's only in town for a couple of days."

Max stepped closer and lowered his voice. "I'm here about what you told me the other day."

Panic seized me. He couldn't be here to have me committed, could he? Had my own past deeds come back to haunt me, because I'd once helped institutionalize the man I loved?

"I wasn't myself that day," I said. "I mean, I don't mean I have psychotic breaks and become another person." I was making this worse. "Let me start over —"

"We all get tired sometimes, Zoe. It's okay. I know you're into this New Age stuff."

I swallowed a nervous laugh threatening to surface. The term "New Age" was entirely backward. Being in touch with nature and our own bodies was as old as the world. It was only in recent times that we'd forgotten about it. But Max's words knocked me back to my senses. "I get carried away sometimes."

"I know you're attached to that statue. That's what I meant about why I'm here. It was stolen, Zoe. The statue was taken from evidence. That's what I wanted to tell you. You must've been right that it's more valuable than we thought."

I kept my mouth shut, the easiest way to avoid lying about what I already knew. I should have known it wouldn't take long for the police to realize their evidence was missing.

"You're in shock," Max said, his voice full of concern. "Can I make you some tea? Or should I get your friend? I'd understand if you wanted me to leave. I told you that you could trust me with your valuable possession, but I was wrong. I hope you can forgive me. But really, I'd understand if you simply want me to go."

When I heard the tenderness in his voice, I knew what I wanted. And it wasn't for him to leave. "Please stay."

"You sure?"

"Very. But you don't look so sure yourself. What is it, Max?"

"I can't let it go. I just — I don't understand what happened."

My heart beat in my throat. "You didn't see the thief, did you?"

Max rubbed his brow. "No. We didn't see them. It was a professional operation."

My body was now completely tense. "Why do you say that?"

"Someone hacked into the security system."

That wasn't what I'd expected him to say. "Really? How do you know?"

"The video only shows a figure *removing* the statue from the evidence locker. They had a blanket draped over themselves so as not to be seen by the cameras. At the door, they picked the lock, again under the blanket. But none of the cameras caught him *entering.*"

People only see what they want to see. It never occurred to the police that a piece of evidence could have walked out on his own, so they assumed it was a much more complicated operation than it was.

"Am I under suspicion?" I asked.

"No. I showed the detective your website. He knows you couldn't have pulled this off."

"Thanks. I think."

"I can't figure out why it was taken." Max paced the length of the small kitchen, from the window box herb garden to the off-kilter back door. "There were no fingerprints or trace evidence on the statue."

"I could have told you that. I keep him — it — well cleaned."

Max stopped pacing and took my hands in his. They were warm and comforting. "I don't like this, Zoe. I don't like it at all. We don't know what we're up against."

"I'll be careful, Max. I promise."

The sound of Tobias's sonorous voice and Brixton's guitar sounded through the door.

"Brixton has gotten really good at the guitar," Max said with a smile that reminded me why I loved having him in my life. "Your friend has a great voice too. He a musician?"

"Not professionally. He's singing to cheer me up. That's why he came to visit. It's been a rough couple of days. I feel like I've aged two years in the last two days."

"I know you've been through a lot, Zoe. Losing your little brother when you were young, and now encountering two violent deaths this year."

I felt my locket against my skin, keeping my brother close to me. "This might sound silly," I began hesitantly, "but one of the things that helps me deal with death is to embrace it. The Victorians, and other cultures, had a custom of having picnics in cemeteries. Would you like to join me for a picnic at River View Cemetery? It helps me clear my head —"

"Have you been going back there again, Zoe?" Max snapped, anger flashing in his eyes.

His outburst was so unexpected that I jerked backward and bumped into the swinging kitchen door. "What's the matter with you, Max? Ever since you got back from China —"

"I'm sorry, Zoe. I shouldn't have snapped at you. I've been thinking about a lot of things differently since that trip to my grandfather's 100th birthday party. I don't want to lose you."

"Why would you lose me? We're just getting to know each other. Why are you being so cryptic?"

Max gave a long sigh. "You know I lost my wife, Chadna, not long after we were married. You asked me before what happened to her, but I didn't want to talk about it."

I thought back to the times I'd been to Max's sparse house. There were only two photographs. A black-and-white one of his grandmother, and one of his wife in vibrant color. His grandmother was photographed inside her apothecary shop in China, her lips unsmiling but her eyes alive. The photograph of Chadna was taken in a field of tulips. Her long black hair flowed almost to her waist, and the loving smile on her face told me Max had taken the photo.

"You weren't ready to tell me," I said. "That's okay, Max."

"That wasn't it. It's not about you. It's that I've always wanted to think about the future, not the past."

That was one of the great things about Max. He didn't press me to tell him about my own past.

I waited for him to go on, but instead he said, "I should go. I'm interrupting your party."

"They seem perfectly happy without me. Is that the Spinners they're singing now? I'd say you've got quite a while before they even realize I'm not in the room. You were talking about not living in the past."

"And I was completely wrong. Grandfather had the traditional big sixtieth birthday party when I was a toddler, here in Portland, but this one was different. He's going to die soon, but he was the happiest I've ever seen him. Family and friends from across the world and from every stage of his life visited over the course of a week. They spoke of being helped by him and my grandmother in ways that couldn't possibly be true. The transformations Grandmother made out of herbs weren't magic. She was an apothecary — just a precursor to a pharmacist. But two of Grandfather's guests in particular made it sound as if my grandparents had transformed their lives with magic. And people Grandfather hadn't seen in seventy years made the trip, so he'd truly touched their lives." He paused. "Looking back *was* looking forward."

"That sounds beautiful."

"It also sounds crazy. What's crazier is that I was starting to believe it."

I squeezed his hand, feeling hope rise within me. Was he closer to understanding than I thought? "It doesn't sound crazy, Max."

"If you really mean that, then I know you're ready to hear the reason why I became so overprotective when you've mentioned going up to the mudslide area.

It's about Chadna." A sad smile consumed his face. "I should start at the beginning. Her older sister died of cancer when she was young. It's why she wanted to become a doctor in the first place. She thought she could channel her grief into something concrete. She was so driven. I met her during her fourth year of med school. In the ER."

"She was your doctor?"

"That would have made a nice story, right? But that's not what happened. A friend of mine called me in the middle of the night, needing to go to the emergency room. I drove him, but I'm no good in the middle of the night, and you know I hate coffee, so I promptly fell asleep. She woke me up." He cringed.

"What's so bad about that?"

"She woke me up with smelling salts. She thought I must have come into the ER for myself and been in such bad shape that I'd passed out. She was brand-new to the ER so she didn't know about proper procedures or anything. She broke the smelling salts right under my nose, and I head-butted her nose. There was blood everywhere."

My hand flew to my mouth and I tried to stop laughing, but my efforts were in vain.

"It's okay," he said. "It's impossible not to

laugh at that story."

"It's a wonderful story, Max. That's the kind of thing that keeps a memory alive."

"It's definitely unforgettable."

"Was your friend you took to the ER injured on the job?"

"No, he wasn't a cop. I hadn't yet joined the police force. I was aimless until I met Chadna. She was the exact opposite of my woo-woo family." He laughed sadly. "I told you my grandmother taught me a lot about herbs when I was kid. She and my grandfather lived here with my family until she died, and then my grandfather returned to China. It was my grandmother who was passionate about herbal medicines, talking about the energy of plants and the intent that goes into creating herbal remedies. I always regretted that, shortly before she died, I told her how stupid it all was." He ran a hand through his thick black hair. "Chadna was nearly finished with her residency when she received her own cancer diagnosis."

"How long did you have left with her?" I asked, wondering if he was acting so strangely because of how sick I looked. Did he think he'd lose me to cancer too?

"She had a year of cancer treatments. She never lost her smile through the whole thing, but it was even brighter when she beat it."

"Wait, she was *cured*?"

He nodded. Tears welled in his eyes. "Two weeks after she received the news that she was cancer-free, we were on a weekend getaway to celebrate. We were hiking. We came across a boulder that looked like it would give us a gorgeous view. We climbed up it, and the stone shifted."

My breath caught.

"She fell," Max said. "We were supposed to have our whole lives together, but in that moment, it was all taken away."

"I'm so sorry, Max. That's why you don't want me trekking around that unstable ground above the river."

"I don't want the same thing to happen to you." He stepped closer and ran his fingers through my white hair that he, like everyone else, thought was dyed. "There was nothing I could do, but I still blame myself, you know?"

"I know. I —" I broke off. Should I try telling Max the truth again? What would he do if he saw Dorian?

"I should go," Max said. "You should get back to your friends."

"Don't go." I put my hand on his arm and took a deep breath.

Thirty-Nine

SAINT-GERVAIS, FRANCE, 1871

As the end of his life grew near, Jean Eugène Robert-Houdin feared for what would become of his not-quite-human son. Inspiration struck one day, out of a tragedy.

A famous personage in France, Robert-Houdin knew others in high society as well as men at the tops of their professions. One such man was a well-regarded chef who cooked *choucroute garnie* with such exquisite results that people traveled for miles to partake of his delicacies. The chef developed an ego, as most men do when told repeatedly how great they are. One day, a grease fire began in the kitchen. It quickly engulfed his establishment. The chef made sure all of his workers made it to safety. He was the last one out. It never once occurred to him that the building would dare injure him. Yet a wooden beam struck him, trapping him inside the burning building. Before he was rescued, the fire scorched his head and hands. He escaped with his life, but without his sight and former dexterity.

As he'd never married, the former chef sat alone in his large house. There was no life in the house, save for the domestic servant who came twice a day to clean the house and bring him barely tolerable food. The chef might have withered and died from desolation had it not been for the occasional interesting visitor, such as his old friend Jean Eugène Robert-Houdin and an odd fellow Robert-Houdin brought with him.

Dorian was introduced as a distant relative of Robert-Houdin's who had been disfigured in an accident and was therefore wary of being seen by people, who could be cuttingly cruel. Oh, how the chef understood the cruelty of men! The people who once adored him would no longer look upon his burned face and hands. The saving grace of his blindness was that he himself did not have to see what his once-handsome face had become.

The chef was the first person aside from Robert-Houdin with whom Dorian had conversed. On one visit, the topic turned to food, as it often did. Robert-Houdin went to the window to look upon the barren trees that swayed in the wind. Winter would be upon them soon. He sensed it would be his last winter in this world.

Robert-Houdin's human son had recently died in the Franco-Prussian War, and the Hessians were threatening Paris. What more did an old man have to live for?

When he pulled himself out of his own thoughts and returned to the sofa, he realized that he had not been missed. Looking between the two outcasts, a flash of inspiration overwhelmed him.

"Martin," Robert-Houdin said. He rose out of habit, even though the chef could not see him. "I have had the most inspired idea. You and my relation Dorian are both men shunned by society through no fault of your own, and you both appreciate eating gourmet food."

"Why must you bring up my failings?" Martin asked, holding up his burned hands. "I can neither see nor hold a knife. I must rely on the vile porridge and stews that wretched woman brings me."

"Yet Dorian," Robert-Houdin said, "has the best eyesight of any man I have met, and is nearly as accomplished at sleight of hand as I. Would it not be possible for you to teach him to cook? He is looking for somewhere to live where he will not need to hide from people who look upon him unfavorably because of his disfigurement. In exchange for food and lodgings, he could cook and clean for you. I cannot imagine a more perfect plan."

And so it was that one of the greatest cooks in France would teach Dorian Robert-Houdin the skills that enabled him to become a gourmet chef.

The war brought challenges that year, but the Robert-Houdin household survived by hiding from the Hessians in a cave. Having gotten his affairs in order, Robert-Houdin passed away that summer, at peace.

Upon the old magician's death, the family unlocked his studio. Everyone was disappointed to find no great creation waiting for them. What had the man been working on all those years? His mind must have left him.

The family was less surprised by a trifling fact of far greater significance. Upon Robert-Houdin's death, his friend Viollet-le-Duc came to pay his respects. He asked if he could see the magician's stage props. Since the architect was not a magician competitor, Robert-Houdin's family saw no harm in allowing an old friend to visit his studio. They didn't expect the elderly architect to erupt in a rage when he could not find the gift he'd given his friend years before. No matter, they thought to themselves. They were sorry for his grief, but could he really have expected that his friend would keep his atrocious gift? When the architect began raving and asking questions, claiming that Robert-Houdin had been an alchemist, they set him straight and politely asked the man to leave.

Forty

"I want to tell you something, too," I said. "So please, don't go."

Max stepped back to give me space, but took my hand in his. I smelled jasmine as he ran his index finger along the life line of my palm, even though I knew his Poet's Jasmine wouldn't be blooming again until summer. "I'm glad you're feeling better after your meltdown the last time I saw you."

Meltdown? I steadied my breathing. As much as I wanted to tell Max the whole messy, unbelievable truth, I'd been overly optimistic that I could tell him everything. He wasn't ready to believe me. Not yet. "Hey, *meltdown* is a bit harsh, don't you think?" I forced a laugh. "There was a search warrant for my house, so I was entitled to a freak-out."

"Fair enough." Max laughed along with me. "What were you going to tell me? After

I told you that embarrassing story of how I met Chadna, you know you can tell me anything."

I couldn't, though. If he thought my talking about a living gargoyle was a meltdown, he'd certainly have his own meltdown if I convinced him it was true. But he was still straddling that line of what he'd let himself believe. One day soon, I hoped he'd be ready. And in the present, it was still true that I didn't want Max to leave. He understood what it was like to lose a loved one under tragic circumstances, and I needed to open up to someone about Ambrose. The memories that had bubbled to the surface were too distracting, and talking with Tobias was no longer an option, since Tobias mistakenly thought he knew Ambrose long after he'd died. Max was who I wanted to talk to, and there was a lot I could tell him that was true. All I had to do was leave out irrelevant details that wouldn't have fit with his understanding of the world.

The sound of melodious guitar chords and a booming baritone continued in the background, lulling me into a sense of safety I hadn't felt in years. Even though the people around me didn't understand all of me, I was surrounded by people who cared for me, and who I cared for.

"It's not only my brother I lost," I said. "There was someone I once planned on spending my life with. I never talk about him either. Until this week, I kept his photograph hidden inside an old notebook. But you're right. When we try to forget them, we're not fully living in the present. I want to tell you about him."

I pulled free from Max's hand. I didn't want him to be able to sense the difference in my pulse when I changed irrelevant facts that would make him question my recollection. As an excuse, I opened a glass mason jar filled with chocolate ginger cookies. I offered one to Max, but he declined. I ate the chewy cookie quickly, barely tasting it. Dorian would have been appalled. He also would have been appalled that I detected a hint of bitterness in the cookie.

"Ambrose was a fellow gardener and herbalist," I said, choosing my words carefully. "Until I met him, I had never really gotten over my brother's death. Not the fact that Thomas died, but the fact that I couldn't save him from the virus that killed him." It was the Plague that had killed my brother in 1704. Dumb luck that a small outbreak swept through France while we were there, and a dumber sister who thought seeking a cure in her alchemy lab could be more useful than simple loving care. "I got him the best care I could, but I should have been there with him."

"You thought you could be a miracle worker with your herbal remedies. I understand the impulse to save everyone, especially those we care about. But I wonder if I could have done something differently that day with Chadna, so I understand how you can still blame yourself."

"I traveled around for several years after that." For over 150 years, if I wanted to be precise. Which I didn't. I ran from my apprenticeship with the Flamels, ran from my alchemy research, and ran from myself. I traveled through the Far East and the fledgling United States of America.

I carried only one satchel, though in my unhealthy state even the single bag was often burdensome. I'd abandoned alchemy when Thomas died, so I was no longer encumbered by the tools of an alchemy laboratory. My bag contained the bare essentials for creating tinctures, tonics, balms, and salves, along with a few items of dirty clothing, a dusty blanket, and stale bread. I walked in the one pair of shoes I owned, with my gold locket around my neck, and kept several gold coins tucked into a hidden pocket. Only in winter did I travel with dried herbs. Throughout the rest of the year, I found plants to work with wherever I went. They were there, if you knew where to look. After many years, I found myself back in France.

"After I got tired of traveling," I continued, "I went to work at my grandmother's shop in Paris — the shop I now run as my online business Elixir. Ambrose was English, but I met him there in France. What are you chuckling about?"

"Ambrose, such an old-fashioned name. I was smiling because it suits you so well. You've always struck me as wiser than your years. *Immortal.*"

I froze.

"Doesn't the name Ambrose mean 'immortal'?" Max continued.

"It does." I relaxed, but I felt my hands shaking. To cover up my nervousness, I absentmindedly bit into another cookie. The meaning of his name was one of the reasons Ambrose had been intrigued by alchemy in the first place. "Ambrose was an aspiring gardener when I met him. You would have been horrified by his sad garden. But he wanted to learn."

One day in the 1890s, when I was bringing an herbal remedy to an ailing household outside of Paris, I came across a striking figure. He wasn't the most handsome man I'd ever seen, but there was something that drew me to him. Something beyond his thick black hair, dark blue eyes, and gently crooked nose.

Next to a cottage along the dirt path, a man was kneeling in the dirt next to a row of unhealthy salsify. The spectacles that adorned his face shone in the sunlight. I watched as he ran a hand through his unruly black hair. Despite the failure of his *potager,* his face showed contentment instead of the frustration I expected. I couldn't resist setting him straight about caring for his struggling garden.

Just as I had never excelled at alchemy involving metals, Ambrose had never been good with plants. Yet he never gave up. In spite of years of failure, he continued to keep a range of plants in his garden and struggled to keep them alive. That was Ambrose. Never giving up. Until the end. We were at once opposites and the perfect complements to each other. *I can't believe I'd have forgotten you, but do we know each other?* Those were the first words Ambrose had spoken to me, on that first day of our acquaintance, when he caught me pausing to look at him. *No,* I replied, *but I know that poor salsify plant you're strangling the life out of. May I show you how to care for it?* After that, we had never left each other's sides.

"Even though I was always good with herbal remedies and healing others," I continued, "I didn't start taking care of myself until I met Ambrose. That's when I began eating the healthy plant-based foods I eat today, to heal both my body and soul. It was a whole new way of life for me, and it was wonderful for a while. Until —" I needed a moment to compose myself. "Until Ambrose killed himself."

"I'm so sorry, Zoe," Max said gently. "The look on your face. It's guilt. You look like you blame yourself for his death too."

"Part of me does." I stopped myself from saying more. That Ambrose had gone insane after hearing that his son Percival had died of old age. He couldn't deal with the weight — the curse — of living indefinitely, so he ended his life.

"When someone takes their own life," Max said softly, "it's about them. Not you."

"That doesn't make it any easier."

"No, it doesn't," Max said, a look of understanding dawning on his face. "That's why you spent most of your twenties on the road."

My twenties. "That's part of it."

"Are your parents still alive?"

I shook my head. "I lost them a long time ago." I'd lost them long before they died. When I didn't adopt the norms of our time and was accused of witchcraft, they didn't support me. If it hadn't been for my brother, I would have been killed before my seventeenth birthday.

"I'm sorry, Zoe. You're so young to have lost so many people."

"I'm not so young, you know." Why had I said that out loud?

"I know. You've been through so much more than most people your age. But . . ."

"But what, Max?" I tapped my foot nervously on the linoleum floor. Why was I so jumpy?

"We're at such different places in our lives. You're just starting out in life. Portland is a fresh start for you. I don't want to hold you back."

"If you're trying to say you're too old for me, I don't care that the age listed on your driver's license is greater than mine." Nor did I care that I'd been born before his great-great-great grandparents.

The older I get, the more I've seen how after adolescence, it's our physical bodies that age us and constrain us. Shared experiences give people within a generation an affinity for each other that makes it easier to connect. While that's a real connection, it's also a superficial one. Aside from my relationship with my brother, all of the other meaningful relationships I've had in my life have been with people — and a gargoyle — who've had vastly different life experiences from mine. Different ages, classes, languages, races, religions, nationalities, occupations, passions. The more I saw people's superficial differences, the more I learned those things weren't important.

In alchemical terms, our bodies are the salt that ages, our spirits are dual-faced mercury that changes with the times, and sulfurous fire is the key to our souls across the ages. Our soul is our true self, regardless of age or history.

One of the reasons I didn't mind falling out of touch with true alchemists was that they often lost sight of their souls. The older some alchemists got, the easier it was for them to abandon their humanity. I sometimes wondered whether I didn't look hard enough for Nicolas and Perenelle Flamel because I feared it had happened to them.

Thinking of them made me fidget even more. That was unlike me. Though I'd been more scattered than usual as I desperately sought out Dorian's cure, my alchemical training has taught me how to focus.

"I wonder if I've been selfish," Max said. "You're only twenty-eight —"

"I'm *not* twenty-eight." I clamped my hand over my mouth, horrified by what I'd admitted.

I looked at the cookie jar. The label on the jar had been typed up on the antique typewriter Dorian used to make the labels I insisted on. These weren't ginger chocolate cookies. They were *coffee* and ginger chocolate cookies. I'd just ingested several cups worth of caffeine.

Max frowned at me. "Are you okay, Zoe?"

"This has been great! Hasn't this been great? Opening up to each other." The caffeine was making me manic. Would it act like a truth serum? I had to get Max to leave before it made me say something I couldn't undo. I took Max's hand and pulled him toward the back door.

"You're trying to get rid of me? What did you mean you're not twenty-eight?"

"Just like you were saying earlier, that I'm an old soul, from everything I've gone through."

"Okay . . ." His furrowed brow said otherwise.

"Old Soul! That's a great name for a band, don't you think? I should suggest that to Tobias and Brixton. They're so talented, don’t you think?”

“Your hands are sweating. Are you sure you’re okay?”

“It’s later than I thought. I should get back to my guests.” I pulled open the back door. “You should go.”

Forty-One

After Max left, clearly displeased by his abruptly requested departure, I gulped two glasses of lemon water. I mentally kicked myself for being so abrupt with Max, but I couldn't trust myself not to say too much. Beads of sweat covered my face. The corner of my lip twitched.

I slammed down the empty glass and stormed into the living room. "Dorian made *coffee* cookies!"

The music broke off with a discordant guitar chord coming to a metallic screeching halt.

"Dorian!" I shouted. "Dorian!"

"I'll go get him," Brixton said, stumbling away from me as quickly as he'd fled from me the first day I met him.

"It was impossible not to hear the piercing banshee wail," Dorian said from the top of the stairs. "I am sorry, *mon amie,* but did you not read the label I created as you asked?"

"I asked you not to bake caffeine into anything, because I knew this might happen." My legs twitched nervously. "Before he left, I let it slip to Max about my not really being twenty-eight. Who knows what I would have told him next if I hadn't gotten him away from me."

"Max isn't still in the kitchen?" Brixton asked.

"I shoved him out the door before I accidentally told him about you lot."

"You're sweating an awful lot," Brixton said. "Are you poisoned? Do you need to go see a doctor?"

"She's got someone better right here," Tobias said, feeling my forehead. He shook his head.

"I'm not poisoned," I insisted. "But I doubt I'll sleep for days."

Tobias checked my vital signs and agreed this was nothing more than a case of an alchemist's reaction to coffee.

"Not cool," Brixton said. "It must suck to be an alchemist. Except for the superhuman part. That's pretty wicked." At fourteen, Brixton was already a coffee convert. I expected that wasn't abnormal in Portland, although the amount of sugar he added to his coffee also explained it.

After he was convinced Tobias was medically qualified and I was all right, Brixton pulled the chocolate-covered blackberries out of the fridge. The kid, the gargoyle, and the former slave ate a simple yet delectable dessert. As for me, I walked up and down the stairs a few dozen times, then lay down on the couch and put a compress over my eyes. Neither worked. Nor did the herbal remedy Tobias insisted I try. I sprang up the stairs to try one more thing.

Brixton was packing up his guitar when I returned with a hula hoop in hand. It was time for him to meet his mom at Blue Sky Teas to help her clean up the teashop.

"You can let your mom know I'm feeling better and can bake pastries for the morning," I said.

"But you're not feeling better," Brixton said. "You said —"

"Since your mom thinks I'm the one who bakes the teashop pastries, we need to keep up the pretense. Now that Dorian has escaped police custody, he can resume his baking." I put the hula hoop around my waist and began moving my hips. The hoop spun around me, with the sound of the tumbler inside following my movements. "I bet he'll make some great items tomorrow, happy to be a free man again. Or, I suppose he's a free *gargoyle,* and it's technically tonight, since Dorian will be baking before any of us are awake in the morning. Except for me. Since I won't be sleeping. For days. Dorian, do you need any ingredients? You must need ingredients. I could go to an all-night market if you —"

"Uh, Zoe," Brixton said, "you're babbling. And you look ridiculous. I'm leaving." With a departing eye roll at the sight of the 1950s hula hoop, he slipped out of the house. Tobias locked the door behind him.

"Well, *mon amie,*" Dorian said. "Now I realize why caffeine is not a method you wish to use to stay awake in the night. You are quite useless at present. Monsieur Freeman, may I interest you in a nightcap before it is dark enough for me to leave the premises?"

"Zoe, do you want to join us?" Tobias asked.

"Can't talk. Hula hooping."

An hour later, I was still twitchy, but I'd calmed down enough to have a sensible conversation. Which was a good thing, because Tobias had to catch a flight the next day. This was our only evening together.

I found him in the attic with Dorian, drinking sherry with the gargoyle out of ornately etched cordial glasses. A nearly empty crystal decanter sat on a silver platter between them.

"You didn't tell me this little fellow could drink me under the table," Tobias said.

"Moi?" The gargoyle chuckled.

"I'm glad you two are getting along so well. Especially since tonight I alienated one of the few friends I've got here."

"Monsieur Liu is not good for you," Dorian declared.

"He seemed like a good man," Tobias said. "We've all been around long enough to be good judges of character. And I judged him to be a kind man who cares for Zoe."

Dorian raised his clawed index finger to make a point. "A good man? Yes. A trustworthy one? No."

"You're just saying that because he's cooked in your kitchen."

"*Mais non!* This is a problem, yes, but I am not being frivolous. Max Liu is the arm of the law. His men locked me up! How can you trust this man?"

"It doesn't sound like that was his fault," Tobias said.

"Yet it would not have happened if Zoe could tell him the truth about she and I!" The dramatic statement was rendered less powerful because it was followed by a hiccup.

"If you two are done determining my love life," I said, "maybe Tobias and I can get back to work on *Non Degenera Alchemia.* Toby, you said you wanted to see more about the Tea of Ashes."

"Catch you later, little man," Tobias said, shaking Dorian's hand.

"It has been a pleasure." Dorian bowed his head.

The stairs creaked under my enthusiastic steps as we made our way down to the basement. We'd left Dorian in the attic with a stack of science fiction books from the library. I wondered what a drunk gargoyle would make of them.

"I wish I could stay," Tobias said as I unlocked the basement's secure lock, "but I've got a shift tomorrow and I'm needed back home. There isn't anyone to cover for me."

"Is your station short-staffed with medical techs?"

"Something like that."

I wasn't up for creating the Tea of Ashes in my present agitated state, or so soon after having done so that week, but I walked Tobias through the process I'd pieced together from the counterclockwise motions in *Non Degenera Alchemia's* illustrations.

"Slow down," Tobias said as I flipped through the pages. "You're going to destroy the book."

He was right. I took a step back. "I should let you handle the book until the coffee is out of my system."

"I don't know what it is about that stuff that messes up alchemists so badly. I'd wager it rivals mercury with its dangerous dual-faced properties. But only for us."

"It's our own faults for being overly connected to nature's transformations."

"Let's get back to these unnatural transformations here." He pointed at the page I'd nearly ripped out of the book. "Jumping right to fire and ash. That can't be good."

"It's not. Each time I light the fire with the intent of practicing backward alchemy, the effects begin. My skin begins to shrivel along with the plants I'm turning to ash."

"The salt of the body. That makes sense."

I nodded. "That's why it temporarily stops Dorian's body from reverting to stone."

"I keep coming back to the gold thefts in Europe," Tobias said. "The ones that you don't believe are thefts at all."

"I'm almost positive," I said. "We looked up the dates of the 'thefts' where the thieves left behind gold dust, and they correspond precisely to when Dorian began to return to stone. The impure becoming the pure — and now transforming back again into dust."

"And they're both connected to this cathedral." Tobias tapped on the page of the book.

"Tobias!"

He jumped back.

"I didn't mean to startle you. I haven't thought much about the crumbling gold since I realized the book illustrations form a cathedral. This means there could be a *pattern* to the gold that's crumbling. It's not that *all* alchemical gold is in danger of disintegrating."

"Are the gold pieces religious relics?"

"Not all of them. They aren't similar pieces. There's no pattern. At least that's what I thought — until now."

"There's a pattern there, Zoe. You just need to find it." Tobias yawned and his eyelids drooped.

I shook his shoulders, even more adrenaline surging through my engorged veins. "Are you all right? Is the book having an effect on you?"

He shook his head. "I worked the night shift right before flying in to see you this morning."

"Why didn't you say so?"

"We don't have much time together. I didn't want to waste it sleeping. But after that sherry . . ."

"Come on, Toby. You know there's no sense working on alchemy when you're so tired. I'll fix up a bedroom for you."

Between the coffee's physical effects and the mental strain of thinking about Ambrose, the cathedral, Dorian's deterioration, and Peter's quest, I knew I'd never sleep. After I saw Tobias to his room, I heard him speaking softly to someone on his cell phone, followed by snoring that was anything but soft. I scribbled a note and grabbed my silver raincoat.

A light misty rain fell from the night sky. I breathed in the scents of fresh rain and blossoming fruit trees as I set off on a brisk pace. I had no destination, but I needed to keep moving. It was early enough in the evening that other people were out, but as soon as the rain began to fall harder, I found myself mostly alone on the sidewalk.

I walked past the restaurants and bars on Hawthorne, past the signs for hand-crafted beer, hand-poured coffee, and hand-made clothing and hats. Turning off the main drag, I passed households watching television for the evening, and parks vacant from the rain. The rainwater streamed down my face, nourishing my unnaturally dry skin. Once my hair was soaked, I began to get a chill, so I came home. The front door creaked loudly enough to awaken the dead bees in Dorian's book in the basement.

"Zoe!" Tobias's voice in the living room startled me. He leaped up from the green velvet couch. "Thank God you're back. You didn't take your cell phone with you."

"I've never gotten used to taking it with me everywhere. What's the matter?" I stood there dripping onto the floor.

"I woke up thirsty after drinking all that sherry, so I went to get myself a glass of water. The house was really quiet. Too quiet, like houses get when everyone is sleeping."

"Dorian doesn't sleep."

"I know. You told me. That's the problem. You said he shouldn't go out this early in the evening — especially now that the police will be on the lookout for a stone gargoyle."

"He's hiding in the attic," I said. "He's probably reading quietly."

"I climbed up to the attic, Zoe. I wanted to be sure, so I checked the whole house. The gargoyle is gone."

Forty-Two

PARIS, 1871

Sleep was not a necessity for the gargoyle. Without knowing any other state of existence, Dorian thought this neither a blessing nor a curse — until his father died. Jean Eugène Robert-Houdin passed away from pneumonia, not long after the tragic news of his son's death due to injuries suffered in the Franco-Prussian War. Dorian found himself more alone than he imagined.

His new employer, the blind chef, understood Dorian's grief at his relative's death. But Dorian could not tell him this was the first person in his life he had lost to death. He had been brought to life only eleven years before, yet with his deep voice and keen intellect, it was important for him to maintain the illusion that he was a much older man. And a man, not a gargoyle, of course.

Luckily, Dorian found himself without much time to be maudlin. Between the distractions of Paris and the cooking lessons from his employer, Dorian could have filled more than a twenty-four-hour day.

At first Dorian objected to the part of the agreement that involved cleaning, but after some grumbling, he found washing dishes and dusting could be contemplative exercises. It was but a small price to pay for the lessons in French gastronomy he received.

The chef could not have been more pleased with how well Dorian took to the demands of French cooking. Dorian did so well that the chef pleaded with him to allow some former friends to come over for dinner parties, as he wanted very much to showcase the gourmet cooking of his successor. Yet Dorian was resolute. He had been traumatized by his disfigurement, he said. Nobody could be allowed to see him.

To keep up the pretense, Dorian pretended to wear the clothes his father had given him for the charade that was to be his life. To add verisimilitude, on his nocturnal explorations Dorian would bring a handful of clothes with him, which he would toss in the dust. Therefore he was able to have his clothing laundered with the chef's clothing without raising suspicions.

Dorian learned not only how to cook everything from creamy *aligot* to succulent *magret de canard,* but also how to find his way through the world without being seen. He learned through trial by fire, as he was in Paris during the short-lived War of 1870.

While the chef slept, Dorian pretended to use the very nice bed chamber created for him, when in truth he was exploring the City of Lights under the cover of darkness.

PARIS, 1881

Ten years later, when the chef approached the end of his life, he wrote Dorian Robert-Houdin a reference so he could be a home companion to other blind people who did not have families to care for them.

Upon Martin's death, a small inheritance was bequeathed to Dorian. The gargoyle was unaware of the money until a letter reached him at the home of his next employer, an *avocate* who had long ago retired from practicing law and had recently been widowed. Not realizing the true form of his disfigured friend, the chef did not have the foresight to give Dorian his gift in person. Now, it seemed Dorian would not be able to claim his inheritance without being seen. But all was not lost. By that time, Dorian, even more than his father, was a master of illusion. His greatest skill was *not being seen.*

Dorian's penmanship was superb. This was not an easy feat, considering his clawed hands, which Viollet-le-Duc had never intended to hold a pen. Holding a whisk and beating eggs was one thing. But it was important for Dorian to rigorously practice writing, for written correspondence was his connection to most of the world.

Upon receiving news of his modest inheritance, Dorian asked his new employer, the barrister, for counsel. Explaining that he was far too embarrassed to show his disfigured face to anyone, Dorian gave the barrister permission to act on his behalf, and the lawyer declared under oath that the tragically disfigured Dorian Robert-Houdin lived at his home and was who he claimed.

It was with methods like these that Dorian made his way in the world.

He moved from place to place with only a small travel case in which he kept a few remembrances of his father, including *Non Degenera Alchemia.* Dorian appreciated art, but he didn't especially care for the illustrations inside the alchemy book. He kept the book because it reminded him of his father, but whenever he opened the book, he felt a strange sleepiness overcome him. He suspected it was his imagination, that it was sadness he was feeling as he thought of the man who gave him life and raised him. The man who was no longer on this earth. His father had explained to him that something in this book had brought him to life, but Dorian was not a philosophical creature. He was a gourmand who appreciated the finer pleasures in life, not a philosopher. If it had been a cookbook, he might have spent time unlocking the book's coded messages. But why dwell on things that had no bearing on his life?

Forty-Three

It wasn't yet ten o'clock. Far too early for Dorian to be out of the house. He never left the house until the dead of night, when fewer people would be around. Did he think that because of the rain it would be safer?

"Maybe he went to hide the knife." I cringed at the thought. One of these days, I was going to have to sit the gargoyle down to talk about police evidence.

"The knife is in the attic."

Great. Just great. All I needed was for the police to raid the house and find a murder weapon inside.

I texted Brixton to ask if he knew where Dorian was. Less than a minute later he texted me back.

HE WENT TO SEE JULIAN LAKE.

I groaned.

"What is it?" Tobias asked.

"He went to see Julian Lake of the Lake Loot. How can he do this? What does he hope to learn by spying on the man whose family heirlooms were stolen decades ago?"

"That's nice of him, though. The little guy is helping Brixton with the magician's quest to clear his dad."

"It's *not* nice. It's not safe for him to leave. His leg is effectively broken, and the police are looking for a missing gargoyle statue."

Another text popped up from Brixton. HE LEFT A WHILE AGO. HE'S NOT BACK YET?

I made a mental note that I should never leave the two of them alone together.

DON'T WORRY, HE'S PROBABLY WAITING UNTIL IT'S LATE ENOUGH TO SNEAK HOME MORE EASILY, I typed. I half believed it. No need for both of us to suffer a sleepless night.

TEXT ME WHEN HE'S BACK, Brixton wrote. We both cared about the gargoyle.

I felt marginally better after I looked up Julian Lake. He was eighty-five years old *and blind.* If Dorian was able to catch him alone, the sightless Mr. Lake would assume he was a man.

Up in the attic, Tobias and I sat on the floor playing gin rummy and drinking cocoa that wasn't nearly as good as Dorian's, while we waited anxiously for his return. With my favorite wool sweaters ruined from the destructive winter storm, I wrapped a blanket around myself to stay warm. As Tobias dealt the cards and light rain tapped at the tarp securing the roof, a comforting familiarity washed over me. I was still worried about Dorian, but the edge was gone from my worry. I had friends who wanted to help.

"You can go back to sleep, you know," I said.

"Not a chance." He paused before picking up the hand he'd dealt. "It's good to be here, Zoe. Even under these screwed-up circumstances, I'm so glad it led you back to me."

"I am too."

For the next hour, we caught up about life and where our travels had taken us. We learned we'd almost been in Albuquerque at the same time, and because we were both on the road so much we'd learned to fix up cars ourselves. Tobias owned fewer possessions than I did, so all his belongings fit into a 1956 Cadillac Eldorado.

"What's so funny?" Tobias asked when I laughed so uncontrollably that I dropped my cards.

"The two of us. Could we have picked more conspicuous cars?"

"In this life we lead, we've gotta take our

enjoyment where we can get it. Though my wife hates that car."

I froze before I could pick up my scattered playing cards. "You're *married*? Why didn't you say so earlier?"

"It's complicated."

"Isn't everything in our lives? Does she —"

"She knows. It would be impossible for her not to."

I no longer felt like playing gin. I looked from Tobias's resigned face to the strewn cards. The King and Queen of Hearts stared up at me. "She's grown older than you."

"So much so that when we moved to Detroit we couldn't tell anyone we were married. I don't talk about it out of habit. Since I'm an EMT, we tell people I'm her live-in companion to help with her health."

"Why didn't you tell me? Is it okay for you to be away from her?"

He chuckled. "I knew you'd be concerned about her if you knew. That's why I didn't tell you when we emailed. I wanted to come see you. And you would have stopped me."

"Of course I would have stopped you!"

"She's okay. One of my friends is looking in on her while I'm gone. And it's just two days. But Rosa is the most important reason why I need to get home."

"What's the matter with her? Is there anything I can do to help?"

"Nah. I've got it covered. And there's no disease or condition to treat." A wistful look passed over his face. "Simply old age."

"When did you tell her?" I asked, thinking of Max.

Tobias stood up and walked the length of the attic, coming to a stop in front of a shelf of antique books on gardening and herbal remedies. "Too late," he said. "I told her too late."

"Once she'd already fallen in love with you."

He gave a single curt nod. "Even though I pretended I gave her a choice, I didn't give her a fair one. If she'd always known, she could have steered clear of me, and had someone to grow old with."

"You seem like you love her very much. Haven't you had a good life together?"

"We have. I would have made the same choice to be with her. I just wish I'd given her an honest choice."

We stopped talking as a faint scratching sounded on the roof. The noise was followed by the appearance of a gargoyle squeezing through the rafters and carefully reattaching the tarp. A cape of black silk was fastened around his neck. It looked suspiciously like the cape I thought was hanging inside my old trailer parked in the driveway.

"Ah!" Dorian cried out when he spotted us. "You wish to kill me by a heart attack, so I will not become trapped in stone?"

"We know where you went," I said.

Dorian stepped to the empty corner of the attic. He unfurled his wings and shook off the rainwater. "*Magnifique,* is it not?"

"No, it is not."

"He is blind, Zoe! It was the perfect mission for me."

"You were able to talk with him?" Tobias asked.

"I thought he didn't take visitors," I added.

"He does not like most people, yet I believe he is lonely. His caregiver is a spiteful woman. And she is a terrible cook." The gargoyle sighed wistfully. "His kitchen is four times the size of this one."

"Hey," I said to the little ingrate.

"He has two refrigerators, each of which is twice the size of this —"

"Dorian."

"You distracted me with your talk of food."

"I didn't mention food. You did."

"Semantics. Where was I? Ah, yes. Not

only was I able to talk to him, but after I presented him with a slice of chocolate cake — my new recipe, which is my best yet, if I do say so —"

"Dorian. I'll grant that the cake is good. Back to Julian Lake."

"*Oui.* I could not carry much with me and remain nimble, but I knew chocolate would be a good choice, because most people favor it. In this, I was not disappointed."

Tobias put his head in his hands. "Is he always like this?"

"Pretty much."

"Impatient Americans," Dorian grumbled, then cleared his throat. "Very well. I learned a very important fact. Monsieur Lake was present on the train Peter's father, Franklin Thorne, was accused of robbing. He has a great memory. He remembers the guard, Burke, very well. It is not possible that the guard was the guilty man. It is as the police reported. Peter Silverman's father was the thief and murderer. The magician is lying about his motive for returning to Portland."

FORTY-FOUR

I texted Brixton that Dorian was home safe and sound, in hopes the kid would get some sleep. I needed more time to figure out the best next steps, and I didn't want Brixton running off doing anything foolish.

If Peter was lying about his motivation, could he also have a motive for murder we didn't know about? Or was he simply an innocent victim who incorrectly believed his father to be innocent? He was only a child at the time of his father's death.

"Something strange is afoot at *Persephone & Prometheus's Phantasmagoria,*" Dorian said. "Do you think he is framing you for the murder of the treasure hunter, so he may find the loot for himself?"

I briefly considered his suggestion that I might have been framed in such an obscure way, but dismissed it as the lingering effects of the coffee. "I don't know, Dorian. That seems pretty far-fetched that he'd find a stone toe in the theater, associate it with me, and leave it in the fingers of the dead body in hopes that it would lead the police to me."

"*Oui,* without facts it is only a theory. But magicians are masters of misdirection. We must investigate!"

"Hold on, you two," Tobias cut in. "I understand that you've been pulled into this inquiry because of Dorian's missing toe, but investigating *yourselves*?"

Dorian blinked his black eyes at Tobias. "Have you not read the works of Agatha Christie? She was an Englishwoman, yes, but her investigative skills are unparalleled. She has taught us that it is the amateur sleuth who is most capable of using his *little grey cells* to solve the most complex of crimes."

"That's fiction," Tobias said. "Anyway, Poirot wasn't an amateur."

"Semantics," Dorian mumbled. "He was not *un flic.* He was not a policeman. Those who work outside of the law are privy to more —"

"The backpack!" I cried.

Dorian grinned. "*Merci,* Zoe, for proving my point."

"What backpack?" Tobias asked.

"Dorian and I saw Peter and Penelope

taking a small backpack out of a trunk in the theater. They were acting in secret, and at the time I believed he was an alchemist, so it made perfect sense that he'd be acting secretively. I didn't give it another thought. But since his secret is that he's Franklin Thorne's son who's looking into clearing his father's name, *what was in the backpack?*"

"I remember thinking," Dorian said, "that it looked like the possession of a child."

"It did. It wasn't a briefcase of research papers. It looked like a child's backpack. I wish I could remember what the two of them said to each other."

"Let us return to the theater," Dorian said.

"No," Tobias and I said simultaneously.

Dorian scrunched his snout. "Dual-faced alchemists! I thought you were on my side."

"I'm so much on your side that it would kill me if you were taken into police custody again. We take no unnecessary risks, which means we don't return to a crime scene."

Dorian's wings slouched. "Your heart is in the right place, Zoe Faust. No matter. It is nearly time for me to return to Blue Sky Teas to bake for the upcoming day. You need not remind me to be careful."

After spending the night in the basement

fruitlessly rereading *Not Untrue Alchemy* from cover to cover, Tobias, Dorian, and I breakfasted on the misshapen leftovers Dorian brought back from the teashop kitchen before sunrise. Today it was a feast of chickpea-flour pancakes. Though his recipe was tasty, he decided pancakes didn't work well for the teashop's glass pastry display cabinet. Presentation was an important last step of Dorian's culinary alchemy. A strong flame under a cast-iron skillet could transform flour, water, ground seeds, and a few herbs into a stack of blissful breakfast. But transformation wasn't always pretty. Dorian didn't think his pancakes were attractive enough to entice people from a display case.

Tobias and I prepared breakfast plates in the kitchen. Tobias inhaled deeply as he fixed an espresso for Dorian, who was waiting impatiently in the attic, then made a pot of tea for himself. I was still drinking my restorative tea blend to combat the effects of creating Dorian's Tea of Ashes and accidentally eating coffee-saturated cookies. This morning I had an extra cup, since I hadn't slept a wink. My large solar infusion batch was nearly used up.

"I wish I didn't have to leave," Tobias said as he lifted a tray of tea and coffee in one hand. “Rosa and the job need me. I’ll think about your problem, though. Maybe I’ll come up with something that’ll help you from afar. I keep thinking that the crumbling gold has to play into this puzzle.”

“I’m glad we found each other again, Tobias.”

“Even if it took a pickle of a mess to drive you to seek out other alchemists, I’m happy you did, too, Zoe. I’m happy you did too.”

I scooped up the second tray, and we joined Dorian in the attic’s safe haven with his escape route in the slanted roof above.

“You carry that tray with such alacrity, Monsieur Freeman,” Dorian said, “that I believe you must have been employed as a waiter in your past.” He took a sip of the espresso Tobias had fixed. “*Oui.* This espresso is *très bon.* I am correct, no?”

“Guilty.”

“You do not look pleased! *Le garçon* is a worthy profession. You help the chef present his creations.”

“You’re an optimistic fellow for a Frenchman, Dorian.”

“But of course.”

“And a great chef. If only you weren’t a gargoyle, you could head any restaurant.”

“You are a sly one, Monsieur Freeman. You are leaving momentarily for a flight, which will not provide edible food. I will prepare a basket of sandwiches and snacks to see you safely home."

Encumbered with enough food for Tobias and his wife to eat all week, I drove Tobias to the airport to see him off. As I drove, he looked through the assortment and chuckled.

"What's so funny?" I asked. "The amount of food?"

"Dragon's tongue, dragon carrots, and even dragon's mugwort. There's a pattern here."

"I doubt it. You're the one who likes patterns, so that's what you see."

"I'm not kidding, Zoe. He's got them all in here."

"I'm sure he does. He loves using Tuscan kale, purple carrots, and tarragon. Texture, color, and flavor."

Tobias rewrapped a fragrant baguette sandwich in its parchment paper. "You've got a point. Gardeners might have even more vivid imaginations than alchemists."

The drive to the airport was far too short. After I saw Tobias off, I couldn't help thinking more about him and his elderly wife. It was the right choice for them. Would I be able to have that for myself? Did I even deserve it? I wasn't even sure I could save my closest friend from an unnatural fate trapped between life and death.

I listened to "Accidental Life" on the drive home, keeping my old friend near me.

When I got back to my house, two unexpected guests were waiting for me: the magicians. They'd made themselves comfortable on the porch in front of my Craftsman. Peter juggled d'Anjou pears that looked suspiciously like ones from a neighbor's tree, and Penelope sat on the top step while twirling a cigar deftly between her long fingers.

I slammed the truck's door. "How did you find me?" Like Peter Silverman, I knew how to stay under the radar. I walked cautiously toward them.

"Your young friend had a card for Blue Sky Teas in his pocket the other night," Peter said. As he spoke, the pears vanished. They didn't drop to the ground, but I didn't see where they could have gone.

"The young woman with bare feet was incredibly helpful," Peter continued.

I groaned to myself. He had to be referring to Brixton's mom, Heather, the free spirit who would never entertain the notion that she was being conned.

"She was so sorry to hear you'd left your locket at the theater," Peter continued.

My hand flew to my locket. It was there. He certainly had the skills to remove it without my noticing, so I was relieved he hadn't actually lifted it as part of his ruse.

"I didn't mean to worry you," he said. "Especially since I came here for help. May we come inside?"

"Now's not a good time." I willed myself not to look toward the attic.

The front and back doors to the house could be opened by a skilled lock-picker, but the attic and basement doors had extra locks on them, so I wasn't too worried about whether they'd already let themselves into the house. Disturbed at the thought, yes; worried by it, no.

"I'm sorry I butted in before," I added. "I wish you luck on your quest, but I can't help you."

"We were looking at your new website," Penelope added.

"My new website?" I said. I'd forgotten Veronica was working on that.

"You've got some antique puzzle boxes for sale," Peter said. From the small backpack I recognized from the theater, he pulled out a carved puzzle box made of sandalwood. It was smaller than the palm of my hand and the irregularly shaped flower carvings told me it had been hand carved.

He handed it to me. The words "ashes to ashes" were carved on the bottom.

Don't engage, Zoe. The box is intriguing, but it's not your problem.

"What's this?" I asked, running my fingertips over the soft wood. A raised rose was carved onto the box, with thorns circling the edges. I'd seen that image before.

"I'm hoping you can help me open it," Peter said. "It has nothing to do with the matter you came to see us about, but being back in Portland to clear my father's name has made me sentimental. This box belonged to him. He made it in his toy studio, and he left it to me."

His father, Franklin Thorne, the supposed thief and murderer, had made the box.

"I know what this is," I said, a disturbing realization dawning on me.

"That's great," Peter said. "I knew you'd know how to open it. Didn't I tell you, Pen?"

"Quite," Penelope said, her eyes never leaving mine.

"Could you show me?" Peter asked.

"I didn't mean that I know how to open it," I said. "I doubt anyone besides the person who put it together could open it without breaking it."

Peter frowned.

"I know that's not the answer you were

hoping for," I said, "because I know you don't want to break what's inside."

"This is ridiculous." The muscles of his lithe body tensed. "How do you possibly know what's inside?"

"I saw the Thorne family crypt at the cemetery," I said. "The carvings on the mausoleum walls are etched into the stone. They're carvings of roses and thorns that match this box. You think this puzzle box contains a key to the Thorne family crypt. But there's only one reason you'd be secretive about your motives —"

"There's nothing secret about my motives," Peter said with false calmness.

"That's where your father's plunder is hidden, isn't it, Peter?" I said. "You know he's the thief — you've *always* known — but you haven't been able to get inside the stone mausoleum to get at his hidden loot."

Forty-Five

Peter stared mutely at me.

"Well," Penelope said, "she's certainly much more clever than we gave her credit for." She stood up and walked down the porch steps, stopping uncomfortably close to me. She was taller than me, so I saw it for the power play that it was. "How did you know?"

"At the time I didn't realize what I'd seen at the cemetery." I stepped away from Penelope and walked a few paces toward the barren elderberry bushes that lined the side fence. Simply being near the garden protector made me feel more in control. "But the Thorne mausoleum isn't too far from the mudslide area."

"The police already searched it after hc was killed," Peter said. "The cemetery keeps a key."

"To the main entrance, sure," I said. "Not the hidden one."

Peter had a fit of coughing.

"Little things you both said didn't add up," I continued. "You didn't approach the police to access the records, but you spent time at the cemetery. The item you were protecting in a locked trunk wasn't part of your research, but a child's backpack containing a puzzle box given to you by your toy-maker father. No, your actions weren't those of people researching historical facts to clear a man's name. They were the actions of the treasure hunters. I didn't put it together until a friend of mine talked to Julian Lake. He said there's no way the guard was involved."

"Nice try," Penelope said. "But Julian Lake is a recluse. He doesn't talk to anyone."

"My friend is good at getting people to open up to him."

Penelope narrowed her eyes at me.

"It's not illegal to search for the Lake Loot," Peter said, recovering his voice.

"No, it's not. You're admitting that you knew your father was the thief all along?"

"It's not Peter's fault his father was a criminal," Penelope said.

"Pen —"

"Oh, do be quiet, Peter. Do you want to resolve this once and for all or not?"

Peter gripped the railing of the porch but remained silent.

"We already told you how Peter spent his whole life running from people's assumptions about him," Penelope continued. "Is it any wonder he wants to at least get something out of it? Returning the jewels to the Lake family and getting a reward will bring him closure."

"Why didn't you just say so in the first place?" I asked.

"After hiding his past for so long, I'm sure you can understand the desire to wrap things up out of the spotlight, so to speak." She gave me an inscrutable smile. "In case he wasn't able to find the hidden loot and return it to the Lake family to redeem *himself,* he didn't want to reveal his identity and open himself up to mockery."

It did make sense. It was an impulse I often felt in my own life. I needed to conceal so many parts of my life that hiding became second nature. But after they'd lied repeatedly, how could I be sure Peter and Penelope's intentions were pure?

"I'm sure you won't mind if the police accompany you to the crypt to open it." I returned Penelope's enigmatic smile.

"Of course not," she said. "But unfortunately, you yourself said there's no way to open it. Without destroying whatever is inside."

"I didn't exactly say that."

Peter dug his fingernails into the wooden railing, and the muscles on his neck looked as if they were going to pop out. "Anyone ever tell you that you like to speak in riddles?"

"I'm not the one who wrote a clue on the box itself."

"It's not a clue," Peter seethed. "I tried every possible letter substitution. It doesn't tell me how to open the box."

"To open a box like this," I said, turning the box over in my hands, "the best way is to know the correct spots to push, in the right order, as you know. The person who built it would know how to do that. But without having a key, the box needs to be destroyed to get at what's inside. Breaking or burning are your options, but if you don't know what's inside, it's difficult to know which would ruin the protected item. If, however, you believe it to be a key, that key won't burn. The box itself tells you that much."

"Ashes to ashes," Peter whispered.

"It was a simpler clue than you imagined. If you want to open the box without breaking the key inside, you have to burn it."

Peter groaned. Before I realized what was happening, the box disappeared from my hand.

On the other side of the porch, Peter applied a putty-like substance to the rose carving on the box. With swiftly moving hands, he peeled it off and handed the putty to Penelope. He jumped over the porch railing, landing gracefully on the stone path, and with a snap of his fingers, a lighter appeared in his hand. He lit the box on fire.

"Wait!" I cried. "It's only a theory."

Peter gave me a devilish grin. "That's why I made an impression of the box carving. Just in case you're wrong."

The box smoldered and caught fire. When the flames extinguished, an iron key was left, its dark metal glowing in the ashes.

"I need your help," I told Max.

I'd pushed aside all thoughts of how I'd shoved Max out the door, and called him. It was the best thing I could think to do.

He sighed audibly at the other end of the line. "You mean you want a recommendation for a psychologist?"

"I'll explain everything later, Max, but I need you to meet me at River View Cemetery. At the Thorne family mausoleum. It's near where the mudslides took place."

Now it sounded like he was choking.

From my front lawn, I explained that I wasn't going hiking in a dangerous area as he feared, but that the magicians had come to me with help on their puzzle box because I had several of them for sale through Elixir. And I told him about Peter's connection to Franklin Thorne and the Lake Loot. I managed to convince Max that since the information wasn't directly related to the murder investigation that another detective was handling, he had every right to accompany me to River View Cemetery to check out my crazy idea.

"He's coming?" Penelope asked.

"He'll be there as soon as he can."

"Good," Peter said. "We'll meet you there."

"We go together." There was no way I was letting the magicians out of my sight. "Your SUV is big enough for all of us."

They exchanged a quick look that confirmed my suspicions that they were up to something. But I'd called someone who knew I was with them, so surely they wouldn't do anything to harm me. At least not here. Not today.

That was the logical conclusion, but people don't always behave in a rational manner. My heart skipped a beat when Peter reached into the backseat before stepping into the driver's seat. It turned out he was grabbing a coat.

Though it was a warm spring day after the rains of the previous night, Peter bundled in the puffy snow coat. That was odd. Perhaps he was getting sick. In spite of the situation, I found myself thinking through the simple herbal remedies from my backyard garden that might help at the onset of a cold, such as one of my mints.

I was more worried about a different danger. A glimpse in the side mirror confirmed that my health was getting worse. I feared that might be the case, but I'd pushed the thought from my mind because I didn't want it to be true. The effects of making Dorian's Tea of Ashes were catching up with me. I had to find a real solution soon.

We parked in the main lot next to the chapel and walked from there.

I was unsurprised to see Earl Rasputin on the steep hillside adjacent to the cemetery, walking methodically with his metal detector in hand. Peter, Penelope, and I continued to the Thorne mausoleum.

Earl must have seen us, too, because as soon as we reached the mausoleum, he wandered over.

"Afternoon," he said, tipping the rim of the baseball cap shielding his eyes from the sun. Peter and Penelope gave no indication of recognizing him. Was their reaction genuine? Earl had remained in the audience on opening night, while his friend volunteered on stage. So if the magicians were telling the truth that they had nothing to do with Wallace Mason's murder, it made sense they wouldn't recognize Earl.

"Let me give you each a flyer." Earl pressed a flyer into my hands: *Baby Bigfoot. Have you seen this creature?*

It was a more detailed flyer than the one he had the day I met him. In addition to the text, this one included a sketch of a hairless gray creature with horns and wings.

Oh, God. Baby Bigfoot was Dorian. He'd been outed by the conspiracy theorists. I groaned to myself, but forced myself to smile as I took the flyer. It was a rudimentary sketch, lacking incriminating details, but it was clearly Dorian, as if seen from a distance.

A normal life, Zoe. You really thought you could have a normal life?

"Do you want me to help pass out your flyers?" I offered. Perhaps if I was enthusiastic enough about the cause he'd give me all of his flyers, and then I could destroy them.

"That's a great idea," Penelope said. "I'd love to help too."

That threw me. Had she seen Dorian moving, too? Was that why she'd been fascinated when I showed her his stone statue?

Earl grabbed a stack of flyers and started to hand them to Penelope. But as he did so, a gust of wind picked up, and the Baby Bigfoot flyers scattered. Penelope and I knelt down to pick them up. The wind didn't make it easy. Moisture from the grass damaged a few of them, but most were no worse off.

The treasure hunter gave his thanks, but lingered even after we retrieved all of them.

"Do I know you?" Peter asked.

"Earl Rasputin. I attended your performance on Friday night. I could tell how you did the ghost trick, you know."

Peter narrowed his eyes. "And I can tell that you're a —"

"Max!" I called out. "We're over here."

We didn't get to hear the end of Peter's comeback, because as soon as he saw Max, Earl said his farewells.

Max apologized for running late, but said that Ivan was back in the hospital for pneumonia and he'd promised to visit him during visiting hours that day. I hadn't realized Ivan was in the hospital. I knew I should visit him as soon as I could too.

I traced my fingers along the intricate carvings on the white granite that belonged to Peter's family. These rose carvings were far older than Peter's father. But if I was right, the toy maker who knew how to carve clever puzzle boxes would have also been able to add nearly-undetectable segments to an existing structure. It's a trick alchemists have employed for millennia. For our work to remain hidden, we learn how to hide things in plain sight.

I focused my intent on the pattern, ignoring the people around me. Besides the main door, nothing on the front of the raised crypt looked like it might fit a key. I stepped back and circled the structure. That gave me the answer. The back wall had aged differently than the other walls. Most people wouldn't have noticed the difference, but I saw it because different plant spores had settled on this surface.

On that wall, I found a tiny hole disguised in a thorn of the rose carving.

"Do you want to do the honors and make this official?" I asked Max.

The slightly charred key fit perfectly.

The key opened a hidden compartment that wasn't connected to the main family crypt. As Peter had previously said, in 1969 the mausoleum was opened by order of the police, but nothing unexpected had been found inside. This hidden compartment was never found because Franklin Thorne had added a *new wall* along the back of the mausoleum, making it two feet larger than its original construction. It was a large enough space to hide stolen items, but was small enough to avoid detection.

The interior of the narrow space was filled with moist dirt. There was no proper floor. Franklin might have been a clever thief and craftsman, but he wasn't a good architect. Rainwater had drastically damaged the hidden compartment. That was how the sapphire necklace became dislodged.

"The Lake Loot," Peter whispered.

Lying in the uneven, damp dirt, half a dozen jeweled necklaces sparkled through their bed of mud.

Peter took a step forward.

"Don't touch it," Max said.

"I was just looking."

But I wasn't paying attention to either of the men. Next to the half-buried jewels, I noticed something else. The dirt in the far corner had been disturbed. An indentation in the earth told me we weren't the first people who'd been there recently. It wasn't a footprint, but rather an imprint, as if an object had been removed.

I looked from the hiding spot to the Baby Bigfoot flyers clutched in my hand. What was going on?

Forty-Six

I dangled the Baby Bigfoot flyer in front of Dorian. "You were seen."

"*Mais non!* How can this be?"

The magicians had dropped me off at my house, where thankfully I'd found Dorian in the attic. He hadn't gone off on any new ill-conceived adventures.

"We're not being careful enough," I said. "Once your foot and leg became a problem, we should have kept you in the house. I'll tell Heather I can't bake pastries for a while —"

"It is not possible," Dorian insisted. "I have been wearing your silk cape over me whenever I leave the house. Even if someone saw me, they would not see me as myself, *n'est pas*?"

"You're wrong," I snapped. "You must not have been careful enough. We have enough to worry about without Bigfoot hunters flocking to Portland."

He stamped his working foot on the creaky attic floor. "You have not told me what has happened! You have been gone for many hours, yet I cannot see or hear anything in this attic. You said you were taking Monsieur Freeman to the airport, yet you did not return. I thought I heard your loud engine earlier, but you did not come inside, so I believed I was mistaken. You expect me to read your mind? Where did this Baby Bigfoot flyer come from?"

My shoulders sagged. "You're right, Dorian. It's been a morning full of surprises. I'm sorry."

"Merci."

"I'm sorry for not having a chance to tell you what was going on this morning," I said. "But I'm not sorry for telling you to be more careful."

Dorian mumbled something under his breath that I chose to ignore, though it sounded suspiciously like the insult *casse couille,* a vulgar way to express irritation.

"What we need," he said, "is a code ring."

"A code ring? To decipher the coded illustrations in the book, you mean?"

"*Non.* I speak of the telephone. You do not wish me to answer it, since nobody besides you and Brixton believe me to live here. I am a clandestine companion. A

lonely lodger. A secret chimera —"
"Dorian."
"Yes, yes. As I was saying, you do not check email on your phone, so we have no way to communicate about urgent matters."
"Normally the house is perfectly safe. We couldn't have foreseen that search warrant from the police."
"No, but who knows what the future holds? We must institute a coded system of telephone rings."
I considered the idea that must have come from one of the Penny Dreadful detective novels he'd read that winter. "That's not a bad idea," I admitted.
"I thought so. We will work out the sequence of rings later. For now, you must tell me what has transpired."
"Remember those treasure hunters you were worried about because they might sully your woods next to River View Cemetery? They're the ones who saw you."
"*C'est vrai?* I do not see how —"
"It's true. Earl, the treasure-hunting friend of the dead volunteer, was passing out these flyers at the cemetery."
"But why did you return to the graveyard in the first place?"
"When I got back from the airport, Peter and Penelope Silverman were waiting for

me here at the house."

Dorian gasped and protectively curled his hands around his ears. "I did not hear you and the magicians downstairs. I am losing my hearing as well!" His wings flew out at his sides in agitation. *"Quelle horreur!"*

I put my hand on his shaking shoulder, careful to avoid his flapping wing. "There's nothing wrong with your hearing. I didn't invite them inside. And they wanted my help, so they didn't aggravate me by picking the lock, even though I'm certain Peter has the skills to do so."

"Excuse my outburst." He folded his wings and sniffed. "I am oversensitive at present."

"We're all on edge. Those magicians aren't helping. They lied to us about being in town to clear Peter's father's name. They've known all along that Franklin Thorne was the murderous thief. Peter wanted to find the loot for the reward and to save face himself."

"The missing Lake Loot."

"It's not missing any longer, Dorian. We found it."

Dorian sputtered and rolled his eyes as theatrically as a stage performer. "You found the *tresor*! Yet this was not the first thing you said when you came home!"

"The treasure doesn't matter. Your safety —"

"Bof." He sat down and patted the floor next to him. "Tell me."

I sat down next to the gargoyle and explained how Peter had a complex puzzle box from his father, like the ones I sold at Elixir, and that I'd figured out it contained a key that opened a secret hiding spot at the Thorne family mausoleum at the cemetery. Franklin Thorne had hidden his stolen loot in his hiding place before the police caught up with him later that day, but not thinking he'd be killed that day, he hadn't had a chance to convey the information about his hiding spot to his wife and son. "But when we went to the cemetery together," I concluded, "I could tell someone had already gotten into the mausoleum, because the dirt inside the secret room had already been disturbed."

"Yet you said there was only the single key," Dorian said. "And you were the one who found it, *non*?"

"Yes. I also took the precaution of going with Peter and Penelope to the cemetery and asking Max to meet us there. That way the magicians couldn't get into the crypt ahead of me. I wonder if I underestimated Earl Rasputin, though. If he saw what we were doing . . . Could he have found another way in?"

The gargoyle drummed his fingers together.

"What are you thinking?" I asked.

"Tell me everything. Every detail, no matter how small." He raised a clawed index finger into the air to make his point.

"To what end?"

"As I said, something strange is afoot with these magicians."

I was wary of my little detective taking things into his own hands. Again. But I could use his insights. I described our trip to the cemetery, from the carving of roses and thorns on the mausoleum to the rose bushes that surrounded the raised crypt, from the tiny hidden room to the indentation in the dirt. I told Dorian how Peter had bundled up like he was cold or feeling under the weather, how we'd met Earl Rasputin handing out Baby Bigfoot flyers with an illustration that vaguely resembled Dorian, that the wind had blown some of the flyers away, and that Max had arrived late at the cemetery because he had to visit Ivan in the hospital.

"It is as I thought!" Dorian exclaimed, jumping up from his perch-like sitting position.

"You know what happened?"

"To test my theory, I have but one question for you." His claws made a crisp tapping noise as he drummed his fingertips together. "When the flyers blew away, whose hands were they in?"

"Earl was handing them to me and Penelope."

"Penelope, eh?"

"We both offered to take some flyers. I wanted to destroy them rather than hand them out, and I was afraid Penelope was intrigued because she recognized you."

"It is obvious what has happened," Dorian said. "Obvious!" He drew his hands behind his back and paced the floor. He was enjoying this. "The magician, Peter Silverman, has stolen something from the crypt."

"That's not possible. I was the one who figured out they had to burn the box. They didn't have the key until then. I was with them the whole time."

Dorian dismissed me with a wave of his hand. "Have I taught you nothing in these last months, Zoe Faust?"

"What does cooking have to do with this?"

He pinched the bridge of his snout. "The magicians! Peter Silverman got into the crypt while you were distracted by his wife and Earl Rasputin."

"You think they're working together?"

"Perhaps, but I think not. Any good magician knows how to read their audience. I believe that because there were two of them and only one of you, they seized on the distraction of Monsieur Rasputin to carry out their deception."

"If Franklin Thorne used the mausoleum as a hiding place for one treasure . . ."

Dorian nodded. "He would have used it for *all* his treasures he wished to keep hidden. This is why the magician was bundled in a heavy coat, though it is a warm day. If he was an even better performer, like my father, he would have feigned illness to complete the deception. But he did not see this illusion through, and you noticed it as odd. Therefore you remembered he was wearing a coat — a coat he used to hide the additional valuables he pilfered."

I groaned. "Peter Silverman didn't want to restore his own good name by returning the Lake Loot to Julian Lake and receiving a reward. He wanted to get his hands on the bigger stash he knew his thieving father had hidden."

Forty-Seven

I called Max to tell him what I thought was going on with Peter, that the magician had retrieved other items his father had stolen. Max said he'd pass along the information to the investigating detective.

Next I texted Brixton to tell him the news, then drove to his high school, where classes would soon be ending for the day. I had no confidence he'd heed my words and refrain from confronting the magicians.

Brixton rolled his eyes when he saw me, but his demeanor changed when he climbed into the truck.

"I'm supposed to help Mom at the tea-shop, but I don't feel like it. Can you drive me home?"

"How about we still go to Blue Sky Teas but I join you for a cup of tea first? It might help."

Another eye roll. "I know you guys think tea solves all the world's problems. But it really doesn't."

I had a good idea why he was upset. "You're disappointed about Peter Silverman, aren't you?"

"He lied to me, Zoe. He never wanted to help his father's reputation. It was all a lie." He stared out the window as we drove past rows of blooming spring flowers. "How am I supposed to trust anyone?"

We drove in silence to Blue Sky Teas. When we arrived, Brixton took his mom's place behind the counter without a word, and Heather joined me at a small tree-ring table. Today, the mason jars were filled with a rainbow of tulips, and the whole teashop smelled like a flower garden.

"I'm worried about Brixton," I said, keeping my voice low. I hesitated. "Can I ask you about his stepfather?"

Heather's eyes lit up. "Abel. He's the best thing that's happened to me since Brix."

"Brixton seems to idolize him, and I know he gave Brixton that guitar he loves. Why won't he talk about what Abel does?"

"What does that even mean, *what we do?*" Heather studied her paint-stained hands for a moment before she looked back up at me. "Such a loaded expression, don't you think? I mean, am I a painter because I paint, even though I don't make much money at it? Or do I work in a café, since that's what I'm doing for money?"

"I wasn't trying to be philosophical. I'm trying to help Brixton. He's really upset, and I think it has to do with Abel."

Heather looked to the counter. "He looks okay to me."

I sighed and tried a different track. "Brixton doesn't have anything to be ashamed of, so why won't he tell me what keeps Abel out of town?"

Heather plucked a yellow daffodil from a braid of her blonde hair and picked the petals off one by one. "It's embarrassing," she whispered.

"Is he in jail or something?"

She crushed the flower stem between her fingers. "In a way, it's worse. If he was in jail, it wouldn't be by his own choice."

I wasn't sure I followed that logic, but I went with it.

"He works for Big Oil," she said, her voice so soft I could barely hear her.

"Oil?"

"Shh. Yes, it's awful, isn't it? I protest them all the time! He doesn't want to do it, but he's great on the oil rig."

I looked up to the faux blue sky above the weeping fig tree and laughed.

"What's funny?" Heather's face flushed.

"See, I'm so embarrassed just talking about it to you. I told Brix it would be better if everyone thinks he's a painter like me."

"I'm so glad that's all it is. And you've just reminded me how easy it is to be wrong about people."

I was too tired to stay awake for dinner that night. I didn't fight Dorian when he brought me a tray in bed and put me to sleep.

At midnight I was awakened, I wasn't sure by what. I'm used to the patter of Dorian's feet on the roof.

I got up to walk through the house. I found the source of the noise almost immediately. Dorian had dropped a hefty notepad in front of my door. There was a note on the top sheet.

You are sicker than you will admit. Ivan is in the hospital, so I have taken the liberty of taking my book to his home library. Do not fear, it is not missing. I am a fresh set of eyes (how American I am becoming!) and will return home with new ideas.

I sighed. *A simple life, Zoe. A simple life.*

I drove my truck toward Ivan's house. It was walking distance, but the truck would be the easiest way to get Dorian home without him being seen.

A plume of smoke rose in the distance,

coming from Mt. Tabor. A bad feeling clenched my stomach. It looked like it was coming from the theater. But unlike the fake fire in the Prometheus and Persephone stage show, this fire was very real. My tires screeched as I turned and headed toward it.

I found Dorian outside the back of the theater, hiding next to a dumpster. His wings flapped in earnest. He was horribly upset.

"I went inside because I thought I heard a voice calling out for help, but it was too hot. I dropped my book! It is inside, burning."

The sound of sirens sounded in the distance.

"Hide, Dorian."

"I know!" he snapped. "I hid from the men in the theater last week, as I will hide now."

He'd "hidden" from Wallace Mason and Earl Rasputin, yet Earl had posters that resembled Dorian. Could it really be that simple?

"Dorian," I said. "I know what happened."

Dorian heard the urgency in my voice and stopped.

"They didn't see you in the woods by the cemetery," I said. "Wallace Mason and Earl Rasputin saw you *in the theater.* Both of them, when they were spying on the magicians just like we were, when they hoped to get inside information about the location of the Lake Loot. That's why Wallace was clutching your stone toe, and why Earl had a knife. They were defending themselves from Baby Bigfoot, and in the confusion and darkness, *Earl stabbed the wrong man.*"

A faint cry of distress interrupted me.

"Merde," Dorian whispered. He gave me one last look, then followed the sound of the anguished cry into the burning theater.

Forty-Eight

ENGLAND, 1925

The flames crackled and burned brightly.

The cloudy mixture bubbled in its glass vessel. The gray bubbles turned to white. The alchemist smiled to himself. He loved watching his transformations take form. He gained a deep satisfaction that his patience and pure intent could transform impure natural substances into something greater than the sum of their parts.

Ambrose looked up from his experiment as footsteps sounded on the stairs leading down to his alchemy lab. The thick wood sagged under the weight of the hefty man entering the secret laboratory.

"Father?" the petulant voice called out. It would have been excusable in a boy, but the boy was now fifty.

"Percival!" Ambrose stood to greet his son. "Good to see you, my boy. I wasn't expecting you until Saturday."

"It *is* Saturday, Father."

"Is it true?" Ambrose extinguished the flame underneath his alchemical creation. All the time and energy he had poured into that vessel, now abandoned at the appearance of his son.

"You forgot about me," Percival said without humor. "I suppose that means you haven't prepared any food for dinner."

"Zoe is gone for a few weeks, and I'm afraid the vegetables miss her touch. I've been eating bread and beer. But we can walk down to the pub for something more substantial."

Percival nodded with approval, his ample chin jiggling as he did so. Even in the dim light from the glowing athanor furnace, the streaks of gray in Percival's hair were apparent. The two men no longer passed as father and son. Percival was now five years older than the age Ambrose appeared to be. In a few years' time, it would look as if Percival were Ambrose's father.

As Nicolas Flamel had warned Zoe Faust many years before, it wasn't possible for one alchemist to transfer their personal Philosopher's Stone to another. Knowledge could be transferred, but transformations themselves were personal. Yet like Zoe before him, Ambrose refused to believe it. He was convinced he could help his son achieve the immortality he craved.

The father and son who now looked like brothers climbed the stairs, then replaced the trap door and rug that hid the laboratory. On the cool autumn day, the cabin was warm with the heat of the burning stove that masked the smoke from the secret athanor furnace of their lab. It was only a short walk from the warm cabin to the local pub. Ambrose had spent many years in France — and he was thankful he had, for it was there that he had met the love of his life — yet he was happy to be back in England. The friendly people in his native land supported each other, and ubiquitous public houses were their gathering spot. He mused that there must have been one pub for every thirty men. He was happy that he and Zoe could live in this welcoming community for at least a few more years before people began to notice they weren't aging like the rest of them.

In a far corner of the dim pub, Percival shoveled mutton into his mouth while Ambrose drank beer and told his son of his latest alchemical discoveries, which he hoped Percival would try. Ambrose did not believe the longer lifespan granted by the Elixir of Life was essential to have a fulfilling life. Yet he considered the quest for the Philosopher's Stone, the penultimate step to the Elixir, to be rewarding for what it could tell a man about the world, and about himself.

"It's useless, Father. I can't do it without your help —"

"We already tried that," Ambrose said, the sharpness in his voice surprising himself as much as Percival. "You know how it turned out."

"You're giving up on me?"

"Of course not, my boy. This very month I found you a new book. An obscure treatise by Roger Bacon. It may help —"

"A book?" the no-longer-young man scoffed. "You think *a book* can help me, Father? Only the apocryphal book you once mentioned could help me. Yet in the same breath you told me it was an unnatural abomination."

"But Percy, surely it's worth a try —"

"If you really wanted to help me," Percival hissed, "you'd find that book created by the sect of alchemists who worked at Notre Dame."

Neither man spoke for a few moments. In their darkened corner, they listened to the boisterous laughter surrounding them, but escaped the attention of the other men.

Ambrose lowered his voice. "I never meant for you to cling to those ideas of backward alchemy. I only mentioned it as part of your education —"

"Then why mention it at all?" Percival straightened his shirt, the buttons straining under his corpulence.

"I found the Elixir by immersing myself in every aspect of alchemy."

"I don't believe you. When you told me of backward alchemy, it was only when that woman was away. *You didn't want her to know.*"

"Zoe is a pure soul." Ambrose's voice was barely above a whisper now. "She wouldn't have understood."

"You don't trust her?"

"It's not about trust. Zoe didn't need to be burdened with this dark knowledge I learned of. She had already discovered alchemy's secrets when I met her."

"Which she didn't share with us."

"You know she couldn't."

"Do I? If you choose to believe that . . ."

"You'd fare better if you believed it too. Then you would be free to gain your own understanding. You could write your own translation of the Emerald Tablet, as every alchemist must —"

"I disappoint you because I'm not a

scholar."

Ambrose knew his son had never possessed the temperament to be a scholar, yet he refused to give up on him. If Percival gave up on his futile quest for the Elixir of Life, Ambrose believed his son could enjoy his remaining years on earth by gaining a greater understanding of this miraculous, interconnected world. But if Percival insisted on seeking out immortality, his father wouldn't deny him. He would simply guide him in the right direction. Wasn't that what a parent was for?

"Knowledge is never a bad thing," Ambrose said. "It gives you the tools to choose what's right."

"More knowledge doesn't always work out for the best. It led to you choosing that foul woman. She ruined our lives the day she forced her way in."

"That's enough," Ambrose snapped.

Percival hefted himself up from his seat. "I need another pint of ale."

Ambrose wondered where he had gone wrong with Percival. The boy's mother had died in childbirth, so he lacked a mother's love. Ambrose had tried to make up for that, but had he gone too far and spoiled him? When Percival was a child, Ambrose hadn't denied his son any comfort he could supply. And as an adult, Percival's indulgent lifestyle was only made possible with alchemical gold from his father.

That was all in the past. Ambrose had to decide what to do about Percival in the present. He knew more of the dangerous backward alchemy book than he'd spoken of. A book created in France, many centuries before, that told of death and resurrection not through the true alchemical process of natural rebirth, but through an unnatural fire that ignored the world around it and quickly created artificial ashes.

Unnatural fire and ash went against everything true alchemy stood for. But it was knowledge nonetheless.

Percival returned to the table.

"My son," Ambrose said. "I have something to tell you."

Forty-Nine

"Can you tell me anything?" I asked the firefighter.

"Everyone got out safely." His face was coated in soot, and his kind eyes showed relief. "Whoever you're worried about, they got out and were taken to the hospital."

I knew the fireman believed he was speaking the truth, but there was no way paramedics had taken a gargoyle to the hospital. I'd been waiting on the outskirts of the blaze, and I hadn't seen Dorian through the thick smoke. Had he made it out? If I sifted through the rubble, would I find the charred remains of a stone statue? I might be all alone in this world once again.

"Zoe!"

I turned and saw Max running toward me. He swept me up in his arms and held me in a comforting embrace. I didn't want to let go, but after a few moments he stepped back and looked up at the smoky night sky.

"Why doesn't it surprise me to find you here?" He took my hand and pulled me farther from the smoldering wreckage. "Are you all right? You look like someone died. It's okay. I heard on the scanner that everyone got out."

"Death and destruction follow me," I whispered.

"Don't talk like that. We've both had our share of —"

I stopped his voice with my lips. He didn't object. Across the street from the glowing ashes, I let myself exist purely in the moment. For a few minutes, I lost myself in the kiss, enveloped in a combination of warmth, caring, and the scent of vanilla.

It was the scent that shattered the dream and brought me back to reality.

"Whatever happens in the future," I said, pulling back, "I want you to know that's how I feel about you."

"What do you mean, *whatever hap—* hey, where are you going?"

I slipped out of his arms and backed away. "I need to check on something."

I didn't trust myself to drive, so I ran home on foot. I heard Max calling after me, but I didn't turn back. With my silver raincoat billowing behind me, the rows of shops and houses passed by in a blur.

I'd traveled around the United States for decades, all alone in my truck and trailer with my window box plants as my only living company. I'd been foolish to think I could stick around Portland for a while, no matter how much the city and its people spoke to me. If Dorian was dead, being back on the road would make it easier to hang onto my fond memories of him, and of Brixton, Max, and the other friends I'd made here.

When I reached my front lawn, I wasn't sure if my heart was pounding so hard from physical exertion or from the fear of returning home to an empty house.

"Mon amie!" Dorian called out as I closed the front door. He flung his arms around my waist, and curled his wings around me. "When you did not return home immediately, I was afraid you had followed me into the theater when I went in because I heard Earl Rasputin's voice. With so many onlookers, I could not return."

I hugged Dorian back, glad he couldn't see the tears of joy in my eyes. "That was brave of you, Dorian. I think you saved his life."

"*Oui.* It is true."

My immodest friend led me to the dining room table, where he was eating a large dinner after exerting himself, and told me what he knew. Earl had indeed been trapped in the theater. But either from the effects of the smoke or from seeing a heroic gargoyle, Earl passed out before he could tell Dorian anything.

"I left him in the back alley," Dorian said. "I could not find you, but I watched until I saw the ambulance. I knew, then, that he would be safe. As for my book — you will see if there is anything that can be recovered?"

"There are too many people there tonight, but as soon as I can, I'll search every inch of the ashes for what we can save. Whatever happens, I'll do whatever I can to save you."

Dorian blinked his liquid black eyes at me. "I know this, Zoe."

I didn't dare tell Dorian I was convinced we wouldn't find anything. As I'd experienced that very evening with Max, living in the moment, however temporarily, could be a wonderful thing.

Now that I knew Dorian was safe, I wanted to return to the theater to get my truck and drive to the hospital. I've always been uncomfortable inside hospitals, because of what they used to be like many years ago with treatments that often did more harm than good, but I wanted to visit

Ivan and find out what had happened to Earl. I checked the clock — I had less than an hour before visiting hours ended.

The optimistic gargoyle insisted that I eat something before leaving the house. I wasn't sure I could stomach anything, so Dorian fixed a delectable consume with freshly toasted croutons.

I hugged Dorian and kissed the tip of his head between his horns, causing his cheeks to turn dark gray with embarrassment, then grabbed my silver coat and slipped out the door.

My own cheeks flushed red when I found Max at the hospital. He didn't bring up my confusing actions from earlier that night, but simply led me to the hospital café. As we drank tepid peppermint tea, he filled me in about what he'd learned.

Earl was awake and recovering. Thankful to be alive, he confessed everything that night. As I'd suspected, he admitted to accidentally killing his friend. The two of them had broken into the theater to spy on Peter Silverman, and Earl spotted a Baby Bigfoot hiding in the shadows. Wallace didn't believe him, so Earl snuck away from his friend in an attempt to find the creature. When Earl felt a hand on his shoulder, he was frightened it was Baby Bigfoot attacking him. He lashed out, only to realize too late that it was his friend.

Earl had spent time in a psychiatric ward in his youth, so he was afraid of what would happen if he came forward with the truth. I thought back on Wallace Mason's obituary, which had mentioned how he took in troubled souls, and how Earl had told me about his rough times Wallace had helped him through.

Earl and Wallace had figured out that Peter Silverman was really the son of thief Franklin Thorne, and they thought he'd have the inside track to recovering his father's lost hoard. Seeing us all at the cemetery, especially with a detective, had spooked Earl. He thought there was additional evidence he'd left behind that the police would put together with him. He set fire to a portion of the theater to cover up his crime, but the blaze got out of control. Earl hadn't realized the flames in the show were fake and that the theater wasn't specially equipped to handle a contained fire.

Earl maintained it was Baby Bigfoot who saved him from the fire. The doctors chalked up his overly active imagination to a near-death experience.

I would have laughed, but I wanted to cry. Dorian's book, and the secret to save him, must have burned down with the theater. It didn't matter that I'd photocopied and photographed the pages. As I'd learned since then, the pages had a life of their own through backward alchemy. It was the book itself that mattered.

"You look exhausted, Zoe," Max said. "Can I drop you at home?"

"I've got my truck here, but thanks."

We walked to the parking garage together, and Max kissed my cheek before he got out on his floor. I hesitated for a moment, then pushed the button to return to the hospital.

It was now the middle of the night, certainly not visiting hours, but I wanted to at least try to look in on Ivan. Max had mentioned where his room was located, so it was worth a shot. I expected I'd find his door closed, but it was ajar. I poked my head inside.

"Zoe, is that you?"

I stepped inside the narrow private room. "I'm sorry to have woken you. I wanted to see how you're doing."

"It's real," he wheezed. "Isn't it?"

"Yes, I'm really here. You're not dreaming. But you should go back to sleep." I moved back toward the door.

"Why didn't you tell me?"

"Tell you about what?"

"About alchemy." His voice rattled. "That it's *real.*"

I froze in the doorway, half of my body in the gloomy darkness of the room, half in the fluorescent light of the sterile hallway. Shivers ran down my spine to my toes. "You're dreaming, Ivan," I said. My voice shook.

"The more I thought about what you did to that book, the more I saw —"

"You *are* dreaming," I whispered. "Go back to sleep."

Ivan sat up in the hospital bed. "Turn on the light." What his voice lacked in strength it made up for in severity. This was a command I couldn't ignore.

I turned on the light and walked to his side. "Whatever you think you saw —"

"You know how I got involved in the study of forgotten alchemists?" Ivan asked sharply.

"You were a professor of chemistry. Alchemists were early chemists."

"I understand chemistry. Science. What you did to that book, at my home, defied the natural order."

"The ashes," I whispered, closing my eyes. After Dorian's disappearance, I'd been so desperate that I'd slipped up and let Ivan see what I was doing. I'd been too upset to think about acting secretly.

"Why didn't you tell me?" The edge was gone from his voice. In its place was disappointment.

"Would you have believed me?"

"If you had showed me —"

"You would have thought it was a magic trick," I said. "People have never been ready —"

Ivan snorted. "You think of me not as a friend but a mindless member of the public?"

"It's because you're a friend that I didn't want to burden you with the truth."

"A burden? You think the Elixir of Life would be a burden to a dying man?"

Now I understood. "I don't know how to find the Elixir of Life, Ivan. I wish I did —"

"But you did find it once, didn't you? You're not simply an old soul, as you always joke with me. Your body is old too."

As much as I wished it were Max who was ready for my secret, it was Ivan who was more than ready to believe me. I nodded slowly. "I don't know how I found the Elixir, though. It was an accident."

"Surely your notes —"

"They're gone."

The look of desperation in his eyes pained me. I didn't know what I could say that would comfort him.

"Non Degenera Alchemia," Ivan said. "You're deciphering it to find the knowledge you once lost?"

"Not exactly." I couldn't tell Ivan about Dorian. That wasn't my secret to reveal. "Backward alchemy is dangerous, and I want to understand what's going on with this book — but *not* use it."

Ivan's eyelids drooped. He nodded. "I must sleep, but when I'm released from the hospital, you will come see me, to tell me what you know?"

"I will," I promised. "But Ivan —"

He chuckled sleepily. "I know what you are going to say. The world has never been ready for alchemy. This is what the alchemists have said for years. Don't worry. I will not speak of this to a soul."

I slipped from the room and flattened my back against the hallway wall. How could I have been so stupid? I had behaved recklessly after Dorian was confiscated, and now Ivan knew my secret. If I thought it could have helped him, I would have told him before. I worried that I'd given him false hope. But maybe, just maybe, false hope was better than no hope at all.

Fire crews were still at the site of the theater fire, so I couldn't yet search for the charred remains of *Non Degenera Alchemia.* Dorian wasn't at home, and after finishing off the last of my solar infusion in the kitchen, the large house felt eerily empty. I tried sleeping, but the stressful events of the day prevented me from nodding off. I popped my "Accidental Life" cassette into the car stereo, and drove around the city that was beginning to feel like home.

Shortly before dawn, I saw that there was no one left at the theater. I parked on a side street and snuck into the wreckage, clinging to my own false hope. A fragment or two of the book might have survived. I didn't care if the roof fell on my head. My best friend was dying.

As I stepped through the smoldering wreckage, the scent of honey wafted through the soggy, charred remains. Was it only my imagination? I followed the scent to its origin in a lump of ashes. Reaching into the sodden mess, I pulled a book into my hands.

Non Degenera Alchemia was intact. It hadn't burned.

It had seemed too much to hope for. A gasp of joy escaped from my lips before I tucked the book under my coat and retreated to the safety of my truck.

I opened the book. It fell open to the page it always did. The scent of honey and cloves overwhelmed my senses so much that I nearly shut the book again. Only one thing stopped me. On the melded cathedral illustration were details that hadn't been there before.

The fire had done more to the pages than the ashes I'd used. Background details appeared on the page, giving life to the cathedral. The intricate stained glass rose window. The island. It was the Île de la Cité. This was Paris in the 1500s. This was Notre Dame de Paris.

And rising up from the cathedral was the outline of a fierce phoenix flying upward, away from the flames. Death and resurrection.

The difference between Dorian and the garden gnome and Buddha statues wasn't their different materials. It wasn't intent. The difference was that Dorian himself was connected to Notre Dame. That was the key.

Fifty

Dorian was so thrilled with the new discovery that he was moved to experiment with new vegan recipes inspired by Paris. He handed me a long shopping list and pushed me out the door.

When I returned from the market close to lunchtime, Dorian showed me what he'd discovered in the news. The police had found Peter and Penelope with a whole stash of riches that had been stolen from several Oregon heists in the 1960s. Also in the magicians' possession was a letter from Franklin Thorne to an associate asking about selling his full "collection." It looked as if Peter's father had been about to retire from the business. If only he'd done so one job sooner, multiple deaths could have been avoided.

Penelope claimed ignorance of the origins of the treasures. Having observed her intelligence, I wasn't inclined to believe her. But neither of them were killers, so I supposed it didn't really matter as much. Peter was arrested, and Penelope told a reporter that she was looking for a fresh start. She'd reinvented herself before, moving from a circus performer to a skilled magician, and I had no doubt she'd succeed in whatever she did next.

Reclusive Julian Lake consented to be interviewed by a television reporter, but the clip we watched online made it clear that he wasn't there to comment on the discovery of his family's lost riches. Instead, he was offering a *new* reward. This time, he sought the help of the public to find the mysterious French chef who'd visited him that week. It was the best meal he'd eaten in years, and he wished to hire the chef.

After Dorian saw to it that I ate every last bit of a roasted vegetable sandwich on fresh-baked sourdough bread with garlic hummus, I called Tobias to let him know what had happened, including my discovery that the illustrations in the book had pointed to Notre Dame Cathedral in Paris. He again apologized for upsetting me by misidentifying the photograph of Ambrose in my alchemy lab. I told him it was all right. I surprised myself by actually believing it.

"One last thing, Zoe," Tobias said. "I

found an old tincture that never worked for me, but my notes say it helps with the symptoms you're experiencing from backward alchemy. I'll overnight it to you."

"And let's not wait another 150 years before we see each other this time, okay?"

"It's a deal."

Brixton made up with his friends. Veronica and Ethan came to the teashop while he was working behind the counter, and they brought him a peace offering: a wind-up gargoyle that Ethan had commissioned from a specialty shop.

Ethan confessed he'd been sneaking around the burned theater after the fire, for kicks, and thought he saw the Baby Bigfoot shown in the posters around town. It made him realize that there might be more going on in this world than he understood. Maybe there *was* a Bigfoot. Brixton went along with Ethan's version of the truth, and didn't give up Dorian's secret.

While the boys caught up at a table filled with Dorian's pastries, Veronica sat with me and showed me my new and improved website on her phone.

"This can't be right," I said. "It looks like I've already sold two of my most expensive items in the last twenty-four hours."

"You haven't checked your email or your bank account?" she asked.

"I've been a bit busy." I'd need to pack up these items right away. I looked more closely, to see which pieces had sold. If what Veronica had showed me was right, I now had enough money to pay Ethan back *and* perhaps enough left over to hire someone to fix my roof. But first, I was buying myself a new wardrobe.

I settled back in my seat and enjoyed the convivial atmosphere. The painted blue sky on the ceiling and the live weeping fig tree in the center of Blue Sky Teas mirrored the sunny spring day outside. Two of Heather's water-themed paintings were now hanging on the walls. Though they'd been inspired by the winter flooding, the dramatic blues and bright whites were in perfect harmony with the spring flowers that filled the café.

"May I join you?" The voice startled me from my thoughts.

"Hi, Mr. Danko," Veronica said. "How are you feeling? I heard you were in the hospital."

"Much better, thank you." Ivan sat down and set a Cyrillic newspaper onto the tree-ring table. He *did* look much better. Perhaps hope was breathing new life into him.

I couldn't say the same thing for myself.

As I caught a glimpse of Ivan's newspaper, I felt as though the life was draining out of me. The sensation was surreal, like being in a dream.

I pointed to a grainy photograph in the newspaper. The focus of the image was a statue on Charles Bridge, the famous stone bridge that stretches across the Vlatava River in Prague. The bridge was lined with statues of saints, but this particular statue didn't match the rest. It was a gargoyle.

"What's this?" I asked, tapping a shaking fingertip on the newsprint image.

"Ah," Ivan said. "That is an interesting story. It seems that a stone gargoyle was found this week on Charles Bridge."

"Why is that weird?" Veronica asked. "Aren't there gargoyles all over Europe?"

"They don't usually appear without warning," Ivan said, "especially not 150 years after they disappeared."

I looked more carefully at the image. Though it didn't look like Dorian, there was something familiar about the style.

"This gargoyle," Ivan continued, "was identified as having been stolen from Notre Dame around the time the Gallery of Chimeras was opened to the public."

Like Dorian, this must have been a carving by Viollet-le-Duc. Was it another piece of the puzzle?

"Wasn't your gargoyle statue stolen, too, Ms. Faust?" Veronica asked. "There's, like, a gargoyle thief on the loose."

"Mine reappeared under mysterious circumstances too," I said, forcing a laugh.

I told everyone that my missing gargoyle statue had been dropped off on my porch during the night. The same "anonymous donor" had returned the murder weapon to the steps of the police station. A security camera video showed only a hunched figure under a black silk cape.

Max was unsettled by the fact that they hadn't caught the thief, but when he found me in my garden the following day, his response surprised me.

"If I had to choose between catching the guy who broke into the evidence locker," he said, "and having your gargoyle returned to you, I'm glad it turned out this way."

"I do believe you're learning to unwind, Max Liu."

He started to speak, but was interrupted by his cell phone. "Damn. I'm sorry, Zoe."

"I know, you have to go."

I had more to worry about than a complicated love life. And also more to celebrate. Dorian was safe from police scrutiny and could go back to being his usual self.

My Tea of Ashes remedy was still taking a toll, so I had opened the package from Tobias with anticipation. I lifted the carefully wrapped dark blue glass jar. The label was faded with age. As Tobias had said, the notes indicated this preparation could help with shriveled skin and hair loss. An accompanying note from Tobias said he'd held onto it for sentimental reasons, because the small man who had given it to him shortly after he met me in 1855 had been another kind soul during that dark time. The tincture hadn't worked for him, which is why he'd never used it up, but because my symptoms were identical to those described, he hoped it might work for me.

I looked from Tobias's note to the label on the glass jar. They had been written by different people, but the writing on the label looked familiar. I found a magnifying glass to examine the label. Was it my imagination, or did a tiny scribble at the bottom of the label say *N. Flamel*?

I sniffed the tincture, then put a drop on my tongue. I'm not sure whether it had a placebo effect or whether it was real, but I felt more energetic than I had in months.

Maybe it was hope that filled me with a renewed energy. I had my first solid lead on Dorian's book. Ivan might be of even more assistance, now that he believed alchemy was real. Now that I knew the book was tied to Notre Dame, I realized something must have changed at the cathedral. What was it that had set in motion the gold statues crumbling into dust and Dorian turning to stone? It had been months since I'd been in Paris. It was time for a trip back. This time with purpose.

I doubted the French customs officers would allow me into the country in my current slovenly outfit, but I was about to remedy that problem. Heather and I had made a date to go to the mall together. The huge department store again overwhelmed my senses, but I allowed Heather to lead me inside. The perfumes, the bright lights, and the endless rows of clothing struck me as unnatural. But on this visit, with a little bit of help, I learned that if you went beneath the surface, you could find the pieces that fit your own unique shape *and* personality. Two hours later, I emerged a new woman. I walked out of the mall wearing the first pair of comfortable jeans I'd ever owned, a green cotton sweater over a tailored white blouse, and silver flats.

I dropped Heather off at her cottage that sat at the edge of a wild field. There in the untamed meadow, the first leaves on the rosebushes were beginning to unfurl.

Brixton came outside before Heather reached the door.

"Hey Zoe, you promised you'd cook me that new dish you're perfecting," he said, giving me what he assumed was a surreptitious look. "Is tonight good?"

"Right. That new dish." Brixton must have been in touch with Dorian.

Heather said she wanted to work on a new painting, but asked if I would send Brixton home with leftovers.

The scent of caramelized onions had thoroughly permeated the house by the time Brixton and I walked through my front door. Dorian cooked a bountiful spring feast for the three of us, and after dinner, he put on a living room magic show with illusions his "father," Jean Eugène Robert-Houdin, had taught him a century and a half ago. Illusions that relied on sleight of hand — or in his case, sleight of claw.

RECIPES

CHOCOLATE ELIXIR

Drink your chocolate in 2 ways:
Hot Chocolate or Chilled Chocolate Smoothie
Serves: 2
Cook time: 10 minutes

Ingredients:

- 2 tbsp cacao or unsweetened cocoa powder
- 1 tbsp coconut sugar
- 1 1/2 cups of your favorite non-dairy milk (e.g., almond, rice, coconut)
- 1/2 tsp vanilla extract
- 1/2 tsp cinnamon, preferably Ceylon
- 1/4 tsp ginger powder
- 1/8 tsp cayenne pepper
- 1/8 tsp sea salt

Directions:

Place all the ingredients in a blender and puree until smooth. For hot chocolate, warm the blended mixture on the stove. For a chilled smoothie, add 8–10 ice cubes to the blender and puree.

Variations:

- Substitute the ginger with cardamom.
- Substitute the coconut sugar with 2 or 3 dates. For easier blending, soak the dates in hot water for a few minutes before adding them to the blender.

Cashew Cream Mac & Cheese

Serves: 4
Cook time: 40 minutes

Ingredients for Pasta:

- 1/2 lb. small pasta, such as elbow macaroni, conchigliette shells, or fusilli

Ingredients for Onion Mixture:

- 1 medium yellow onion, diced
- 5 cloves garlic, diced
- 1 tsp olive oil
- 1/4 tsp salt

Ingredients for Sauce:

- 1 cup unroasted cashews, soaked in water overnight (or for at least 4 hours) and drained
- 2 tbsp tomato paste
- 1 tsp salt

- 1/4 tsp black pepper
- 1 tsp smoked paprika
- 1 tsp turmeric
- 1 tbsp yellow mustard, powdered or liquid
- 1 tbsp nutritional yeast (optional; add extra 1/4 tsp salt if not using)
- 1 tbsp corn starch
- 1 1/2 cups water

Directions:

Preheat oven to 375. Start a large pot of boiling water and cook pasta according to package instructions.

While the pasta is cooking, sauté the garlic and onions with 1/4 tsp salt for approximately 10 minutes. When the onion mixture is translucent and slightly browned, remove from heat and set aside.

Combine sauce ingredients in a blender. Add half of the cooled onion mixture to the blender mixture. Blend for a few minutes, until creamy.

In a large bowl, combine the cooked pasta and sauce. Add the pasta and sauce to an oven-safe baking dish (a 9-inch glass baking dish works well). Sprinkle the remainder of the onion mixture on top for a flavorful topping that will crisp in the oven. Bake for 15 minutes.

Variations:

- Want to add vegetables to the recipe in a way that makes the sauce even creamier? Cauliflower works great with the flavors in this recipe. While the onions are sautéing, break a small head of cauliflower into florets and steam for 10 minutes. Add the steamed cauliflower to the sauce ingredients in the blender. Follow the rest of the instructions above.
- Don't want a crispy onion topping? Use a smaller onion and blend the whole onion mixture into the sauce.

Roasted Asparagus & Brussels Sprouts with Tarragon Avocado Sauce

Serves: 4
Cook time: 20 minutes

Ingredients for Roasted Spring Vegetables:

- 1 lb. asparagus
- 1/2 lb. Brussels sprouts
- 2 tsp olive oil

Ingredients for Sauce:

- 1 large avocado (or two small ones), peeled and pitted

- 2 tbsp olive oil
- 2 tbsp fresh lemon juice
- 2 tbsp water (more or less, depending on desired thickness)
- 1 tbsp fresh tarragon, chopped
- 1/4 to 1/2 tsp salt, to taste
- 1 tsp granulated garlic or 1 large garlic clove
- 1/4 tsp black pepper

Directions:

Preheat oven to 425 and prepare a baking sheet with parchment paper. Cut off the tough ends of the asparagus, and cut the remaining spears into 2-inch pieces. Quarter the Brussels sprouts. Toss the vegetables with 2 tsp. olive oil, then spread evenly on the prepared baking sheet. Roast for approximately 15 minutes.

While the asparagus is cooking, prepare the sauce. Put all the sauce ingredients into a blender and puree until creamy. Toss the roasted vegetables with sauce.

Variations:

- Asparagus and Brussels sprouts are a nice combination of seasonal late-winter and spring vegetables, but if you feel like making the dish during the winter, the sauce works well with potatoes. Cut 1 lb. of potatoes into 1/2-inch pieces (red or Yukon gold potatoes work well, either peeled or scrubbed), toss with olive oil, and roast for about 30 minutes. Toss potatoes with sauce.

- For a more garlicky dish, toss several smashed garlic cloves with the roasted vegetable mix. Roast along with the other vegetables. The garlic will be softer if you leave the skin on while roasting, but remember to peel the skin off before serving.

AUTHOR'S NOTE

The Masquerading Magician is a work of fiction, but the historical backdrop is real.

Jean Eugène Robert-Houdin (1805–1871) is the French stage magician known as the "Father of Modern Magic." The astonishing history of his life in *The Masquerading Magician* is accurate except for the following: he was not known to be a book collector, he never possessed the fictional alchemy book *Non Degenera Alchemia,* and he was not given a gargoyle by his contemporary Eugène Viollet-le-Duc (1814–1879). Viollet-le-Duc was the architect who created the Gallery of Chimeras on Notre Dame, including the carving Dorian is based on. As far as history recorded, the two famous men did not know each other.

Records suggest that alchemists used to meet at Notre Dame many centuries ago, and there are theories of a backward "death rotation" in alchemical transformations.

However, as far as I can tell, there never existed a break-off sect of backward alchemists.

It's true history that the façade of Notre Dame de Paris was defaced during the French Revolution, and there is indeed evidence that alchemical codes have been carved into Notre Dame in the past. My addition of *Non Degenera Alchemia* to the façade is fictional. As for the real carvings that once existed, some scholars have attributed them to fourteenth-century alchemist Nicolas Flamel.

Nicolas Flamel and his wife Perenelle claimed to have discovered the Philosopher's Stone, granting them the power to transmute lead into gold and extend their lives. Is there any truth in this assertion? The Flamels did possess an ancient alchemy book, donated large sums of money to charity, lived exceptionally long lives for the time, and when their graves were unearthed the coffins were empty. The less fanciful interpretation of these facts is that Nicolas Flamel was a bookseller who owned many books, his wife was wealthy and had money to donate, and graves in the fourteenth century were not especially secure. But doesn't it make for great fiction?

Dorian the gargoyle was inspired by the

many mysterious gargoyles I've visited over the years. My gargoyle photography can be seen on the Gargoyle Girl blog at www.gargoylegirl.com.

Though Dorian is fictional, his culinary alchemy is based on my own exploits in the kitchen. A cancer diagnosis challenged me to completely transform the way in which I ate, and instead of giving up meals I loved, I challenged myself to learn how to cook healing foods from scratch that would nourish both my body and soul.

In addition to the three vegan recipes in the back of this book, recipes are included in each book in the Accidental Alchemist mystery series, plus more recipes can be found online at www.gigipandian.com/recipes.

ACKNOWLEDGMENTS

Huge thanks to my amazing publishing team: At Midnight Ink, my editors Terri Bischoff, Amy Glaser, and Nicole Nugent; publicist Beth Hanson; cover designer Kevin Brown; and cover illustrator Hugh D'Andrade. At the Marsal Lyon Literary Agency, my agent Jill Marsal, who pushed me to turn an amorphous idea into the Accidental Alchemist mysteries.

This book also wouldn't exist without the insights of readers Emberly Nesbit, Nancy Adams, Adrienne Bell, Ramona DeFelice Long, and Susan Parman, or the moral support from my local writers group, the Pens Fatales.

And as always, I count my blessings for James and my parents, who have always believed in me, and who only occasionally grumble about the long hours I spend absorbed in my writing.

ABOUT THE AUTHOR

Gigi Pandian is the *USA Today* bestselling author of the Accidental Alchemist mystery series and the Jaya Jones Treasure Hunt mystery series. A breast cancer diagnosis in her thirties taught her two important life lessons: healing foods can taste amazing, and life's too short to waste a single moment. Gigi spent her childhood being dragged around the world by her cultural anthropologist parents, and she now lives in the San Francisco Bay Area with an overgrown organic vegetable garden in the backyard. Find her online at www.gigipandian.com.

The employees of Thorndike Press hope you have enjoyed this Large Print book. All our Thorndike, Wheeler, and Kennebec Large Print titles are designed for easy reading, and all our books are made to last. Other Thorndike Press Large Print books are available at your library, through selected bookstores, or directly from us.

For information about titles, please call:

(800) 223-1244

or visit our Web site at:

http://gale.cengage.com/thorndike

To share your comments, please write:

Publisher
Thorndike Press
10 Water St., Suite 310
Waterville, ME 04901